'Whatever are you thinking *now*?' she demanded.

'This.' Crispin moved quickly. Their closeness made it no great matter to slide his hand behind her neck, to cup the back of her head through the layers of her thick hair, and draw her the short distance to his body. He took her lips in an open-mouthed kiss that tempted and tested.

She was more than up to the challenge, responding with a fierceness that rocked Crispin to his core. Her tongue tangled with his, and she sucked hard on his lower lip, grazing the tender skin with her sharp teeth. At length, she pulled back, a knowing smile on her lips. 'Well, I suppose we can all be thankful for small miracles.'

'What would that be?' Crispin gave a smile. This was more like it. Women were usually impressed with his kisses. He stepped forward, ready to claim more.

She stepped backwards towards her mount. 'At least you kiss better than you ride.'

AUTHOR NOTE

I had a great time with each of the Ramsden brothers. They're all a bit different: there's Paine, the youngest, who by birth order has the opportunity to dabble in business to make his fortune abroad in exotic India, since there's no chance he'll inherit. There's Peyton, the heir, born to be the Earl and the patriot. Then there's Crispin, who's born to be wild. He loves horses and women and shuns commitment—until he meets Aurora Calhoun.

Crispin's story was fun to write. My favourite section is the part at the St Albans Steeplechase. England is mad for horses, and historical records are quite thorough. I was able to find a list of the horses and riders that ran in the 1835 race, and a report of the race itself—who finished and who fell. It's all accurate, so pay special attention to the race and know you're reliving history.

Crispin's tale was meant to be the last, but it's not necessary to read the three stories in order. Be sure to check out Paine's story in NOTORIOUS RAKE, INNOCENT LADY and Peyton's in THE EARL'S FORBIDDEN WARD. There is also a short story— GRAYSON PRENTISS'S SEDUCTION—giving Julia's cousin her own romance (available on the www.millsandboon.co.uk website), which runs concurrently with Julia and Paine's story.

Thank you for all your interest in the Ramsden brothers. I enjoyed getting your emails and the comments you left on my blog, urging me to get those Ramsden books on the shelves.

Readers can reach me at
www.Bronwynswriting.blogspot.com,
or at my web page: www.Bronwynnscott.com

Stay in touch!

UNTAMED ROGUE, SCANDALOUS MISTRESS

Bronwyn Scott

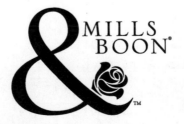

First published in Great Britain 2010.
This edition 2012
by Mills & Boon, an imprint of Harlequin (UK) Limited.
Harlequin (UK) Limited, Eton House, 18-24 Paradise Road,
Richmond, Surrey TW9 1SR

© Nikki Poppen 2010

ISBN: 978 0 263 22911 0

Harlequin (UK) policy is to use papers that are natural,
renewable and recyclable products and made from wood grown in
sustainable forests. The logging and manufacturing process conform
to the legal environmental regulations of the country of origin.

Printed and bound in Great Britain
by CPI Antony Rowe, Chippenham, Wiltshire

Bronwyn Scott is a communications instructor at Pierce College in the United States, and is the proud mother of three wonderful children (one boy and two girls). When she's not teaching or writing she enjoys playing the piano, travelling—especially to Florence, Italy—and studying history and foreign languages.

Readers can stay in touch on Bronwyn's website, www.bronwynnscott.com, or at her blog, www.bronwynswriting.blogspot.com—she loves to hear from readers.

Previous novels from Bronwyn Scott:

PICKPOCKET COUNTESS
NOTORIOUS RAKE, INNOCENT LADY
THE VISCOUNT CLAIMS HIS BRIDE
THE EARL'S FORBIDDEN WARD
A THOROUGHLY COMPROMISED LADY
SECRET LIFE OF A SCANDALOUS DEBUTANTE

and in Mills & Boon® Historical eBooks
***Undone!*:**

LIBERTINE LORD, PICKPOCKET MISS
PLEASURED BY THE ENGLISH SPY
WICKED EARL, WANTON WIDOW
ARABIAN NIGHTS WITH A RAKE

and in Mills & Boon® eBook:

PRINCE CHARMING IN DISGUISE
 (part of *Royal Weddings Through the Ages*)

To Suzanne Ring.
Thanks for your support of the
South Sound Titan's swim club annual auction.
Thank you also for your personal friendship.
Your commitment to the community is inspiring.

Chapter One

Early February 1835

Crispin Ramsden never saw it coming. One moment he was trotting peaceably down the dirt lane that led to the turn towards Dursley Park, savouring a countryside he hadn't seen in three years, and the next he was flat on his back, having been unceremoniously spilled from his stallion, who was even now rearing and flailing his dangerous hooves in reaction to whatever had spooked him.

Straining against the pull of a sore hip and buttocks that had taken the brunt of his fall, Crispin levered himself into an upright position to take in the scene. He saw the cause of the accident clearly: a tall, slender youth and his horse, an impressive-looking bay hunter that went at least sixteen hands. Even with a sore hip, Crispin noticed such things. The youth was standing in the road, managing to calm Crispin's highly strung stallion.

'Miraculous,' Crispin called out, hoisting himself to his feet carefully. He'd only ever met a handful of people who could handle Sheikh.

'That's what I was going to say about you.' The youth turned from the horse and faced Crispin, hands on hips, and Crispin realised his mistake. It was no youth who'd calmed his horse, but very clearly a woman; a woman with long athletic legs shown off to advantage in riding breeches that did nothing to disguise the delicious curve of her rear-end and high breasts that rose and fell provocatively beneath a man's cut-down white shirt.

'Miraculous? I can be.' Crispin sauntered towards Sheikh, doing his level best to not limp, wince or otherwise indicate the fall had left him in need of a hot soaking bath. This woman didn't appear to be the type to appreciate infirmities or she would have run straight over to him first and seen to the horse second. He reached out a hand and stroked Sheikh's quivering flank.

At this close proximity he could make out the long braid of dark hair tucked down the back of her shirt. In fact, it was quite amazing he'd mistaken her for a young man at all.

She shot him a hard look with eyes the colour of summer grass, a deep verdant green. 'I meant it was miraculous you didn't hear me shout when I entered the roadway. I called out twice to warn you of my presence. You had plenty of time to get out of the way. What were you thinking?' she snapped.

He'd been thinking how nice it would be to get home, to see his brother, Peyton, to see his twin nephews, who had been born two years ago, and the new baby, who had arrived a month early in January. He'd been thinking about settling the inheritance that had finally compelled him to stop making excuses and come back to the Cotswolds.

His attention might have been errant in regards to his surroundings, but Crispin Ramsden didn't like being taken to task by anyone and certainly not by a black-haired virago dressed in men's clothing a mile from his home.

Crispin folded his arms over his chest and faced her squarely. 'The better question is—what were you thinking? You're the one racing a horse into a country lane out of nowhere. In case you haven't noticed, this is a public thoroughfare. Any number of people or conveyances could have been on this road and you would have bowled right into them.'

'How dare you impugn my abilities as a horsewoman,' she shot back, boldly stepping forwards so that now they stood toe-to-toe, her dusty riding boot touching his. It was hard to tell whose was dirtier. 'You have no right to pass judgement on my skills when you were as absentminded as the vicar's grandmother. You could have ruined that fine animal of yours.'

Not only were they toe-to-toe, they were nearly nose to nose, give or take a few inches on her side, Crispin observed. He appreciated the benefits of her height. Being a tall man himself, he'd always had a preference for taller women—better compatibility when it came to dancing, which he abhorred, and bed sport, which he liked quite a lot.

He knew he should at least feign attention to the dressing down she was giving him, whoever the hell she was, but it was deuced awkward to concentrate when his mind was giving her a dressing down of another sort. Who could blame him when those luscious breasts heaved with indignation mere inches from his chest? When those grass-green eyes of hers flared with passion for her subject? It was rather difficult *not* to imagine how those eyes might fire with another sort of passion that had nothing at all to do with horses and everything to do with those long legs wrapped about his waist, locked in the throes of ecstasy, and those inky tresses spilled across a pillow, free from their confining braid.

He had himself thoroughly aroused by the time she drew a deep breath and brought her scolding tirade to an abrupt halt. 'Whatever are you thinking *now*?' she demanded, obviously alert to the fact that his thoughts had wandered from her lecture.

'This.' Crispin moved quickly. Their closeness made it no great matter to slide his hand behind her neck, to cup the back of her head through the layers of her thick hair, and draw her the short distance to his body. He took her lips in an open-mouthed kiss that tempted and tested.

She was more than up to the challenge, responding with a fierceness that rocked Crispin to his core. Her tongue tangled with his, she sucked hard on his lower lip, grazing the tender skin with her sharp teeth. At length, she pulled back, a knowing smile on her lips. 'Well, I suppose we can all be thankful for small miracles.'

'What would that be?' Crispin gave a wolfish smile. This was more like it. Women were usually impressed with his kisses. He stepped forwards, ready to claim more.

She stepped backwards towards her mount. 'At least you kiss better than you ride.'

Small miracles indeed! Crispin was still fuming over the encounter by the time he arrived in the drive of Dursley Park. She'd pricked his pride and ridden off without a backwards glance. She could not know, of course, that he took great pride in his horsemanship. It was the one thing he did better than anyone he knew and he knew many fine equestrians.

Her blind arrow had hit the mark perhaps more intensely than she'd meant. Crispin would love nothing more than to find the minx and show her just how wrong she was. However, he was grateful that his stinging pride had given his body something else to focus on the last mile home. It wouldn't do to show up at Dursley Park after a three-year absence with a painfully obvious erection straining his trousers and no good explanation for it.

Crispin jumped down from Sheikh and tossed the reins to a groom who'd come running from the stables the moment he'd been sighted. He mounted the wide steps to the front door, taking a moment at the top to survey the park spread out around him. The place looked the same as it always had: the lawns neatly manicured, the hedges that bordered the gardens impeccably trimmed, flowers blooming when and where they should. He chuckled to himself.

Even nature in late winter obeyed Peyton and Dursley Park was clearly Peyton's domain; well-ordered and peaceful.

There was comfort in the knowledge that such a place as this existed in a chaotic world. But that comfort came with a price Crispin knew all too well: boredom. Just as he embraced the comfort of Dursley Park at the moment, he already knew two or three months from now he'd be chafing to get away.

His knock was answered by the butler who immediately ushered him in and went to inform Peyton. It was four o'clock in the afternoon. If he knew Peyton, he'd be in his study. Like the clockwork Crispin had bet on, Peyton emerged from the study ahead of the butler. His brother crossed the entry in three long strides and surprisingly pulled him into a firm embrace.

That was new.

Crispin could not recall the last time Peyton had *hugged* him and this definitely qualified as a hug, not a mere embrace done simply to make a show of expected, scripted affection.

'Crispin!' Peyton said at last, stepping back, his hands still gripping Crispin's forearms as if he were reluctant to let him go. 'Why didn't you tell us you were coming?'

'I didn't know I was coming until I got here,' Crispin said truthfully. He'd thought to come home so many times in the past three years. He'd even mentioned returning in a few of his letters, but then he never had. Something had always come up; some new adventure claimed his attention and he put off returning yet again. After a while, he stopped making any mention of coming home for fear of letting everyone down when he failed to appear.

Peyton nodded, perhaps understanding him as well as anybody did. 'It doesn't matter. You're here now. Tessa will be glad to see you and you have to meet the boys.'

With uncharacteristic informality, Peyton led him to the nursery on the third floor, the noise from which would have made it easy to locate even without a guide.

On the floor in the centre of a large, braided rug, two identical-twin boys wrestled and yelled in their excitement. Not far from them, Tessa sat in a rocking chair, holding a blue-blanketed bundle and watching the boys' antics, good-naturedly putting up with their noise.

'Tess, look who's stopped by,' Peyton called over the racket. 'Boys, come meet your Uncle Crispin. Crispin, this is Nicholas and Alexander.'

Two little dark-haired boys bounded over to them with no trace of shyness, two sets of piercing blue eyes looking up at him in curiosity. The boys were Ramsdens through and through. There was no mistaking the trademark dark hair and the blue eyes for anything less. Crispin dropped down to his haunches and met the boys at eye level. 'Want to see a trick?' The boys' heads nodded vigorously. Crispin made a show of flexing his hands and then slid one hand over the other to create the age-old illusion of his thumb separating from his hand. The boys' eyes grew large and they howled with laughter. Crispin ruffled their hair and stood up. 'They're Ramsdens all right.' He smiled at Peyton.

'Here's the newest one.' Tessa joined them, proudly holding up the blanket bundle to reveal another baby boy bearing the same genetic imprint, this one named Christopher and as healthy looking as the others in spite of his early birth. Crispin laughed and slapped his brother on the back. 'Three boys! It's you, me and Paine all over again. Probably serves you right, you old devil,' he teased, but he could see the obvious pride and love in his brother's face.

'I'll have tea set up downstairs,' Tessa said once the initial excitement of Crispin's arrival passed. She handed the baby to the nurse and shepherded the boys into a quieter activity.

In the drawing room, Crispin studied Peyton while Tessa made general small talk and poured out the tea. Peyton appeared the same as always: tall, fit, in prime health. But if he looked closer, Crispin could see subtle signs of change. His brother's Ramsden-dark hair showed brief signs of silver at the temples. Tiny lines faintly etched the corners of his blue eyes and the brackets of his mouth.

Very small variations on the usual theme, to be sure. He shouldn't be surprised. Peyton would have turned forty-one last August. Forty-one wasn't so terribly old. All in all, Peyton was ageing wonderfully, but Crispin still hated to think of Peyton as getting old simply because it meant he was getting older too. If Peyton was nearing forty-two, that made him thirty-eight and far closer to forty than he'd care to be.

Tessa passed him a teacup. 'Do you still take it plain without sugar?'

'Yes.' Crispin took the teacup, thinking how delicate, how fragile it was. He'd not drunk from such a frail vessel since he'd left home. Dainty teacups were not practical in the places he'd been.

'So you're home to settle the inheritance,' Peyton remarked, referring to the property a few miles away that Crispin had inherited from an aunt on their mother's side. Peyton took a teacup from Tessa. 'The manor is in great shape. I've been over several times to keep an eye on things, but the steward is doing an outstanding job. He's a younger fellow, highly capable and eminently trustworthy. I think you'll be pleased, Crispin. The stables are in prime condition; lots of light and big stalls. There are not any horses there at present, of course.' He smiled knowingly over the rim of his cup, taking a sip.

Crispin shifted slightly in his chair. He'd had months—a year really if anyone was counting—to mentally come to grips with his inheritance. It wasn't that he was ungrateful. Second sons rarely had anything to call their own if there wasn't some kind of settlement from the maternal side of the family. But after all this time, he still hadn't reconciled himself to the notion that he was a landowner with all the responsibilities therein. He'd already decided it would be better to sell the property. A wanderer like himself had no business owning land he had no intention of supervising.

'I'm not sure I'll be keeping the estate.' Crispin steeled himself for a cold scolding from Peyton. Peyton would think him most ungrateful.

Peyton merely raised a quizzical eyebrow. 'Perhaps you'll have a better idea of what you'd like to do after you've seen it. Woodbrook is an attractive piece of property for those who are horse-minded. Regardless of what you decide to do, there are a few papers that need your signature and some other minor points in the will to settle.'

'We can ride over tomorrow and take a look at things,' Crispin offered by way of a subtle apology. The least he could do was go look at the property. Peyton was no doubt disappointed he'd not immediately declared his intentions to set up a home and embark on establishing a superior stable. Such a goal had long been Crispin's dream in childhood, but these days, he had little desire to be tied down in the way such an enterprise would demand.

'Woodbrook is a bit too far for me to stable my horse there on a daily basis, I was wondering if I could put up my stallion in your stables, Peyton?' Crispin shifted to a safer topic.

'Of course, if we had room. However, we're full up just now for any long-term boarding,' Peyton said regretfully. 'But I'm sure we can think of something.'

'What about boarding the horse over at Rory's?' Tessa suggested. 'It's close by.' She shot a look at the mantel clock. 'You could go over and see about making arrangements. Rory will be done giving lessons in a half-hour.' Tessa reached for a scone and added, 'Petra's taking riding lessons over there. You can walk home with her.'

Crispin smiled. 'How is Petra these days? Has she survived her London début?' Of all the Branscombe girls, and there were plenty of them—four counting Tessa—he liked Petra the best. Although there was a large difference in their ages, Petra and he shared an affinity for horses that made for enjoyable conversation. He'd genuinely enjoy the chance to talk with Petra and show off Sheikh.

Peyton grinned. 'You know Petra—she put up with London for our sakes, but was happy to come home. It's where her heart is, quite obviously in this case. She's engaged to the squire's son, Thomas. They'll be married here at Dursley Park this autumn.'

'One down, Peyton. Two more Branscombe girls to go.' Crispin laughed, offering his congratulations. 'If you give me the directions, I'll head over to this Rory's and see about boarding my horse. I'll have Petra back for dinner.'

Peyton rose too. 'The groom can show you the path, it's just across the valley.' He paused and smiled. 'It's good to have you home, Cris.'

'It's good to be home, Peyton,' Crispin said, knowing his simple words to be entirely sincere.

Peyton turned to his wife after Crispin had gone. 'You're quite the minx, my dear.' He smiled and wagged a scolding finger in her direction.

'Whatever can you mean?' Tessa feigned innocence, busy stacking the teacups on the tray.

'You know very well what I mean.' Peyton fixed her with a laughing stare. 'You didn't bother to mention that Rory is a woman.'

Chapter Two

Aurora Calhoun shot a considering eye at the heavy grey clouds looming ominous and low overhead. 'Good work today, ladies, let's get the horses unsaddled quickly so everyone can get home before the rain sets in.'

The five young women in the equestrian arena, all wearing trousers, dismounted and began moving their mounts towards the long stone stable, Petra Branscombe leading the way with her grey-flecked hunter. Petra had ridden well today, taking even the highest jumps with ease. It was a point of pride for Aurora to watch Petra blossom from a horse-mad girl into an expert horsewoman over the past two years under her tutelage. Petra was no longer the quiet girl she once was. Her confidence on horseback had translated into confidence in other areas of her life as well.

Aurora frowned, surprised to see the other horses moving around Petra at the gate. She narrowed her gaze and found the source of the disruption. A man lounged against the gatepost, engaging Petra in conversation. Even at a distance, Aurora could tell the man in question wasn't Petra's fiancé.

Aurora wiped her hands on her dusty riding trousers and strode forwards, ready to protect Petra. Strangers were unwelcome at her riding school and unannounced gentleman callers even less so, not to mention that she'd had enough of men for the day after her encounter with the arrogant man in the road. She wouldn't mind another look at the man's stallion, but she could do without the rider and the hot kisses that went with him.

There'd been a disturbing aura of wildness about the man, a feral quality about his bold, blue eyes, and the unconventionally long dark hair that had hung loose about his shoulders, to say nothing of the fact that he kissed like sin itself. *That* kind of man boded ill for any woman no matter how enticing he was in the moment.

Apparently this was not to be her lucky day. After eight years on her own, Aurora Calhoun knew enough about men to know trouble when she saw it. And she saw it now. The man from the road was leaning against the gatepost and chatting up Petra Branscombe with an obscene amount of familiarity. How had the blasted man managed to find his way to her stables of all places?

'What are *you* doing here?' Aurora approached the man and Petra with firm authority. From the looks of things, she was just in time. Petra was appearing far too at ease with him and it had only been a matter of minutes. Aurora had rather hoped the usually sensible Petra would prove to be less susceptible.

A slow smile spread across the man's rugged features, softening them slightly as recognition struck him. 'So this is where careless horse riders come home to roost.'

Petra knitted her eyebrows, confusion setting in. 'Do you know each other?'

'We met on the Dursley Road this afternoon quite by accident,' Aurora explained tersely, her displeasure over his presence obvious.

'*Literally* by accident is a more accurate retelling of our encounter,' the man put in, his blue eyes flickering with challenge and something else, quite possibly humour. 'I am looking for Rory Calhoun. I need a place to board my horse. I was told he might have a stall to lease.'

Aurora was torn. It wouldn't precisely be a lie to say *he* didn't have a stall to lease. After all, Rory wasn't a man. She couldn't imagine anything more disturbing at the moment than having this man underfoot on a daily basis. Then again, there was the allure of having that splendid beast of his in her stables where she could study it up close. Perhaps she could even convince him to put the stallion to stud with her mare. She thought the stallion carried Arabian bloodlines. Mixed with her standard-bred mare, she could produce an excellent jumper. In the end temptation won out, but not without some parameters.

Aurora crossed her arms. 'Let's be clear. First, it's not "he". It's "she". I'm Rory Calhoun to my friends, Aurora to the rest. You'd be in the latter group in case you were uncertain on that account. Second, I do have a stall you can lease, but there are some stipulations. Foremost, you cannot interfere in any way with my riding academy. The horses, my pupils, and my lessons are off limits. In fact, I'd prefer that you not schedule any of your time here during the afternoons on lesson days. You can come before or after lessons, but not during.'

'Don't want the village knowing the women ride astride and in trousers?' he queried with keen insight.

'We have trouser days just as we have habit days here at my school. Riding astride is a much safer way to learn the jumps,' Aurora countered fiercely. She did not care to have her methods challenged or her secrets exposed. It was not public knowledge the girls rode in trousers on occasion, or astride. It was one of the reasons she banned unannounced outsiders from practices.

Petra moved past them with her horse, leaving them to sort out the details. Smart girl, Aurora thought. She'd like to leave too. Better yet, she'd like him to leave. Once the girl was out of ear-shot, Aurora delivered her next dictate. 'She's off limits. I will not have you behaving as you did with me in the road this afternoon. I don't want to catch you with her, not walking with her, not talking with her. Nothing.'

The man had the audacity to laugh. 'That might be a bit difficult. Petra Branscombe is my sister in-law.'

Aurora's mind did the genealogical maths at rapid speed. 'Then that makes you...'

'The earl's brother,' he finished for her.

'The Honourable Crispin Ramsden?' Aurora said drily. It seemed the height of irony that this rough-around-the-edges, broad-shouldered man would bear such a title.

He seemed to think so too. 'Technically speaking.' A slow smile spread across his mouth, highlighting the lips that had kissed hers only hours ago.

Crispin raked her form with a gaze that seared as it travelled down every inch of her in deliberate contemplation. 'I would have thought someone like you would be less tempted to judge, Miss Calhoun. It appears you have already catalogued and classified me. I wonder? Should I do the same to you?' He chuckled at her overt reaction. 'That's what I thought. You don't care to be pigeonholed any more than I do.'

He took a step towards her, his strong gaze holding hers with a teasing glint of challenge. 'So, you think you know all about me after our brief acquaintance?'

He didn't look honourable so much as rakishly unprincipled. Not even the moment he'd taken at some point to pull his long hair back with a leather thong into something more orderly could give him an added measure of respectability. Aurora made a special effort not to back up under the onslaught of his advance. 'I've met men like you before, earl's brother or not.'

He had a seductive smile for her alone as he leaned close to her ear and whispered, 'I doubt it, Miss Calhoun. There are no other men like me.'

Four hours later, Aurora was ready to concede Crispin Ramsden might be right. She'd succeeded in getting him out of her stables, but not her mind. Aurora stretched her long legs out, feet resting on the fender of the fireplace absorbing the warmth of the flames in her converted apartments at the back of the stable. By rights, this was her favourite time of day. The horses were bedded down, their quiet snuffles keeping her company as she ate her dinner. But tonight, the usual peace the evening routine brought didn't come.

She was restless. She'd made endless excuses to herself: it was the rain drumming on the roof that made her restive, it was because she had a new horse in the stables. But she'd been out to check on Sheikh twice now and the visits hadn't alleviated her agitation. Neither the rain nor the horse was responsible for her current state. It was Crispin Ramsden that made her uneasy.

Perhaps it was nothing more than like recognising like. She'd certainly seen more than one set of horses test each other out before mating, nipping and biting. Their methods weren't all that different than Crispin Ramsden's. Aurora thought of Crispin's kisses in the road and blushed, glad no one else was there to see her. There had been plenty of nipping and biting involved that afternoon.

Aurora bent forwards and stirred the fire, forcing her mind to focus on more pleasant issues. There were tomorrow's lessons to plan. The rain would make the outdoor arena too muddy to be useful or safe. The Wednesday class would have to ride in the indoor arena. Eleanor, one of the girls in Petra's class, had wanted to talk with her after the lesson today, but by the time she'd dealt with Crispin Ramsden Eleanor had left. She'd have to make a point to speak with Eleanor on Thursday when Petra's class returned.

She knew what Eleanor wanted to talk about. The girl's father, Gregory Windham, was a very wealthy gentleman who wanted a title for his daughter. He was dead set on seeing her married to an impoverished baron who led a dissipated life. Eleanor was frankly against the match, but Aurora could feel the girl weakening under her father's pressure.

Eleanor wasn't the only student with needs. Young Mrs Twilliger was new to the area after marrying an intimidating older man who clearly had her cowed. Catherine Sykes was worried to death over her impending London Season this spring, fearful she'd be a wallflower, and Lettie Osborne spent most of her days dreaming up ways to bring the new, single vicar up to scratch.

Whatever their needs were, the riding school was a place to start. Here, Aurora gave them a place in which they could discover their own power and build their confidence. If one could master a horse, one could master a man. That was Aurora's philosophy. Perhaps a lucky few would do more than master a man. Perhaps a few would find a true partner for life if they had the confidence to do so.

It was the same principle with riding. She'd ridden two horses in her life that had been her partners. When she rode, she and the horse were equals. Nothing could compare with that. The other horses had been mounts to be mastered. She could get them to do what she wanted, but ultimately it hadn't been about giving and taking with them, it had been about control.

Aurora understood the enormity of the task she'd set herself. Her girls came here to learn to ride, to learn the art of looking pretty in the saddle, their habits spread out behind them, the traditional teachings of young English womanhood firmly ingrained in their minds. Aurora wanted to change that for them, wanted to show them how to think on their own. On a horse there was no one to think for them; they had to rely solely on themselves. If they could do it on a horse, they could do it in other places in their lives.

She didn't pretend her task was an easy one or an acceptable one by the standards of most people. It had been her experience that the local men wherever she'd been weren't receptive to her lines of logic regarding male and female behaviour. On more than one occasion she'd been forced to leave a village once word got out that she was imparting more than horsemanship to the women she instructed. She wondered what Crispin Ramsden would make of that? Would he be a man who supported tradition or a man who could open his mind to the possibilities of equality between the sexes?

Crispin Ramsden. Again. Apparently she'd not been successful in directing her thoughts away from the earl's brother. She gave herself a mental scolding. This was not the time to be considering any kind of flirtation. There were more important concerns. The St Albans steeplechase was coming up in March. She'd trained hard, her hunter, Kildare, was ready. Kildare was the best horse she'd ever ridden, better even than her beloved first stallion, Darby. If she could win, it would garner a great amount of prestige for her fledging stables, opening the gateway to good breeding opportunities.

There were difficulties to be worked out, not the least was how a woman was going to legally ride in a gentleman's race. She could always hire a rider, but the thought of turning Kildare over to another rider filled her with trepidation. The other option was to risk all and ride in disguise. She'd done such a thing before, but only in small venues with very little at stake.

If she were caught, she'd be disqualified and made the fool. Her stables' prestige would be sacrificed. But where would she find a rider that could work intimately with Kildare in the short time remaining? Rebellious images of Crispin Ramsden and his midnight stallion threatened the edges of her mind. Aurora rose from her chair and stretched. She'd do best to leave those contemplations for another day or she wouldn't sleep at all. It was time for bed. Morning always came early at the stables.

Dinner came early in the country, but it was still half past seven before the Dursley clan was assembled at the long dining room table. As Crispin had expected, Tessa turned his sudden arrival into an excuse for an impromptu dinner party, which explained the slight lateness of the meal. Even on short notice, the Dursley clan managed to fill up the table: Petra and her fiancé, Thomas; Annie, Tessa's youngest sister who was thirteen now; and Cousin Beth, who had run Peyton's household for years before Peyton married Tessa.

'Where's Eva?' Crispin asked, taking a mental roll call in his head once they were all seated and realising one of the four Branscombe sisters was missing.

'She's in London with Aunt Lily,' Tessa answered from the foot of the table.

'Isn't that a bit early?' Crispin had never liked the Season and it was beyond him to imagine why anyone would go up to town earlier than necessary. That Eva had gone months in advance bordered on the point of ludicrous.

Tessa smiled. 'She'll come out this year. She turned eighteen immediately after Christmas. She and Lily wanted to get a good start on her wardrobe.'

Crispin wondered how his brother did it, acting as a legal guardian for Tessa's three sisters; three Seasons to put together and then weddings to follow if those Seasons were at all successful, extra Seasons to follow if they weren't. Either way, there would be more endless twaddle. The very thought of all that frippery and nonsense was enough to put a man off his oats. Yet, Peyton looked as if he'd weathered the first two débuts quite well. In fact, his brother looked to be a well-satisfied man, sitting comfortably at the head of his table. There'd been a time not long ago that Crispin had doubted Peyton's ability to embrace such a life. Then Peyton had fallen in love with Tessa and that love had changed him, as it had his other brother, Paine.

Crispin took a bite of excellent roasted beef and suppressed a shudder. He was not falling in love. He had no desire to be changed. It was all right for his brothers to change. But he had no intentions of giving up his wandering and adventures. He liked his life just the way it was. All he needed was a horse beneath him and the wide world spread out before him. Women had other expectations.

Still, coming home for a while felt good. Crispin ate the well-cooked food with gusto and enjoyed the conversation flowing around him as everyone brought him up to date on events in the family. Although there were several family members at dinner, there were others missing besides Aunt Lily and Eva. His brother Paine had taken his family to visit his wife's cousin, Greyson. Greyson was interested in Paine's opinion on some new investments and Greyson's wife, Elena, was expecting their second child in late spring. Petra and Thomas had set the date of their wedding for September particularly out of consideration for them. Crispin wondered if he'd still be here for it.

At last, Tessa rose, giving the signal for the women to join her in the drawing room. Thomas rose too. 'I'll join the women tonight, Dursley, and leave you alone with your brother. No doubt there is still more to catch up on and I don't wish to intrude,' he offered graciously.

'He's a very nice young man,' Crispin commented as the group trooped out of the room.

Peyton nodded with a smile. 'We couldn't be more pleased for Petra. They're very happy together and well-suited.' Reaching for the decanter, he poured them each a glass. 'Cheers, brother.'

'Ah, this is the good stuff.' Crispin drank down the brandy with relish. 'I can't remember the last time I had brandy of this calibre.'

'The perks of being home,' Peyton offered cryptically. 'Did you work out an arrangement with Rory?'

Crispin chuckled. 'Tessa could have told me Rory was a woman and a sharp-tongued one at that. A little forewarning wouldn't have gone amiss.'

Peyton grinned. 'Aurora Calhoun is strong minded.'

'To say the least.'

Peyton poured them each another glass. 'Tessa likes her. She and Petra helped her get the riding school started a couple of years ago.'

Crispin eyed his brother over the rim of his snifter. He wasn't surprised to hear that Tessa had championed the unconventional Miss Calhoun. Tessa might look like an English angel on the outside, but he knew his brother's wife well enough to know it was merely a façade. 'Do you know what goes on out there?'

'You mean the riding astride and wearing trousers part? Yes, I am quite aware of it, although I must caution you that it is not common knowledge. Don't tell me you're shocked? You're the most untraditional person I know besides Tessa. I would have thought you'd applaud her. A woman's lot alone in this world is almost impossibly difficult, yet, against all the insufferable odds, Aurora Calhoun has found some degree of success. As much as she can hope for, I think, given the circumstances of her gender and situation.'

Peyton's remark was quite telling. Crispin took a moment to digest the layers of his brother's comment. His brother was devoted to his wife. He would tolerate his wife's eccentric friends for her sake. But Peyton's comment implied he did more than tolerate Aurora Calhoun; he respected her and, for that reason, was willing to make exceptions on her behalf. Such a concession from Peyton made the interesting Miss Calhoun all that more intriguing.

'I don't care what she does. She's entitled to her own eccentricities,' Crispin said shortly, realising it was true. It wasn't the unconventional nature of her school that bothered him. It was simply *she* who had him all churned up inside for reasons he couldn't quite put his finger on. She definitely stirred his blood.

'I rather thought the two of you would be good friends. She knows horses as well as you do,' Peyton was saying. 'That black of yours looks exotic. She'll be interested to hear about him. For that matter, I'd be interested to hear about him too.'

Peyton fixed him with a friendly stare and Crispin knew what was coming next. Inquiries about the 'exotic' nature of the stallion were Peyton's prelude to the bigger question. Whatever else changed about Peyton, this one thing would not: Peyton would always be his older brother.

'So, Cris, before we rejoin the others, why don't you tell me what you and my government have been doing for the last three years? The short version, of course.'

Crispin grinned and drew a deep breath. It was good to be able to talk with someone who appreciated the depth and importance of his work. This was something Peyton understood with extreme clarity. 'Let me start with the Eastern Question...' he began, his passion for his work evident in his recitation of events and astute analysis of the many evolving situations on the Continent.

At last, Crispin leaned back in his chair, balancing it on its two hind legs, and drew his report to a close. 'And that, dear brother, is the short version. I haven't even begun to tell you about British interests in America. There's another powder keg just waiting to ignite.'

Peyton nodded noncommittally at the implied reference to a future posting. 'Well, you've done your duty for Britain. Perhaps it's someone else's turn this time.'

'Perhaps,' Crispin replied vaguely, knowing the direction of his brother's thoughts. Tonight was not the time to discuss his next assignment. When the posting came, Crispin was almost certain it would be an assignment to the American South, a place he was itching to explore on a personal as well as political level. Such a posting would make the sale of Woodbrook imperative. He'd be in America a very long while, more of a relocation than a temporary assignment. Crispin reached for the decanter. There'd be time to quarrel with Peyton over that later. Tonight he simply wanted to enjoy the peace of being home.

'The long and short of it is, I am running out of time.' Gregory Windham leaned forwards across the cherrywood desk in his estate office, pushing a small leather pouch of coins across the desk's highly polished surface to the man on the other side. The black-smith, Mackey, had been the one villager he'd been able to actively recruit to his side. The others remained quietly neutral with regards to Aurora Calhoun. Damn them.

His *laissez-faire* strategy had not worked. He'd patiently waited for Aurora Calhoun's own unique situation to work against her. He'd originally thought the local gentry and the villagers wouldn't tolerate such a 'modern' woman; a woman who ran her own business and sauntered around in men's clothing. But Aurora had proved wily in that regard, keeping her trousers and lifestyle heavily obscured from the local populace. It had not helped matters that everyone knew she was an especial friend to Dursley's countess and Dursley's ward.

Aurora had lived out of sight and out of mind and the villagers had been happy enough with that. Such contentment needed to change. The villagers had to be rattled out of their complacency. He needed to force Dursley to make a stand. Dursley might quietly countenance such a friendship for his wife if no one complained about it. But the earl was also a traditionalist at heart. Windham thought it would be rather interesting to see what Dursley would do if there was a fuss over Aurora Calhoun.

It was time for a more direct approach if he meant to succeed in launching himself as a respectable horseman and sending Aurora Calhoun down the road of ruin. He tapped his long fingers on the desk.

'The St Albans steeplechase is a month away. That race is mine to win. I won't have her and that hunter of hers interfering.' He possessed a stake in the well-favoured horse, The Flyer. The stake had been an expensive purchase, but money was no object. The Flyer might not be *the* favourite in the race, but the horse was poised to be a contender if not a winner in the prestigious steeplechase.

'What do you propose we do?' The big man across the desk hefted the coin pouch in a meaty hand. 'I could make items disappear around the stable, or plant a burr in a saddle...?'

Gregory Windham dismissed those suggestions with a wave of his long hand. 'Those are the second-rate tactics of an amateur.'

He pointed to the bag of coins. 'Take the money and buy drinks tomorrow night at the tavern. Tell everyone what really goes on at the riding school of hers.' It was time to reveal his daughter Eleanor's confession and lift the veil of obscurity Aurora kept around her lifestyle at the stables.

The big man thought for a moment. 'I'm scheduled to go shoe her horses this week. Won't it look odd if I'm spreading those rumours and still doing business out there?'

'You won't be doing business there any longer.' Gregory Windham drew out another pouch and slid it across the desk. 'This should more than suffice to cover your losses in that regard.' He held the blacksmith's hard eyes with a cold gaze of his own. 'There's more money for you when she leaves town and even more when the horse I've invested in wins St Albans.'

The blacksmith grinned. 'I'll be a rich man by the month's end.'

And Aurora Calhoun will be ruined, Gregory Windham thought silently as his henchman departed. It was no less than she deserved. The woman was a threat to all he'd spent years accomplishing. He'd used his money to buy his daughter a titled match with a baron and to establish a small but prime stable a nobleman would respect.

He was hovering on the brink of acceptance into the ranks of the peerage. His future grandson would have a title. Even now, Eleanor rode at Aurora Calhoun's academy solely because the earl's ward rode there. Originally, it had been a good social-climbing opportunity. Now, such an association endangered his dreams. Eleanor had become obstinate over the match, spouting too many philosophies she hadn't learned at home. Windham knew exactly where she'd learned them. They were the same philosophies Aurora Calhoun had spouted when she'd rejected his attentions the one time he'd thought to recruit her to his side. He'd offered her the position of his mistress. She had all but bodily thrown him out of her stables.

Gregory Windham shifted uncomfortably in his seat. Just recalling how that hellcat had railed at him, spitting furiously at his offer, brought his arousal to life. His cheek had borne a bruise from the flat of her hand for days. She'd been magnificent in her anger, her eyes like emerald flames, her dark hair loose about her, an exquisite flowing curtain.

It would bring him great pleasure to subdue the wildness she exuded. Wild things were meant to be tamed. Aurora Calhoun, that tease of a siren, was going to pay. Women had a place in this world. He would make sure Aurora Calhoun knew hers.

Chapter Three

Crispin blew in his cupped hands and rubbed them together vigorously as he entered the relatively warmer interior of the Calhoun stables. Mornings were colder in England than he remembered and certainly colder than the ones he'd most recently experienced in the south of Europe. Crispin strode towards Sheikh's stall, anxious to see how his horse had fared during his first night in his new home.

Horses whickered as he passed and a few poked their long faces out into the aisle. Even though it was early, the horses were alert and had already been fed. One stall was empty. He recognised it as the stall belonging to Aurora's horse. Perhaps she was out on a morning ride, although Crispin thought it was too foggy yet for that to be a safe option. He'd been glad he'd walked across the valley this morning instead of riding. It would have been too easy to overlook a rabbit hole or a soft piece of land; too easy for a horse to take a misstep and be rendered lame or worse. Well, if Aurora was out that was her business. At least her absence meant he wouldn't have to encounter her.

Crispin slipped a halter over Sheikh's head and led him into the wide aisle of the stable for grooming. Crispin picked up a curry brush and began the morning ritual. He liked grooming Sheikh as much as Sheikh liked being brushed. Not usually a patient horse,

Sheikh stood exceedingly still for brushing. Crispin found the ritual soothing. He could lose himself in thought, letting his mind wander freely. The stables were a place of peace for him, any stable. The smell of horses and leather tack were familiar no matter where.

He finished grooming Sheikh and quickly saddled him. Through the stable windows, he could see the fog starting to lift. He was eager to get back to Dursley Park and the hot breakfast that waited. Beside him, Sheikh shook his mane. Now that grooming was done, he was ready to be off too. Crispin fished in the wide pocket of his greatcoat and pulled out a few slices of apple. Sheikh snapped them up as Crispin led him out into the morning.

The fog had definitely lifted, Crispin confirmed. He could actually see the indoor arena across the stable yard now. The faint sound of a horse's nicker drew him that direction. He knew what he'd find inside before he and Sheikh arrived at the door. Aurora had not opted for a dangerous, foggy ride. She'd brought her horse to the arena for a morning workout.

Crispin manoeuvred himself and Sheikh into the shadows of the wide doorway to watch her practise. The arena was set up for jumping and she was executing the fences expertly. She finished the last jump in a corner and made a clean cross through the centre of the arena to the opposite corner and started again.

Magnificent, Crispin thought, his gaze focused on her hands and thighs, appreciating the subtle pressures each of those parts used to communicate with the horse. Her movements were so completely synchronised with the flow and bunching of the horse's body that it seemed she barely moved at all. Crispin had no idea how long he'd stood there, but at last Sheikh gave him an impatient nudge and Crispin withdrew from the scene. He didn't worry about being heard. From the look on her face when she'd drawn close to the entrance where he stood, Crispin knew she was in another place altogether. Her thoughts were entirely with her horse; when to move, when to ask for the leap in order to get the most height for the jump.

Where had she learned to ride like that? Surely such skill was not acquired haphazardly.

The question plagued him all the way home across the valley and at the breakfast table until he finally blurted it out to Peyton and Tessa. It was a complete non sequitur. They'd been discussing a bill in Parliament and he'd set down his coffee cup and said suddenly, 'Where did Aurora Calhoun study riding?'

Tessa looked at him rather startled. 'I think she said somewhere in Ireland,' she replied vaguely; too vaguely for Crispin's tastes. After making a career out of reading people, Crispin knew without effort that Tessa was withholding details. If Peyton knew the specifics he did nothing to fill in the gaps and the conversation quickly reverted back to the bill under earlier discussion.

But Crispin wasn't willing to give up his inquiries. Once he and Peyton set out on their short jaunt to Woodbrook, he tried again. 'I happened to catch part of Aurora's workout this morning when I was saddling Sheikh. I'd be interested to know where she was trained.'

'Then you should ask her,' Peyton said levelly in a tone that suggested that topic of conversation was closed. Peyton was more eager to discuss the merits of Woodbrook, which he promptly began to do the moment the first property marker came into view. He continued to elucidate the fine points of the property right up until they dismounted in the stable yard and Crispin could see for himself what an excellent inheritance he'd acquired.

Peyton had not exaggerated. The manor house was a modest, twelve-room affair, hardly more than a cottage compared to the grandeur of Dursley Park. But to Crispin the stone manor was plenty.

'What would I do with twelve rooms?' Crispin remarked halfway up the stairs to see the other six, all presumably bedrooms.

'You could marry and fill the house with children,' Peyton laughingly suggested. 'Within three years, you'd be enlarging the place, declaring how you'd outgrown it.'

Crispin knew Peyton meant well, but all the same, the thought of being somewhere for three years, let alone a decade or a lifetime, sent a quiet shudder up his spine. Children couldn't be dragged around the world every year or so to satisfy his whim for adventure. Children needed the stability of a permanent home, of permanent parents. His own childhood was a testament to that. With two absent parents, Peyton had been the closest thing he and Paine had had to a father growing up. In his darker hours, Crispin often thought it was his worries of turning out like his parents that kept him from pursuing a family of his own, although his brothers had certainly proved such worries to be groundless. Both of them had become model family men.

Crispin made a quick tour of the upstairs rooms and returned downstairs. 'Perhaps Paine and Julia could make use of the manor.'

Peyton shook his head. 'There's plenty of room at Dursley Park for them when they visit. Tessa has a whole wing set aside for them these days. Besides, they spend most of their year in London. Paine's too busy with his banking investments to make use of a country house on a more regular basis.'

They walked out to the barns, which were just as impressive as the house. There was no outdoor work area for horses yet beyond a paddock, but the room for establishing a training arena was readily available in the wide, open spaces around the barns. Crispin could easily imagine setting up an equestrian centre here. The old dreams came to him as he walked the wide aisle of the barn, counting stalls. He had Sheikh to stand to stud for a pricey fee and to race. He could build a legacy from Sheikh.

Peyton stayed close, continuing his verbal tour of the facility.

'There's stalls for fifteen horses. The windows provide good light.' Peyton pointed overhead. 'There's plenty of hay storage in the lofts above. The tack room can easily support all the riding gear you'd need for that many horses. The roof is fairly new. There aren't any serious repairs you'd have to make. All of your attention could be on improvements and additions.'

Peyton had been a dangerously compelling diplomat in his day, knowing exactly when to push, when his opponents were most open to persuasion. To be honest, that was precisely where Crispin was now; wondering, in spite of his earlier inclination to sell the property, if this place was what he needed to conquer his wanderlust or even if he wanted to conquer the wandering spirit that drove him.

Crispin let a hand drift idly across the half-door of a stall. Commitment begot commitment. It wouldn't stop at committing to the stables. There would be grooms to employ who would count on him for pay and for work. There would be social obligations. The community would expect him in church and at their gatherings. Women would expect him to marry, if not someone from London because of his family, then certainly a lady from their part of England. Peyton was right. Manor houses were expected to be filled.

He was too much of a realist to believe he could stop at just one commitment. One commitment was merely a gateway to other commitments he felt less compelled to make. The commitments would not happen overnight. They would form a slippery slope that would erode slowly over the span of several years. It would occur gradually so that it didn't appear to be a life-changing overhaul, but single small steps taken in isolation from one another until, one morning, he'd wake up and realise it was too late to go back.

Crispin tamped down hard on the old dream of his own stables. It was a startling discovery to find the dream was far more potent than he'd realised. He'd come home, thinking to sell the property. He would stay with his original plan. He had his work. It was only a matter of time before a summons arrived from London. He would not give in, he would not change his course, no matter how much Peyton talked.

They emerged out into the daylight, Peyton's well-rehearsed tour complete. To his credit, Peyton pressed for nothing. He merely gestured down the road where a rider had turned into the drive. 'I've invited the steward to go over the books,' he said simply.

Crispin fought back a chuckle. Of course Peyton had invited the land steward. His brother had this visit orchestrated perfectly for maximum effect. All the same, Peyton would be disappointed. He wasn't going to stay. He couldn't. It just wasn't in him.

Several hours later, Crispin knew one thing. He needed a drink and he needed a drink *alone*. He'd been surrounded by a horde of well-meaning people since his return home. For a man who was used to operating solo and keeping his own counsel, such attention was unnerving. Well, he had to rephrase that. He'd been surrounded by *Peyton*. In all fairness, Tessa, Cousin Beth, Petra, Annie, the twins and the new baby had all kept at a respectful distance. They'd done nothing more than make him feel welcome.

But Peyton knew what he wanted from Crispin and he was wasting no time in trying to extract it. Crispin could see his brother's vision clearly. His brother wanted him to embrace the stables, settle down, take a wife and raise a family. For Peyton that had been the clear road to happiness once he'd found the path. Crispin understood it was only natural for Peyton to want that same happiness for him. However, Crispin doubted that path would work well for him. Crispin understood too that Peyton was trying not to be oppressive, certainly a harder task for him than for others. Peyton was well used to being obeyed. But Peyton could not make him into a man he could not be.

He and Peyton swung up into their saddles, thanking the steward for his time and his conscientious adherence to every detail.

They turned their horses towards home, riding in much-appreciated silence; Crispin's head was full to bursting with all he'd learned.

Crispin was amazed Peyton had stayed quiet for as long as he did. He'd bet himself Peyton wouldn't make it a mile before asking what he'd thought of the manor. Tessa's influence must be powerful indeed, Crispin mused. But he could see the effort the restraint cost his brother. Peyton's mouth was tense; on two occasions, Crispin felt Peyton was on the verge of bringing the subject up, but then thought better of it.

They reached the fork in the road, one turn leading to the Dursley Road and the other going on a short distance to the village. 'I think I'll stop in for a pint or two,' Crispin said off-handedly.

'I'll come with you,' Peyton offered, making a quick check of his pocket watch.

'That's all right. I'd prefer to do some thinking in private.' Crispin hoped Peyton understood. He needed a kind of privacy he wouldn't find at Dursley Park and he'd have no privacy if he turned up at the inn with the earl in tow.

'And dinner?' Peyton asked cautiously. 'Shall I tell Tessa to expect you?'

Crispin nodded his head. 'Probably not. I'm not sure how long I'll sit and think.'

'It's no trouble to set an extra plate if you change your mind,' Peyton said graciously. Crispin could see that his absence wasn't what Peyton had hoped for, but that his brother guessed at how monumental the day had been, how many things needed thinking over.

Once inside the inn, Crispin lost himself in the crowd, taking a small table by the window. Word had not yet spread of his return and he was thankful for the anonymity. Around him, the work day was ending. Large groups of local workers filed in for a pint before heading home for the evening.

Crispin studied this crowd unobtrusively. These men worked the fields as hired labour or in various other occupations in the village. They were journeymen and artisans, a few apprentices among them. They would drink and go home to supper and wives. The rougher crowd, those without familial commitments, would come in later after the supper hour and stay until closing; drinking, wenching, perhaps brawling if it suited them.

The men here now, though, would be the men he'd fraternise with if he took the manor. They'd be the men who would work his stables. They'd be the men who he'd drink with on occasion. Their lives would be interwoven into his.

Crispin took a swallow of his ale, trying to imagine his life as a gentleman landowner. It seemed so far from the things he'd told Peyton over brandy the other night as to be laughable.

These men didn't care about the nationalist revolutions sweeping Europe, about water-routes to faraway places they'd never visit, about fighting over lines on a map. Their lives were about wheat crops and sheep, cattle and corn. If he threw his lot in with them, his life would be too. Everything to which he'd devoted his life in the first twenty years of his adulthood would cease to matter— every nebulous peace he had brokered, every boundary dispute he had negotiated, would carry little weight in that new life. It would be tantamount to erasing who he was and remaking himself in a new image. The soldier, the warrior-diplomat, would not fit into this new world of quiet landownership.

The thought sat poorly with Crispin. He rather liked himself just as he was. Of course, there were plenty of people who didn't. The *ton* didn't know what to make of him. He was too bold, too loose with the rules of proper society for many of the matchmaking mamas to trust him with their daughters. Yet, he had a certain appeal with his brother's connections, his brother's wealth, and his brother's affection behind him. Any woman who married him would be well looked after under the Dursley banner. Proxy polygamy, he called it. The only reason anyone would marry him would be because they were marrying Peyton by extension. If he stayed in England, he'd have to decide in whose world he fit.

Without appearing to eavesdrop, he listened in on snatches of nearby conversations, trying to put himself in the frame of their world. Could he come to care about the issues they cared about? Could he empathise with the problems that plagued their lives?

Snatches of one conversation rose over the rest. 'The Calhoun woman was in today to buy some shovels. It's not natural, a woman buying tools. There's strange things going on out there,' a beefy man said loudly, drawing all the room's attention. Crispin tensed. In the silence of the inn, the man let his news fall on expectant ears. 'I've found out that the girls in her stables ride in trousers *and* they ride astride.'

Shock and outrage exploded at the announcement; questions were shouted over the din. Crispin stifled a groan. That could hardly be what Aurora wanted. But what followed was worse. Crispin slouched anonymously in his chair and listened.

The big man, named Mackey from what Crispin could gather, hushed the upset crowd. 'Aurora Calhoun needs to go. She's no good for our village, teaching our womenfolk to ride astride. Who knows what kind of ideas she'll plant in their heads next? We don't want our women turning out like her.' There was a loud roar of agreement. 'One of her is enough. She's had two years to prove she could fit in. We've left her alone and look how she's repaid us! The only thing she's proved is how out of place she is.' There were other comments too. 'We should have paid more attention…' 'Should have known it wasn't natural from the start…'

Good lord, the man was creating a witch hunt. Crispin half-expected the men to pick up torches and march out to the stables then and there. Crispin had heard enough. He'd end up fighting with someone if he stayed. Crispin slapped a few coins on the table and made a quiet exit, opting to exercise his authority when cooler heads prevailed, including his.

Dusk was in its final throes when he swung up on Sheikh. He could still make dinner at Dursley Park, but he wasn't ready to go home. More to the point, he wasn't ready to go to Peyton's home. He couldn't expect Peyton to keep silent about the manor forever. But Crispin wasn't ready to talk about it yet, at least not with his brother. He could only think of one place that might suit his needs. In the fading light of day, Crispin turned Sheikh towards Aurora's stables.

The stable lanterns threw a welcoming light into the yard and the fresh smell of evening hay assailed his senses the moment Crispin led Sheikh through the stable doors. Horses neighed, acknowledging Sheikh's presence among them as they passed stall doors. Crispin stopped outside Sheikh's stall and removed the saddle. With one hand, he stroked Sheikh's long neck, soothing the horse. With the other, Crispin groped for the kit holding the brushes. The kit should have been right behind him on the nail hook outside the stall where he'd left it that morning.

'Are you looking for this?' The voice startled him. Crispin whirled around; releasing a breath when he saw the voice belonged to Aurora.

She held the kit out to him. 'I didn't mean to give you a start,' she apologised, taking one of the brushes and moving around to Sheikh's other side. She began to curry the horse.

'You've had a long day. I noticed Sheikh was gone when I came back this morning. You must have been here early and now it's dinner time,' Aurora commented.

'Peyton and I rode over to see some property,' Crispin said, surprising himself with the truth. He could have answered the question just as easily by saying he'd waited until lessons were done. Such an answer would not have given away any particular information about his whereabouts and it certainly wouldn't have invited any further conversation. His chosen answer, on the other hand, invited all nature of possible comment, none of which Aurora opted for.

'Your brother is eager to see you settled,' she said, meeting his eyes for an instance over Sheikh's back.

Of all the things she could have said, he'd not expected that. He'd expected the usual; 'Do you mean to settle here?' 'Where is the property?' 'What do you plan to do with it?'

'I suppose he is,' Crispin replied, bending over and clicking to Sheikh to lift his hoof.

'How do you feel about that?'

Crispin answered honestly. 'The property is enticing, but I'm not the right man for that kind of life. I'll sell the property outright and then I'll be on my way.' He finished picking the hoof and stood up, stretching his back. Aurora was nearly finished brushing Sheikh's opposite flank.

'I know what you mean,' she said casually. 'I've been here longer than I've been anywhere else. I'd always taught on a property owned by someone else. But Tessa talked me into leasing this one. Actually, in all truth, Tessa wanted me to buy it, but I couldn't go that far. A lease was as permanent a commitment as I could make.' Aurora stopped brushing and shook back her hair, which had fallen forwards over her shoulders as she worked. An awkward silence fell between them as if they both suddenly recognised they'd said too much to someone they didn't know.

Crispin met her eyes over the back of Sheikh and nodded in the awkward quiet; a wealth of understanding passing between them in that single look. He could well imagine all the trappings of permanence to which she referred, trappings that went beyond owning the actual structure.

Buying the property would have meant applying for a loan. She wouldn't have had any money of her own. She would have had to have relied on Peyton's support. Support Peyton would have provided based on the comments Peyton had made at dinner, but she would have been indebted to him. She couldn't have left until that obligation was fulfilled. Once again Crispin's hypothesis proved true. Permanence bred obligation. It was odd to think how much this stranger's situation paralleled his own in spite of its own unique circumstances. It begged several questions.

How had a strikingly beautiful woman come to own a riding academy in the unlikely middle of sheep country? How was it that a stranger he'd never met until yesterday could sum up in a sentence his precise feelings over the property? She could empathise with him on this issue while his brother, who knew him better than anyone, could not.

Aurora cleared her throat in the silence. 'It's late and I'm sure you haven't eaten yet.'

Ah, the audacious woman was dismissing him. Of course. She'd want to get to her own meal. It had been a long day for her as well. She'd been up jumping before he'd even arrived that morning. It had been a long time since a woman had dismissed him.

'I'm sorry to keep you. I'll just see to Sheikh and be going.' Crispin piled the brushes into the kit, disappointment unexpectedly swamping him. He hadn't been ready to leave the stables. Or perhaps he hadn't been ready to leave her. They'd got off on the wrong foot yesterday. This brief exchange had been a pleasant contrast, but perhaps that was too much to hope for. Perhaps she was merely being nice.

'No, don't go.' Her words rushed out. 'I was going to suggest, before you interrupted me, that you stay for dinner.'

There was that sharp tongue he remembered. Crispin stifled a laugh on behalf of the truce they seemed to have struck. But he noticed she couldn't help sneaking that small rebuke in—'before you interrupted'. What might have been an invitation had now been turned into a suggestion, which everyone knew was just a step below a command. He was very familiar with 'suggestions'. Peyton made a lot of them.

But she wasn't Peyton and Crispin found he'd like nothing more than to have dinner with the intriguing Aurora Calhoun, who was less like his brother and perhaps more like him; a wanderer, a straddler of worlds. A kindred spirit? It was far too early in their acquaintance to draw that conclusion. There was too much unknown about her for him to make such leaps of logic. Still, it couldn't hurt to find out and Crispin intended to explore the potential.

Chapter Four

What was she thinking to invite the earl's brother to dinner? Because that's what he was, when all was said and done. Men with that kind of power were dangerous to her freedom. One word from him and Dursley could shut her down with a single sentence dropped at a dinner party.

She needed Crispin Ramsden to keep his distance. But, no, she'd invited a potential danger right to her dinner table. It didn't matter that he wore plain clothes and didn't put on aristocratic airs. It didn't matter that she wanted to see if he was worthy of riding Kildare. He was still brother to the earl.

In retrospect, she was amazed she hadn't seen the resemblance instantly. He had the earl's raven-black hair, the earl's dark-blue eyes, but not the earl's urbane demeanour and that made all the difference, distinguishing them from one another in spite of their inherited physical similarities.

Dursley carried his confidence like one born to it. Everything Dursley did was done with a polished veneer of sophistication. Not Crispin. He exuded a rough worldliness. She was certain his blue eyes had seen things that would render most men cynical about the world they lived in. The tanned skin of his face and hands suggested he was a man who knew how to work. The rugged planes of his face and the breadth of his shoulders affirmed this was a man used to hard living. He was no pampered prince of the *ton* regardless of who his brother was.

That was why she'd invited him to dinner. Like her, he knew a world outside the circles of rarefied society, he'd lived in its milieu and, like her, he'd been a participant in that world beyond the drawing rooms. When their eyes had met across the back of his stallion, she'd felt a connection; two wayward souls contemplating the merits of landowning against the odds of their natural tendencies. It would be somewhat comedic if the connection hadn't been so strong.

Aurora laid out the dinner things, setting the earthenware plates down on the plank table with a harder thud than she'd intended. She tried to remember anything, everything, Petra or Tessa might have mentioned in passing about Crispin. There was very little she could recall. She could hear his boots coming down the short hall from the stables. In moments he'd be there in her meagre rooms, thanks to her impetuous offer, and she would have to live with it.

'Smells good.' Crispin ducked into the room under the low-beamed door. He was all male, all six foot two and change of him. He positively radiated potent masculinity and Aurora wondered what other impetuous decisions she might be tempted to make before the night was over.

Crispin had taken time to wash off at the pump outside in the yard. Leftover droplets of water glistened at his neck where his shirt opened in a V, offering a small glimpse of his chest. She smiled at the interesting dichotomy he posed; a man who cared enough to wash before dinner, but had no use for the finer rules of gentlemanly dining that demanded he eat with a waistcoat and jacket on. Aurora doubted one ever caught Dursley dining in his shirt sleeves.

'Stew and fresh bread,' Aurora announced, placing a pewter plate laden with slices of dark country bread on the table. 'Sit down, I'll have the stew on in a minute.' She was suddenly conscious of his eyes on her, following her movements. She told herself it was to be expected. Her quarters were small—where else was he supposed to look? It was only natural to be interested in the one moving object in the room. That object just happened to be her.

Crispin straddled a bench on one side of the table and politely tugged off his boots to save the floor from dirt. 'You live here instead of the house?'

Aurora put a pitcher of ale on the table. He was referring to the cottage at the end of the drive. She'd never lived there even though it was part of the lease. 'I like being close to my horses.'

She turned to the fireplace and the hob where the stew pot hung, feeling his eyes peruse her backside. 'The cottage is too much work for me to keep up and run the stables on my own.' She set the stew down and began ladling it into bowls.

Crispin nodded. 'I like these rooms. They're cosy.' His gaze stole past her to the small bedroom. Aurora wished she'd taken time to drop the curtain that separated the bedroom from her main room. She wished she could read his mind as well as she was following his gaze. What was he thinking about her invitation to dinner? Was he thinking it was an invitation to something more? Did he think because he was the earl's brother and she a woman without rank that he was entitled to something more? Aurora rather hoped not, but her experience with Gregory Windham had proved that hope was often misplaced. She was now fully regretting her impromptu decision to invite Crispin Ramsden to dinner and the finer philosophies that might have motivated it. She had convinced herself last night this wasn't the right time for a flirtation. She should have stuck with that. But those resolutions had been quickly trampled.

'This is good,' Crispin said between mouthfuls. 'There's nothing like hot stew on a cold night.'

Aurora watched him thoughtfully throughout the meal. He ate much like regular people ate, people who were conscious of the cost of food and the effort it took to prepare a meal. He used a piece

of bread to sop up the remaining stew, making sure not a spoon-
ful went to waste in his bowl. It was odd to think of him as a man
who knew hunger, who knew of the simple things it took to survive the day when he could have chosen otherwise. His brother's
table was always set with plenty.

Aurora had not meant to pry, but the question was out of her
mouth before she could stop it. 'What do you do, Crispin? I mean,
where have you been for three years?'

Crispin set down his bread crust and fixed her with his sharp
gaze, a small smile playing at his lips. 'How badly do you want to
know?'

Aurora smiled back, recognising the game afoot. 'Ah, so it's to
be twenty-questions?'

'Precisely. I'll answer your questions, but you need to answer
mine.' Crispin reached for another slice of bread and buttered it.

'I work for the British government when they have need of me.
Before that, I used to be in the cavalry. I found I didn't enjoy the
life of a half-pay soldier. It was too dull for me. I saw some action
in the early twenties after Napoleon's defeat. But then my regi-
ment came home and I spent far too much time being Dursley's
brother.' Crispin swallowed some ale. 'There wasn't much to do
as Dursley's brother, as you can imagine. Peyton doesn't need any
help and, frankly, I'd rather be my own man. I didn't relish the idea
of being defined as the "spare". I was at a loose end. So, Peyton
introduced me to some friends at the Foreign Office and off I went
to look after British interests abroad.'

'Where did you go?' Aurora asked, feeling as if she'd been told
everything and yet nothing.

Crispin winked across the table. 'Princess, I could tell you, but
then I'd have to kill you.'

'You were a spy?' she asked evenly, deciding to push the boundaries of his disclosure.

'More like the government's best-kept secret,' Crispin corrected with equal seriousness. 'Suffice it to say that I've been places that don't exist on maps. I wasn't responsible for the kind of diplomacy that goes on in the glittering mansions of Vienna.' He drew a deep breath and steered the conversation away from himself. 'Now, it's your turn. Where did you learn to ride?'

'Ireland,' Aurora said shortly. She'd expected a question along that vein, but, like Crispin, she wasn't ready to divulge all the details. 'Now, as for my next question—' she began, leaning forwards on her elbows. But Crispin had no qualms about interrupting a lady.

'No, Aurora, finish your answer,' Crispin said shortly, arms crossed over his chest. 'You have to say more than that. Where in Ireland? I saw you jumping this morning when I came to get Sheikh. No one rides the way you do without extensive training.'

He had been watching. She'd thought she'd glimpsed someone at the entrance to the arena, thought she'd felt his presence. When no one had materialised, she'd chalked it up to silliness on her part. Of course no one could really feel another person's presence.

'I lived near Curragh in County Kildare. My father was head groom to a wealthy family.'

'You don't have an accent,' Crispin said pointedly as if judging the truth of her answer.

'Accents can be bred out of you.' Among other things. Once upon a time there'd been such hopes for her, thanks to the status of her mother's family. A moment of foolishness had dashed those hopes. Aurora rose from her bench and began collecting the dishes. The conversation was heading in a direction she was distinctly uncomfortable with. There were things Crispin didn't need to know about her. Those things could make no difference now. She'd negotiated her own peace with the past and accepted the consequences of her decisions, as lonely and as costly as they were.

She reached to take Crispin's bowl, but his hand shot out and his fingers closed around her wrist. 'Why did you invite me here,

Aurora? You won't tell me anything about yourself, so, clearly, getting to know each other was not the purpose.'

Aurora tried to pull away, but his grip held firm. 'You're hardly the epitome of a forthcoming gentleman,' she replied tartly. 'You can't or won't tell me anything about yourself either.'

'Perhaps that gives us something in common.' Crispin's voice was husky. 'Two people with mysterious lives.' His eyes moved to her mouth and back to her eyes.

Aurora's temper rose. 'Did you come here to seduce me?'

Crispin laughed softly. 'How could I do that? I had no idea I was coming to dinner until you invited me.' Silence rose between them. Aurora was acutely aware of the crackle of the fire, of the light drum of rain on the roof, of the intimate play of firelight on her walls, the only light in the room.

Crispin released her wrist and ran the back of his knuckles gently down the side of her cheek, skimming it low where cheek met jaw line. 'Would it be so bad if I did?'

'Did what?' Aurora's concentration waned, heat surging in her belly at the stroke of his hand against her cheek. She could not delude herself now. She had not asked him here for Kildare. She'd asked him here for herself.

'Seduced you, hmm?' His tone was languorous. He shifted on the bench, straddling it to draw her down to him. She went willingly, cognisant of her growing need. She'd been alone too long. It had been ages since she'd taken a lover. No one had compelled her. Even the ones that had were few and their appearances in her life had been irregular at best. Men were a luxury she could not afford. They'd shown themselves to be fickle companions on the path she trod.

Why not play his game a while? It's just one night and he's already said he's not planning to stay around. It won't upset your plans, a wicked voice in her head prompted. It was the perfect night for love, or what temporarily passed for it: English rain on the roof, a fire in the fireplace, a handsome man who knew the rules of this sort of engagement, a man whose hot kisses in the road had already proven he was a master of pleasure, a man who was the master of his own destiny just as she was of hers.

Crispin's lips replaced his hand against her cheek. He trailed a line of gentle kisses to her mouth where all gentleness ended. Intuitively, he seemed to know she would not tolerate being seduced. Seduction implied that she was somehow not an equal participant in the activity, that she needed to be led. Aurora revelled in the aggressive action of his mouth on hers.

She pulled his shirt loose from the waistband of his trousers and pushed the linen up, her hands running underneath the fabric, caressing the expanse of chest beneath the cloth. The man felt magnificent, all sculpted muscle beneath her fingertips.

He gave an appreciable shudder as her hands ran over his nipples. 'Perhaps I should be asking you the question. Did you invite me here to seduce me?' Crispin said.

Aurora gave a throaty laugh and repeated his earlier words. 'Would it be so bad if I did?'

'No,' Crispin breathed against her neck. 'It wouldn't be bad at all.'

But Aurora had no illusions about being in charge of the seduction. Crispin Ramsden was very clearly a man used to being in charge. He would let her participate; in fact, he gave every indication so far of liking a partner who was actively involved, but he would call the shots. Still, Aurora thought she'd see just how far she could go before he rebelled.

She shifted back on the bench and stood up, tugging on the neck of his shirt. He had little choice but to rise and follow her. Once on his feet, Aurora tugged him closer, pressing a full-mouthed kiss on his lips. She reached a hand between them to the front of his breeches. Her own aroused state grew at the feel of him, hard and ready behind the cloth.

'God, Aurora,' Crispin growled at the intimate contact. He propelled her backwards until she made contact with the wall. He grabbed both her hands and raised them over her head, manacling them in position with his strong grip. His eyes were dark and wild now, his hair erotically loose about his shoulders. There was an immediacy to his actions that warned Aurora they weren't going to make it to the bed. He was going to take her rough and fast against the wall.

A tremor of anticipation, of pleasure at the very thought of his impending actions, surged through her, firing her passion. The core of her was weeping already. She rattled her arms beneath his grip, wanting her hands free to touch him, to push his shirt off his shoulders, to drag his pants down his hips.

'Not yet, my impatient one.' Crispin was all seductive huskiness. His free hand deftly slipped the buttons of her shirt free. He pushed the folds of her shirt aside, only momentarily foxed by the presence of her thin chemise. He would have to let her arms go now, she thought gleefully. But Crispin surprised her. He bent his mouth to the chemise and held a bit of it between his teeth and ripped with his hand. The fabric gave easily, releasing her breasts to Crispin's hot gaze. He cupped them, one at a time, his breath coming in gratifying rasps. His arousal was full and complete. Only then did he release her arms, letting her work the fastenings of his trousers as he worked hers.

Aurora kicked out of her breeches, feeling his naked member brush against her thigh as she did so. She bit her lip to keep from crying out, so intense was her longing. It was time. Her body knew it was time. No part of her wanted to wait a moment longer. Crispin was lifting her, his hands fitted beneath her buttocks. She wrapped her legs about his waist, gripping his shoulders for balance. Crispin took her weight easily.

'Oh, God, you're so ready.' Crispin's member teased at her entrance, testing, planning its entry. She moved slightly, forcing him inside, taking all of him without a qualm. He slid deeply. For a moment, Aurora savoured the feeling of fulfilment his presence brought. Then he began the exquisite rhythm. This time she did cry out as he pleasured and tortured by turn. The roughness she'd anticipated came and she welcomed it. His mouth seized hers in a bruising kiss even as his body claimed hers against the rough-hewn wall.

Crispin was her only source of stability. She clung to him, feeling her body's passion crest, feeling his own need peak alongside of hers. He shuddered his release into her shoulder moments after she gave voice to her own. She was drained, so completely sated that coherent thought eluded her. The wildness of the interlude had gone, replaced by something more peaceful.

She tried to tactfully disengage her legs, sure that even Crispin's strength must be waning beneath the extended weight of her, but Crispin murmured a soft denial in her ear. Still buried deep in her, he carried her, carried them, to the pine-framed bed just beyond the doorway. He lowered them down on the soft blanket. She could feel his member stirring inside her, could see his body towering over her, possessive and primitive in the echoes of firelight from the other room. Her breath caught; her desire rose again.

'This time, we'll go slowly,' came Crispin's whispered promise in the firelit darkness.

Slowly or roughly, on top of her or underneath her, the night could not outlast Crispin, nor the insatiable desire he raised in her and fulfilled repeatedly until dawn when at last Aurora fell asleep, deeply and wholly sated with a pleasure beyond any she had felt before. She had to admit privately as she drifted off to sleep that when Crispin Ramsden had boasted there weren't men like him, he just might have been right.

Crispin dozed beside Aurora, more awake than asleep, savouring the languorous peace that held him in its thrall. The intense night of love-making had left him feeling unusually complete. The concerns he'd carried throughout the day were securely tucked away at the back of his mind. His thoughts were centred on the black-haired beauty breathing softly next to him.

She had been boldness personified the prior evening, matching him relentlessly in their passionate explorations. No lover he'd ever taken had been as compelling, as beguiling. Aurora moved against him in her sleep and Crispin felt himself harden yet again at the merest touch.

Perhaps what made her so appealing was that she'd established herself as his equal thus far. Last night she had taken what she needed and given him what he needed in return without him having to ask. There had been women who'd purported to be capable of such loving, but all had fallen short when put to the test.

That test wasn't complete, Crispin reminded himself. There was still the morning to contend with. He'd bedded women too who had no expectations of further commitment in the night, but who were suddenly struck with a need to attach themselves to him come the morning.

His gaze drifted the length of Aurora's form, half of it under the warm plaid blanket, the other half encased only by his arm. He knew her, and knew her not. He could no more predict what Aurora Calhoun would do when she awoke than he could predict next month's weather. The woman in his arms was a marvellous mystery. In most cases, he'd be happy to let a woman's mysterious history lie untouched. Not so with Aurora. He found he wanted to know everything about the groom's daughter from Curragh.

Aurora gave the semblance of waking, her body stretching against his. Crispin decided to encourage that behaviour, his curiosity getting the better of him. What would she do when she awoke? He didn't want to wait any longer to find out. Neither did his rising member, which apparently had a mind of its own and was fairly certain what it thought Aurora's response would be. Crispin pulled her firmly against him, letting his not-so-bashful erection greet her buttocks. He pressed a gentle kiss to her shoulder, his hand tenderly massaging a naked breast.

'Good morning,' Aurora murmured in appreciative, husky tones. She turned in his arms to face him, her hair spilling thickly around her in a morning mess of tumbled curls. He watched her study him through sleepy green eyes, the beginnings of a smile flirting on her lips. Then she tugged at him, pulling him on top of her, her legs parted, ready to take him into her. 'I want you, but we'll have to be quick. The horses need to be fed.'

Crispin laughed softly. 'They can wait a few minutes more, Princess.' He entered her, finding her slick and eager even after their night. He quickened at her welcome, his body throbbing with the intensity of his need. This coupling would indeed be swift and urgent. Such an outcome would please them both. Crispin could sense the fervent urgency in her body as well. She was impatient in her desire to achieve her ecstasy, like a child who couldn't wait for Christmas morning. Beneath him, she cried out.

'Almost, hold on, Princess,' Crispin groaned, his own pleasure about to overwhelm his sensibilities. Somewhere in his passion-addled mind a distant jangle of sound registered. He crested and let his release swamp him.

With a surprising amount of haste, Aurora squirmed beneath him. 'The horses are fine, they can wait,' Crispin repeated.

'I know they can,' Aurora said tartly. 'But the blacksmith cannot.' She gently pushed him aside and leapt out of bed, grabbing up clothes from where they'd fallen the previous night.

Crispin rolled over and folded his arms behind his head, appreciating the view of Aurora dressing at rapid pace. She struggled into her boots and strode out of the rooms into the stable. Crispin gave full rein to the smile he'd sought to suppress. He let out a low whistle and raised his eyes to the low-beamed ceiling. He could not recall having ever been thrown over for a horse or a blacksmith before. It was quite a novel experience really. He couldn't blame her. In her position, he would have done the same. Clearly, this was his kind of woman.

Chapter Five

Reality pierced the morning and Crispin suddenly remembered. The blacksmith wasn't coming. The realisation served to hurry Crispin out of bed. He dressed hastily. If that wasn't the blacksmith, then who was it in the stable yard? Recalling the conversation from the tavern made him worry for Aurora's safety.

Crispin moved into the dim hallway between the apartment and the stable, still tucking his shirt into his breeches. If he had to make his presence known, he didn't want to do it half-dressed and broadcast to everyone where he'd spent the night. Until then, he'd wait and watch. From his vantage point in the hall, he had a good view of Aurora in the yard.

'Where's Mackey?' Aurora stood her ground, arms crossed, disgust evident in her expression. Crispin could see that Mackey had not come. Instead, he'd sent one of his assistants, a drunken lout named Ernie who still looked hung over.

'He sent me to tell you he's not coming. He said to give you this.' Ernie fished a crumpled sheet of paper out of his pocket with grimy hands.

Aurora scanned the note, fighting to keep her temper in check. Mackey wasn't just not coming today, he wasn't coming again, ever. Well, she'd see about that.

'Shall I tell Mr Mackey anything?' Ernie sneered.

Aurora's gaze hardened. 'I'll tell him myself. Now, get off my property.' She turned hard on her heel and swept past the hallway where Crispin stood, not seeing him in the dim light of the passageway. She threw open the first stall door she came to and swung up bareback on the sturdy gelding. Her intentions were clear. Crispin could read her thoughts plainly. If she went cross-country, she'd beat the worthless Ernie back to the forge and get Mackey out of bed with a wake up he wouldn't soon forget. Crispin couldn't allow that to happen. Such an action would be more damaging than helpful.

Aurora flew out of the stables, urging the gelding to full speed. Concern spurred Crispin into motion. She had no idea what she might be riding into. She hadn't heard the anger directed at her last night at the tavern, but he had.

Crispin flung open the door to Sheikh's stall, not bothering to go back for a coat. 'Come on, boy, we've got to stop her.' He led the stallion into the aisle and leapt up on to the Arabian's lean back. Aurora hadn't taken time to tack up, so he couldn't either.

He sighted her veering off the Dursley road and followed, pushing Sheikh into a hard gallop. Aurora's gelding might not be fast, but she had a head start. Crispin had ground to make up. With sure feet, Sheikh overcame the distance.

'Aurora, hold up!' Crispin shouted over wind and hooves, pulling alongside the gelding.

The gelding slowed slightly in response to Sheikh's presence. Crispin grabbed for the reins and missed. 'What do you think you're doing?' Aurora railed.

'Saving you from yourself,' Crispin shouted, angrier than he'd recognised. 'You're a stupid fool if you think you can ride into the village and call the blacksmith to account.'

'Why is that?' Aurora's eyes flashed a lethal green. She urged the gelding to more speed. Crispin matched her.

'Because they mean to pillory you. Your secret's out. Mackey told everyone who would listen last night. I was there at the inn when it happened.'

That brought her to a full stop, the gelding's sides heaving from exertion. 'What secret is that?'

'The girls ride astride,' Crispin replied, choosing not to acknowledge the implication of her response. She had more than one secret. He wondered what they were? He would have to tread carefully if he meant to unearth them all.

'How did he know?' Some of the fire had gone out of Aurora's eyes, replaced by a sense of betrayal. 'Who would have told him? None of the girls would have. We're all sworn to secrecy. They know it would be the end of the academy.' She shot him a chilled look. 'Was it you? Did you tell him?'

It had not crossed his mind that she would suspect him. The idea that she would was a slap in the face of his honour. 'It wasn't me,' Crispin said defensively. 'It doesn't matter who told him. What's important is that you don't go charging into town and live up to their expectations. They're ready to think the worst of you and ranting at Mackey will only prove it.'

Aurora looked out over the fields, away from him. 'I haven't a choice. If I don't confront him, it will only serve to encourage him and others. They will think they have power over me, that they control what I do.'

Crispin stared at her. Had she not heard what he'd said or understood its importance? 'I hardly think it's a question of supply and demand. It's larger than that. Someone means to see you run out of business and out of town if possible.' He related what he'd heard at the inn.

Aurora snorted and fixed him with a baleful stare a lesser man might have shrunk from. 'Do you think I don't know that? Do you think this is the first time something like this has happened to me?'

The weariness in her voice cooled Crispin's anger. 'If you know what people are up to, what will shouting at the blacksmith solve?'

She didn't have a ready answer for his question. 'It will make me feel better.'

Crispin nodded. 'Breakfast might make you feel better too.' He was starting to feel the chill in the air now that the heat of emotions had been banked. He turned the horses in the direction of the stables.

Aurora put up one last effort at resistance. 'Breakfast won't solve the problem.'

Crispin grinned. 'No, it won't, but I always think better on a full stomach. I imagine you do too.'

Crispin stood at the hearth, making breakfast, intent on the cast-iron frying pan he held over the fire and presenting Aurora a glorious view of his backside encased in tight, buttock-hugging riding trousers. This morning was her turn to do the perusing, but the opportunity was lost on her. She might have found the sight arousing if she hadn't been so angry. Empirically, there was something positively alluring about a man cooking breakfast. She was just too upset to appreciate it at the moment. Her mind was reeling with questions and conclusions. The battle had begun. She knew this pattern well, but what had provoked it? Crispin was wrong about one thing—it *did* matter who'd told Mackey.

Aurora drummed her fingers on the table, trying to follow the twisting paths of her thoughts. Who had spilled the secret to Mackey? On his own, Mackey wasn't ambitious enough to care what went on at her stables.

'Someone's behind Mackey, using him,' Aurora spoke her thoughts out loud.

'A phantom puppeteer?' Crispin asked.

The very notion gave Aurora chills. 'It's the most likely reason.' She shrugged, trying not to let it show how much the idea bothered her. 'Mackey has no reason to know such a thing or to share it. Someone has given him a reason and the information.'

'Any ideas who might want that information spread around?'

'None comes to mind,' Aurora said quickly. It wasn't true. One *did* come to mind, but surely he had come to terms with her rejection long before this? Surely he would not stoop to such levels?

Crispin turned towards the table with the frying pan in hand. 'I've managed a fry-up of sorts.' Crispin scooped eggs and sausage from the pan and popped them on to two wooden plates. 'There's toast too.' He reached for the slices of bread he'd placed on a rack in the hearth, juggling them so as not to burn his hands as he placed them on the plates. 'And coffee.' He retrieved the tin coffee pot from the embers of the fire where he'd left it to heat.

'Delicious.' Aurora took a bite of the eggs, more than half-expecting they wouldn't taste as good as they looked, but they did. 'Where did you learn to cook like this?' It was better talking about food than potential enemies.

'The military,' Crispin said between bites. 'Most useful skill a soldier can have besides knowing his weapons. A soldier can't fight on an empty stomach, although most quartermasters I've known have been hard-pressed to believe it.' Crispin winked. He bit into his toast and sobered, returning to the earlier conversation. 'You should tell Peyton.'

Aurora shot him a hard look. 'If I went running to the earl every time someone troubled me, I'd never convince anyone I was anything more than the earl's lackey. How could people take me seriously as a horse breeder, a horsewoman, if I couldn't manage my own business? I would think you of all people would understand why I won't mention it. You don't strike me as the type to let your brother fight your battles.'

'*Touché.*' Crispin tossed her a wry smile. 'Still, don't let pride get in the way of your security.'

Aurora sensed a stalemate and tacitly returned to her eggs, but

Crispin wasn't content. 'Are you sure one of the girls didn't let it slip?'

Aurora shook her head. 'I am sure.' She gave him a hard stare. 'It is unconscionable to doubt my students.' Even as she said it, an uneasy suspicion crossed her mind. Her students *would* keep the secret to the best of their abilities, but she didn't expect them to withstand extreme punishments or worse in order to protect it. They were gently bred young women after all and had little experience with the darker side of life. Except for Eleanor Windham. The poor girl! Could Gregory Windham have extracted such a confession from her, his own daughter?

Crispin leaned across the table, answering her with equal steel. 'In my experience, Princess, secrets are leaked by those on the inside. Very rarely does an outsider stumble upon a secret and expose it. Don't be naïve, Aurora. In all likelihood, one of your girls told someone. Don't ignore the reality simply because it is unpalatable.'

Aurora rose from the table, pushing her unpleasant thoughts to the back of her mind. 'You presume too much on too short an acquaintance, I think, Lord Ramsden.' She gathered up the plates. 'Thank you for breakfast. I am sure you have responsibilities elsewhere that demand your attention.'

His hand seized her wrist. 'I will not be dismissed so easily.'

'Unhand me.' This was how it had all started last night; a quick touch, a little flirting, and she'd talked herself right into bed with the earl's brother. Now she had Sir Lancelot in her kitchen wanting to do good deeds.

'We're not finished. If you won't talk about the potential danger you're in, then we can talk about last night.'

Aurora groaned. The only thing she wanted to talk about less than the stables was last night. Conversations that began with 'about last night' never went well.

'What is there to mention?' Aurora sat down hard on the bench.

'I thought we were doing rather well not mentioning last night at all.' That was the way she preferred it at least, which was one reason she so seldom took a man to her bed. Worthy men always wanted to complicate matters afterwards with feelings of obligation. With feelings of obligation came feelings of ownership. Aurora fought back a shiver. She did not belong to any man. Not any more. Not ever again.

'What is there to mention?' Crispin repeated coolly. 'Surely it hasn't escaped your notice that we didn't take any precautions.'

Aurora looked him firmly in the eye, her tone brisk. 'I did not consider you a traditionalist in that sense. There won't be any complications. You needn't worry. Now, if you'll excuse me, I have classes to prepare.' She moved to go past him.

He put a staying hand on her arm. 'This discussion is not over,' Crispin said warningly. 'Peyton has set up a meeting with my steward today, but I'll be back and this discussion will be continued.'

Mackey finished his report and Gregory Windham rubbed his hands together in satisfaction. 'And the rest? Was your man, Ernie, able to scout out the stables last night?'

Windham preferred to believe that his indirect attempt to stir the villagers against her would be all that was required. However, in the event that failed by the month's end, he needed a back up. He'd hired Mackey's assistant to find out the night schedule of the stables in case more direct intervention, such as an injury to Aurora's prize horse, was needed. Such drastic measures were only to be used in desperation. He didn't want to risk anyone being caught in the act and have them lead the authorities back to him.

Mackey shuffled his feet. 'Ah, no, sir. She had company at the stables last night and we weren't able to get close without fear of being spotted.'

Windham steepled his hands, pretending apathy. 'Oh? Who might the visitor be?'

'Ernie says it was Crispin Ramsden, sir. Dursley's brother. I've never met him before, so I have to take Ernie's word on that,' Mackey hedged.

'I'd heard rumour he was home. You could have waited until he left. I pay you enough to wait all night if need be. Everyone has to go home some time.'

Mackey coughed, embarrassed. 'That was the problem, sir. He didn't go home. Ernie said he stayed all night.'

Envy shot through Windham in hot bolts. The Jezebel! She'd shunned his offer only to take Dursley's rakehell brother to bed instead. It sickened him to think of her with another, doing the things he'd dreamed of doing to her.

Windham carefully schooled his features to not give away any hint of his inward turmoil. Ramsden certainly complicated matters, especially if he was welcome in the hoyden's bed. Yet, this last transgression provided another nail in the proverbial coffin, proof that Aurora Calhoun was no better than she ought to be. It was his experience that women living alone without a man's guidance were prone to illicit behaviours. He would make sure that was the village's experience too. When he finished with her, no man would want her again except for him and she would be glad to welcome his attentions. When she was broken, finally, she would see that only he could save her.

'Did you know?' Crispin fixed Peyton with a challenging stare over the decanter of brandy in the empty dining room. He'd dined at Dursley Park that evening, but the excellent food and company had done little to appease his dark mood. The day had gone steadily downhill after leaving Aurora's.

The meeting with the land steward had been less than satisfactory.

'That the estate was entailed?' Peyton clarified. 'Yes, I knew.

I hardly thought it mattered since I assumed you'd be taking the property on permanently. If you kept the property, the entailment is irrelevant.'

'You knew I was thinking of selling. I told you as much over tea,' Crispin ground out. 'You could have mentioned that little detail then.' Entailed property was under legal restrictions with regard to how it could be treated or managed. Entail regulated what could be sold and what remained intact. In this case, the inheritor of the property was not allowed to sell it in whole or part. Such a restriction put quite a crimp in Crispin's plans.

'But that was before you'd seen the property,' Peyton dismissed the complaint easily.

'Yes,' Crispin groused. 'Before I'd seen it, before I was treated to your exquisite tour and well-calculated visit with the steward. You thought you could change my mind.'

Peyton shrugged. 'I thought *you* would change your *own* mind if presented with the right arguments, if you could be persuaded to see past your own stubbornness.'

'My dreams aren't yours, Peyton. They never have been. I am not a landowner like you or a banker like Paine,' Crispin said in a dangerously quiet voice. He didn't want to fight with his brother, but neither did he wish to build up Peyton's hopes with half-truths.

'What are your dreams, Cris? Surely you don't expect to work for the government the rest of your life.' Peyton's tone was hard with hurt.

'No, but I do like to travel. There's an exciting world out there, full of changes, and I want to be part of that. I'd prefer to consider the subject closed before I say something I'll regret later.' Crispin drew a deep breath. 'So, speaking of changes, is there another blacksmith in the area?'

Peyton raised an eyebrow. 'What's wrong with Mackey in the village? I've found him quite adept.'

'Let's just say I don't like his attitude,' Crispin answered.

Peyton thought for a moment. 'Thomas's father uses a smithy closer to Woodbrook, named Durham, I think. You can ask Thomas tonight for his direction.'

Crispin rose and took the opening. 'I will, then I think I'll head down to the inn for a pint.' He could not believe his small bit of good luck. Peyton wasn't going to call him on the carpet for not coming home last night. As well he shouldn't. His brother had to learn he was a thirty-eight-year-old man, not an adolescent with his first beard any longer.

At the door to the drawing room Peyton reached out a staying hand. 'By the by, Cris, you didn't say anything about Aurora's stables. Are they to your liking?'

'Yes.' Damn. He wasn't going to get off as easily as he thought. He heard the unspoken question behind his brother's casual query, but Crispin offered Peyton nothing more. If Peyton wanted to play lord of the manor, he would damn well have to ask the hard questions if he wanted answers.

When Crispin volunteered nothing more, Peyton meted out careful words. 'She is Tessa's friend. I would not want any awkwardness to drive a wedge between them. Even so, I would caution you. Aurora's past is full of shadows. She is a hard woman to know, I think.'

'I know someone very much like that: myself.' Crispin gave a wry grin, silently acknowledging that Peyton could have said much more. Once upon a time, Peyton *would* have said much more.

Crispin had made his way to the inn shortly after their brotherly exchange in the hallway. The other blacksmith's name was indeed Durham and Crispin planned to put that piece of information to good use. He ordered a pint at the bar and sauntered over to insert himself into the large group of people surrounding the blacksmith who'd disparaged Aurora the night before.

'Are you the local smith?' he asked as the loud conversation waned for a fraction. Crispin took a swallow of ale from his tankard.

'I am. My name's Mackey. You have a horse that needs shoeing? I shoe everybody's horses around these parts,' Mackey boasted. Someone gave a nervous laugh. The man was awfully bold. Crispin attributed his boldness to his ignorance. The man was new to the area since he'd left three years ago. It was obvious to Crispin the man hadn't attached a name to his face.

'Then why didn't you shoe Miss Calhoun's horses this morning?' Crispin asked bluntly. 'Is it the shoddiness of your work that causes her to seek out Durham? I'd like to meet this Durham fellow. My stallion will be needing shoes soon. Sounds like he might be quite the smith if she's willing to make the effort.'

His tone was friendly, but the implication of his comment spread through the room on a wave of whispers. If Dursley's brother was going to use Durham, perhaps Dursley's patronage would shift too. And if the Ramsdens used Durham, maybe the rest of them should as well.

Mackey's eyes narrowed—the insult was not lost on him. He understood the risk to his business even if he didn't understand with whom he spoke. 'If you understood anything, you would understand that I don't care to do business with "Miss" Calhoun. That woman is a slut in trousers.'

There was an intake of breath and the space around Mackey widened. Many might agree with Mackey when it came to Aurora Calhoun, and Crispin knew for a fact that they did. He'd heard the cheers when Mackey had made similar comments the night before. But to make those comments to the earl's brother's face about a woman rumoured to be the countess's friend was to invite trouble.

Old timers in the village who'd watched him grow up knew

Crispin Ramsden was a good man in a fight and the speculation about what he did during his years abroad only heightened that belief.

'You slander a woman whose only crime is to make her own way in the world,' Crispin said calmly. True, he didn't know Aurora that well in their short association, but that much he felt sure of and his gut instinct was seldom wrong.

The blacksmith grunted, rolling up his sleeves with a snort. 'Ah, a Lancelot is among us.' He spat on to the floor. 'Who do I have the honour of pummelling tonight?'

Crispin grinned, setting aside his coat. He didn't usually enjoy throwing his title around, but tonight was an exception. 'Crispin Ramsden. *Lord* Crispin Ramsden.'

To cover his surprise, Mackey snarled, 'That explains it, then, why you're willing to take a beating for the whore. You're defending her because you're infatuated with her. Rumour has it you spent the night between her legs.' Mackey swung a giant fist at Crispin.

Crispin neatly dodged the blow and came up lightly on the balls of his feet, his fists up and ready. 'I'm defending her because a lady should never have to beg.'

Crispin planted the man a facer and the fight was fully engaged.

A few broken benches later, Crispin shouldered into his greatcoat, tossed some coins on the bar for the damages and headed out into the night, leaving the blacksmith passed out under a table. He swung up on to Sheikh's back. It was late. He'd stable Sheikh and be on his way back to Dursley Park. Aurora would be asleep. In spite of his promises to continue their conversation from the morning, he wouldn't bother her.

That was the plan at least, but it was a hard plan to follow when his mind seemed obsessed with conjuring up images of Aurora as she'd been last night, all hot passion in his arms, her dark hair hanging down her back, her hands on him, her body answering him with its pleasure.

This was turning into one devil of a homecoming. When he'd stood atop the stairs at Dursley Park, thinking how serene and orderly everything had looked, he had no idea such turmoil would lurk beneath the surface: an estate he couldn't sell, a village looking to run an independent woman out of town, the very same passionate, stubborn woman who had landed in his bed. Crispin smiled to himself, remembering last night. He'd made his bed, he'd happily lie in it... And he'd thought he'd be bored.

Chapter Six

'Rory, can I talk with you?' Eleanor Windham asked tentatively on her way to the tack room, a saddle in her arms after lessons.

Aurora turned from the horse she was currying with Petra. She smiled fondly at the girl. 'Of course, Eleanor. Come to my apartments after you've put your saddle away.'

The girl nodded gratefully and hurried off. Aurora was glad Eleanor had persisted in speaking with her. She'd known Eleanor wanted to talk, needed to talk, but she didn't relish the upcoming conversation. Eleanor's situation was a difficult one. It would take an inordinate amount of character and courage on Eleanor's part to change the outcome. Additionally, she suspected Eleanor held a certain amount of hero-worship for her, that the girl saw her life as being considerably more alluring than it was. If Eleanor thought she was going to tell the girl to run away and forsake the marriage Windham had arranged, the girl would be disappointed.

Aurora had tea going by the time Eleanor had put away her tack and come to the apartments. 'Now, tell me everything.' Aurora offered her a mug and motioned for her to take a seat across from her.

Eleanor gratefully took the mug. 'I can't stay long, though. My father will be angry if I'm late.'

If Gregory Windham hadn't been so concerned with losing a chance for his daughter to ride with the earl's ward, Aurora knew he would have withdrawn Eleanor from the riding school out of spite if nothing else after her pointed rejection of his indecent proposal.

'He watches me all the time now.' Eleanor nervously sipped from the heavy mug.

Beastly man. Such controlling behaviour had been at the core of Aurora's dislike. Couldn't the man see that managing his daughter in this strict manner was having the opposite effect? The harder he tried to rein her in, the harder Eleanor strained to get away.

Aurora's temper began to simmer. She wanted to march straight up to the Windham place and give Eleanor's father a rather large piece of her mind, the piece that demanded women not be treated as chattel. Yet that would do Eleanor no good, nor would it help the other girls if she got herself expelled from yet another village.

With a calm that hid her inner turmoil, Aurora said, 'Does this have to do with the engagement?'

Eleanor nodded, her face pale. 'My father and the baron feel a woman's place is in the home.' She looked down at her hands and shrugged. 'It's understandable, of course, there's a lot to be done. I have my trousseau to put together. There's linens to be embroidered and invitations to be penned.'

'You don't have to excuse them, Eleanor,' Aurora said softly, but there was unmistakable steel to her voice. 'A woman's place is where she wants it to be. If embroidering your trousseau gives you pleasure that's fine, but if it is an activity that is used to make you a captive in your own home, then that's wrong. There's no excuse for it.'

Eleanor looked up and offered a wan smile. 'Perhaps I am being too emotional. My father says that I am. Perhaps I haven't given the baron a fair chance. It's true that I hardly know him. Perhaps when I am mistress of my own home, with my own family to look after, things will be different.'

Aurora put down her mug and reached for the girl's hands. 'That's an awful lot of "perhaps".' The baron was much older than Eleanor, an heirless widower with a less-than-pristine record about town. 'Don't you think you should find out if the two of you are compatible before the wedding instead of after?'

'Father and the baron think whatever rough edges exist between us will be worn away with time,' Eleanor offered the empty platitude.

Aurora could hear the doubt in the girl's voice. Tessa had told her how Eleanor's father had scoured London for an unmarried peer of any rank who'd be willing to take an attractive daughter of a wealthy gentleman off his hands. The Windhams were landed gentry, but nothing more; they'd coveted a title for generations. Now they would have it, at the expense of Eleanor's happiness.

'What do you think, Eleanor? Do you think that is true?'

Eleanor's usually soft gaze hardened with something akin to bitterness. 'What does it matter what I think or if I think? If I disagreed, what could be done anyway? It's a woman's lot to be thankful to marry at all. I'll have to make the best of whatever my marriage brings. At least for once I will have done something to please my father.'

Eleanor's despair swamped Aurora. She knew that feeling of hopelessness all too well. She knew how overwhelming and complete it could be, this giant abyss that swallowed you up whole, body and soul, until you forgot who you really were. But what could she say to the girl?

Difficult was an incredibly inaccurate word to describe her own journey away from a marriage that had nearly destroyed her. In good conscience, she could not advocate running away. Eleanor was clearly desperate and would jump at any option. In her desperation, Eleanor wouldn't see the long-term costs such a choice entailed. Yet, she did not want to let Eleanor down. To tell her to give in to the marriage, to give up being true to herself, was counter to everything she'd taught her students.

A little of the bitterness receded and Eleanor pushed back a length of blonde hair that had come loose. 'Tell me what to do, Rory. I want to be like you. You go where you want, you do what you want, you live on your own, with no cares, no responsibilities beyond your horses. No one owns you. Tell me how you did it.'

Her passionate outcry invoked a level of panic in Aurora. She had to be honest with her. She'd not told her students much of her own story. Indeed, she seldom told her tale to anyone. Eleanor had to be made to see the grim realities of Aurora's own choices.

'No, you don't want this, Eleanor.' Aurora shook her head emphatically. 'There's a price for my freedom. Choosing to be on your own is not an easy sop to your problems. You're not just on your own, you're alone, Eleanor. Alone.' She never misrepresented her choice as an easy elixir to the choices women faced. Leaving Ireland and her father had been the most harrowing choice she'd ever made.

'I know that doesn't mean anything to you right now,' Aurora continued. 'I didn't fully grasp what being alone meant when I first decided to leave Ireland. For me, it meant a chance to start over, to be my own person.' Aurora shook her head. 'I learned there's no starting over, Eleanor. There's only going forwards. I will never marry. I will never have a husband. I will never have children. There's no man who wants a woman who has put herself outside society.'

'But you have Tessa and Petra,' Eleanor protested.

'For now,' Aurora said quietly. 'Eventually I will move on, that's the nature of my life.' She didn't bother to elucidate the finer points as to why she'd have to move on or that in most cases it was an issue of force.

'You have your horses,' Eleanor continued to argue.

'For now,' Aurora repeated. 'I will have them for as long as I can afford to care for them and for as long as I can ride them. Some day, I'll be too old.'

She met Eleanor's gaze squarely, wanting the girl to see the naked emotions in her eyes, wanting her to see that she spoke a deep personal truth. 'That some day scares me, Eleanor. There will be no pension for me when I'm too old to work, no family to take me in, no husband to guarantee my financial security. You're right. I have my horses. My riding is all that stands between me and abject disaster. It's a very thin bulwark, Eleanor, and I know it will not last. I know what awaits me and I would not willingly send you down that path.'

'You're saying you would have chosen differently if you could do it again?' Eleanor knit her brow, clearly perplexed by this surprising disclosure.

'I didn't get to choose,' Aurora replied evenly. Jonathon had decided to discard her. It had not been her choice at all. She had loved him and he'd only thought he loved her. To be fair, he had loved her, just not enough.

'Then what I am to do?' Eleanor asked.

'I can't tell you what to do.'

That made Eleanor angry. She rose in a huff, tears threatening. 'It's not fair. You tell us to be true to ourselves. You tell us to be masters of our futures and now you sit there and tell me to accept this marriage. You taught us to think for ourselves!'

'Yes, Eleanor. I've taught you to think for yourself. You should no more look to a man's opinion to decide your future than you should look to mine,' Aurora answered her firmly, sternly, rising to meet the angry girl. 'I've taught you to trust yourself, to trust in your own strength. One doesn't have to forsake society to be strong. You're a far stronger young woman than the one who first came to me. Embrace that strength now.'

The reference to her growing skill brought a smile to Eleanor's face. 'I could hardly ride when I first started coming here.' Her rage started to ebb as Aurora's words penetrated her thoughts.

Aurora nodded. She remembered vividly Eleanor's father marching the timid girl into the stables and demanding she be given training. The boorish man had originally liked that the instructor was a woman. No inappropriate, unvetted male would be working with his daughter, laying his hands on her. All that had changed once she and Windham had taken each other's full measure and found the other lacking.

Eleanor was calmer. She wiped at an errant tear on her cheek. 'Thank you, Rory. I understand things better now. You've given me some hope. I must go home and think what to do.'

Aurora walked Eleanor to the stable yard and saw her off in the pony trap, then was surprised to see Tessa riding down the drive. She smiled, glad to see her friend. Tessa hadn't been out since the newest baby had arrived and Aurora had missed her visits.

'Hello, Tess. What brings you here today?' The sky was overcast and Tessa could have picked a nicer day to come over if this was a social call. Aurora hoped her friend didn't bring bad news. 'I think I saw Petra still in the stables.'

'I'm sure you did. I can hardly pry her away from Peyton's stables when she's not over here.' Tess swung down from her saddle with ease and hugged Aurora. 'It's been a long time. It feels good to be out on my own a bit.'

'I can imagine.' Aurora smiled. 'You look wonderful. Motherhood agrees with you. I would never guess you'd just had a child and a third one at that.' Tess really did glow, Aurora decided, taking in her friend's appearance. Her dark-blue habit showed off her eyes and her figure to best advantage. Tessa Ramsden was clearly a happy woman.

Aurora did not begrudge her friend an iota of that happiness, but a twinge of regret kicked at Aurora's insides. She would never be a happy mother, escaping for a few hours from a house full of boisterous boys. Aurora tamped it down. She was being maudlin because of her discussion with Eleanor.

'Let's go inside. I have hot water on already for tea. We can chat while Petra finishes up,' Aurora offered. 'Tell me what the boys are up to.'

They made small talk about the nursery antics of the Ramsden twins until Tessa's tea was ready. Then Tessa settled herself in a chair and got straight to business. 'Was that Eleanor Windham I saw leaving?'

'Yes, she's distraught over the engagement.'

'Understandably so.' Tessa sighed into her tea. 'That man her father has picked out has little regard for anyone, not even a wife. He'll get an heir on her if he can and tuck her away in the country while he goes straight back to London to spend her fortune.' Tessa's tone was brittle.

'At least he'll leave her alone for a good part of the year.'

Tessa raised her eyebrows. 'That doesn't sound like you, my dear, willing to settle for a marriage of absence.'

'I told her the truth, that this life of mine is not as desirable as it might look from the outside, and gave her the usual talk about her rights; that her opinion matters, that she's entitled to her own life.' Aurora shook her head. 'I do not know if Eleanor has the fortitude for making such a choice.'

'Few of us do.' Tessa nodded in agreement. 'I could have Peyton talk with her father. If it's not too late, I could send her to London to stay with Eva and Aunt Lily. With the right kind of Season, she might find someone she cares for and who might also appeal to her father. Her father's idea of combing the marriage mart was a bit heavy-handed. With Lily's guidance, the search might go better.'

'That would be most kind, Tess.' Her friend's offer was heart-felt, but Aurora doubted it would make a difference. Eleanor's arrangements were too far gone for Windham to back out now. Still, she would not cheat Eleanor of a chance, no matter how slim.

Tessa poured another cup of tea. 'Now that's settled, I came to tell you that Peyton and I are throwing a party, a small ball.' She drew an invitation out of the small bag she carried. 'It's in official honour of Petra and Thomas's engagement and it will be a chance to celebrate Crispin's homecoming. He's been gone so long there are lots of new faces to meet, especially if he's going to take over Woodbrook.'

Aurora focused on the invitation in her hand, the heavy cream paper, the crisp black ink in Tessa's precise hand. Better to look at the invitation than to give anything away in regards to Crispin. The last thing she needed was Tessa playing matchmaker. 'You don't want me there. This will be a formal affair. I'm not sure your guests will want to fraternise with the local riding instructor.' She usually eschewed formal invitations to Dursley Park. Dressing up and pretending to be someone other than the head-groom's daughter hadn't worked out for her in the past. She had no desire to repeat such foolishness.

Tessa shrugged as if oblivious to any of the rumours that swirled around Aurora. She wasn't, of course. Tessa knew exactly what the neighbourhood thought of a woman setting up on her own. It was only through Tessa's tenacious sponsorship that the school had become acceptable. Aurora knew too that many of her pupils came from families who hoped for a chance to enter the earl's social circle by riding with Petra, his ward. That dangling carrot and the effort she'd taken to keep any breath of scandal from her name had worked wonders. Now, the episode at the inn threatened to undo her hard-won peace.

Tessa leaned forwards reassuringly. 'I want you there, Rory. Petra wants you there to celebrate her engagement and surely Crispin would appreciate you being there.'

Aurora snorted at the last. 'Why would he care? He hardly knows me.' Surely Tessa didn't know what had transpired between her and Crispin.

Tessa fixed her with a knowing gaze. Aurora knew she'd come to the heart of the visit. 'I am told Crispin broke Mackey's nose at the inn last night. He threw in a black eye for good measure.'

Aurora took a sip of tea to disguise her surprise. That was bad. Clearly Tessa attributed the brawl to her and that was worse. 'Men tend to brawl.' Aurora shrugged, hoping she sounded compelling in her apathetic response. 'Perhaps Mackey spilt his beer.' So, that's where he'd been last night. Not that she'd expected him to return last night, she hastily reminded herself. They had no claim to each other beyond their one night.

Tessa arched her brows and Aurora knew her ruse of objective nonchalance hadn't worked. 'It wasn't about beer, Rory. I have it on good authority it was about you. I must say, my dear, you do have quite an effect on men.'

Aurora choked on her tea. So much for hiding her surprise. How could she have misjudged him so badly? She'd thought she under-stood Crispin Ramsden. She never would have taken him into her bed if she'd thought he'd feel compelled to brawl on her behalf. She'd wanted a lover, not a hero.

It was the height of hypocrisy to warn her off confronting Mackey and then go and do the very same thing himself. He could be quite sure there would be a reckoning when he returned to the stables. Whatever possessed him to behave like that?

Tessa studied her over the rim of her teacup. 'Crispin's more of a gentleman than he leads most of us to believe. If a lady's honour were at stake, he would not hesitate to defend her. He was raised by Peyton, after all.' She set her cup down. 'What's going on, Rory?'

'Mackey announced to everyone at the inn that my students ride astride and wear trousers.' Aurora explained.

Tessa reached for her hand with a comforting squeeze. 'I'm so sorry, my dear. I know how hard you've tried.' She paused and then asked quietly, 'Do you know who told him?'

Aurora nodded and confessed her suspicions. 'I think it was Windham. It's unlikely Mackey would discover anything like that on his own. I fear Windham may have bullied the secret out of Eleanor. I know she wouldn't volunteer that information readily.'

'Is that all?' Tessa probed gently. 'Is that the sole reason Crispin broke Mackey's nose? Goodness knows it's enough.'

'It's the most significant, but Mackey also refused to come out and shoe my horses.'

'That must be why Crispin wanted the name of another black-smith at dinner the other night,' Tessa mused in a considering tone. 'He's certainly put himself forwards as your champion in such a short time.'

Aurora experienced a moment of panic. It was bad enough to discover Crispin had broken a nose over her. 'Tessa, I don't like where your thoughts are headed. This is not the time for me to be pursuing a relationship. You know how important the race at St Albans is to me. I cannot afford a distraction.'

Tessa laughed. 'I am sure you're the only woman who has ever referred to Crispin as a distraction. Most of them find him to be something more.'

Aurora shot her a stern look and Tessa stood up, correctly assessing that Aurora could not be pushed further on the subject. Tessa brushed at her skirts, 'Right. Well, I'll go fetch Petra and we'll be off before the rains come.'

'It was good to see you, Tess.' Aurora hugged her friend again.

'I'll see you this weekend for the horse fair,' Tess replied. 'And you have to come up to the house for dinner soon. The table seems empty with Eva gone.'

Aurora gave a non-committal nod, seeing the invitation to dinner for what it was. She would have to make it very clear that she had no permanent designs on Crispin Ramsden no matter how many noses he broke.

* * *

Aurora waited until she heard Crispin moving about in the stables later that night, helping Sheikh to bed down. She squared her shoulders and marched out to meet him. There was no sense in waiting. She began without preamble, 'I don't need a man to defend me.'

Crispin turned to face her with equal solemnity, unbothered by her blunt approach. 'I disagree.'

His cool response fired her anger. How dare he stand here in *her* stables and second-guess what *she* needed? He should not have insinuated himself into her affairs. He should not have tried to manage her business. He should not have told her to do one thing and then gone and done another. There were so many things he should not have done she could scarcely list them all.

'Why should I worry about making a spectacle of myself when I have you to do it for me?' she stormed. 'You had no right to go down there and beat Mackey to a bloody pulp because he didn't show up, no right at all when you'd counselled me against taking action.'

'I didn't punch him because he missed his appointment. I told him you were thinking of using the smithy closer to Woodbrook.' Crispin's voice was calm, neutral against her indignant tones. 'I suggested that if the smith, Durham, was to your liking I might shoe Sheikh there as well. I think it made him nervous to think that he could lose the Dursley patronage and in turn lose some business in the village.'

'Why did you punch him?' She'd already heard Tessa's answer to that, but she wanted to hear Crispin say it.

He fixed her with his blue stare. 'He called you a whore in no uncertain terms.' Crispin's gaze did not waver from hers.

Aurora fought the urge to flinch. She'd been called such harsh names before, but that didn't make them any easier to digest. She paced the short length of the room. 'He's entitled to his thoughts.'

'Not when he voices them out loud,' Crispin retorted.

'No, *then* he's apparently entitled to your fist in his face,' Aurora argued fiercely. She had to make this man understand that one night did not entitle him to any claims or require any obligations.

'Why are you defending him? Do you want him to turn the village against you? Do you not care that you're slandered?' Crispin's cool demeanour was fading.

Aurora wanted to blurt out it was the only option open to her under the circumstances. She'd badly misjudged Dursley's brother. She'd thought the rumours of his devil-may-care lifestyle meant he had little regard for responsibility, that he'd be less like Dursley. If she'd known he'd react this way, she might have found the fortitude to resist. She did not need a responsible man in her bed no matter how virile he was. The very thought was nearly as disturbing to her as the growing situation in the village.

'Let me be clear, I don't welcome your interference, no matter how well intended it may be. Did you stop to consider that by standing up for me you proved to them that I was all they believed? You cannot defend me and not expect people to think there's something between us.' Aurora slapped her hand against her thigh in agitation. 'Why couldn't you leave well enough alone?'

Crispin studied the woman pacing before him. They weren't exclusively talking about the situation with the blacksmith any longer. Leaving well enough alone extended to the nature of their liaison. They'd tacitly decided there were to be no expectations, no obligations, and now there were, put there by others who would make assumptions about their relationship. He could see the world through those jaded, conservative eyes. In their narrow minds, it would be quite a coup for a woman like Aurora to keep the earl's brother in her bed.

Regardless, he'd not been raised to allow a woman to be treated with the disregard Mackey had shown Aurora. Even amid the shambles of his parents' marriage, there had been some semblance of courtesy between them as a matter of honour.

'Are you going to answer my question?' Aurora snapped.

'Not to your satisfaction, at any rate. I will not apologise for acting chivalrously on your behalf,' Crispin said staunchly.

'Chivalry is dead,' she ground out before turning on her heel and stalking out of the room.

Crispin watched her go, chuckling softly under his breath. He understood why she was angry, although he disagreed with her sentiments. What he didn't understand was why she was so adamant about being left alone even at the cost of her own reputation. Anger was often a convenient mask for fear, but he had no inkling what she might be afraid of. For that matter, he had no inkling as to why he'd behaved as he did on such short acquaintance.

True, Aurora Calhoun was a rare beauty and a confident lover. Both were appealing qualities to him, but those qualities alone did not make her unique. He'd had plenty of affairs with attractive, assertive women before. There was something deeper that drew him to her, that nebulous connection of understanding that had driven him to her two nights ago instead of going home to Dursley Park. In all his experience, he'd never felt such an immediate and intense connection to anyone. It was both novel and frightening. But he was not one to shrink from an adventure and that was exactly what Aurora Calhoun was proving to be.

Chapter Seven

She was supposed to be mad, Aurora reminded herself two days later, cantering side-saddle beside the Dursley carriage on a well-dispositioned sorrel mare from her school string. But it was hard to remember that when the weather was fine and she was on her way to a horse fair.

The reason for her hard-to-remember anger rode casually beside her, chatting easily with the occupants of the coach and acting as if they hadn't quarrelled at all. He should be apologising.

To her.

He'd overstepped his boundaries and interfered unnecessarily. Such a breach of their arrangement had to be addressed. One night didn't entitle him to any claims. But it was difficult to hold on to that reasoning when Crispin looked so handsome with his dark hair sleek and pulled back, accentuating the striking planes of his face, and his clothes so well turned out. He didn't look like the dusty traveller she'd met in the road with his rough clothes. Today he was dressed like a lord in clean buckskin riding breeches, white linen and an expensively tailored dark-blue riding jacket that left no doubt as to the natural excellence of his physique.

He'd be an incredible specimen of manhood if it hadn't been for the little issue of his over-protective, misguided 'chivalry'.

'Sheikh's a prime-goer, no doubt about it.' Crispin was saying to Peyton, who rode inside the carriage with Tessa, Thomas and Petra. Inside was where Crispin was supposed to be as well. She'd ridden the sorrel mare expressly for that reason. She'd thought to avoid his company.

'I had to win him twice. The nomad chieftain who'd wagered him had second thoughts about parting with him, after he lost of course. Seems our nomadic friends have different notions of fair play than we do.'

'Did you steal him back?' Petra asked, looking pretty in pale blue and leaning out the window. Aurora hadn't meant to be sucked into the story, but it proved irresistible. She leaned forwards to hear better in spite of her resolve to the contrary.

'No, we had a knife-throwing contest and I was much more prepared, shall we say, for that competition.' Crispin gave a light chuckle that belied the underlying danger of the situation. Aurora could well imagine a darker scenario than the one Crispin alluded to.

'Then the horse is an Arabian,' Peyton put in.

'Yes, and about nine years old, just coming into his prime. I was thinking of racing him. The larger Arabian nostrils enhance his ability to breathe. That gives him an advantage in endurance races. He's ripe for steeplechase and for stud.' Crispin shot her a naughty look and Aurora flushed, letting her horse fall behind the carriage while she fought images of a stallion of another sort who seemed quite ripe for stud too. It appeared horse and master had a lot in common.

She didn't have her privacy for long. Crispin's horse soon dropped back to join her. 'You were supposed to be riding in the carriage,' Aurora said without preamble.

'So were you.'

'That's why I didn't,' Aurora's answer was short.

'You wanted to avoid me,' Crispin said. 'I guessed as much.'

'You're a wicked man to upset a lady's manoeuvring.'

'You're still upset about the other day,' Crispin charged.

Aurora kept her gaze straight ahead on the back of the Dursley carriage. 'You over-reached yourself.'

'I don't feel the need to apologise for defending a woman's honour.' Crispin's answer was simple. 'However, I do regret any inconvenience my actions may have caused. It was not my intention to imply that something untoward existed between us.'

Aurora struggled not to grin. 'You're absolutely right. That's definitely not an apology, not even close, but it's probably the best I'll get.' Her anger was vanishing rapidly.

'Probably,' Crispin affirmed, then adroitly changed the subject. 'Are you looking or buying today?'

'Buying, I hope. I need a good jumper for intermediate riders. My girls' skills are growing beyond the school horses I have.'

They made no move to catch up with Peyton and Crispin was happy to have Aurora to himself. When had he ever found a woman so compelling? Crispin was well aware how mundane that question really was. In their days apart, he had become more certain that he'd never encountered a woman that held anything like the level of Aurora's appeal. However, he was usually quite careful not to give women a chance to become too alluring. A quick bedding sufficed to quell any penchant for attraction that he might be tempted to feel for a woman. Not so with Aurora.

His regular method of disposing of potential attachments had soundly failed in her case. The early physicality between them had merely served as a gateway to increased desire—a desire his body had recognised immediately and his mind was only now beginning to acknowledge; he was definitely interested in what lay beneath the surface of Aurora Calhoun's lovely face and exquisite body. Today, that exquisite body was neatly showcased in a dark-green riding habit and proving that Aurora was as capable on a side saddle as she was riding astride.

'I wouldn't mind picking up a horse with Irish bloodlines.' Aurora's conversation broke into his daydreams.

His mind was decidedly not on horses at the moment. Crispin dragged his thoughts away from peeling Aurora out of her riding habit and applied himself to the conversation. 'The lines of an Irish draughthorse give a hunter a strong chest for jumping.' Maybe his fascination with Aurora was due to their mutual interest in horses.

Aurora gave a smug laugh. 'That's a pretty good answer for someone who wasn't paying attention. Just where were your thoughts, Crispin Ramsden?'

'I was admiring how lovely you look today.' Crispin opted for the gentleman's version of the truth.

'In my habit or out of it?' Aurora gave a coy sidelong glance.

'Well, out of it, if you must know.' Crispin leaned towards her and said in a low voice, 'What's the point of imagining you in it when I can see that for myself?'

The fair was early in the year, but no less attended because of it. Dedicated horse lovers had thronged to the wide, flat plains of the fairgrounds, eager to see a fine display of horseflesh outside of Tattersalls and Newmarket. Crispin deduced almost immediately as they strolled the venue that the event was definitely designed to appeal to a higher calibre of horse aficionado. The men who had horses to sell here were professional breeders. This was not a random event open to all and sundry, but a well-planned affair for an exclusive group.

Aurora must have guessed in advance. It explained why she'd opted for the habit instead of her usual attire. She must have known some modicum of social conformity was in order. The habit wasn't all that Crispin noticed about Aurora. She moved with grace and confidence, not the least intimidated by the wealthy surroundings or the elite calibre of horseflesh. She could have passed as a peer's lady. Indeed, when she walked next to Tessa it was hard to tell which one was the countess. He would not have guessed it of her, although seeing her today, the demeanour fit her perfectly. It was no sham, adding to the beautiful mystery of who was Aurora Calhoun?

The fair offered a perfect opportunity to delve into that mystery, to remind Aurora of his interest in her, and Crispin did it most subtly. His hand provided a gentle pressure at the small of her back, guiding her through the rows. He took every opportunity to murmur comments in her ear or to touch her arm. The public would see nothing untoward in these small gestures, but Aurora would not mistake the attentions his body paid hers. He would make sure of it.

Crispin stopped to watch her assess the legs on a bay hunter. She ran an expert hand down the fetlock and picked up the hoof to inspect it. Daughter of an Irish groom? Her expertise certainly suggested it. He thought of her comment about accents being bred out of you. What of her mother, then? Perhaps a woman of some rank who had the misfortune to fall in love with a man of inferior station? Aurora had clearly been educated in horses and in much else that women of common birth did not bother with. She had enough knowledge of bookkeeping and finances to run her own business. Both skills suggested education in mathematics and literacy.

'What does this horse eat?' She stood up and faced the owner squarely.

'Clover, alfalfa.' The owner shrugged.

'Too much clover, is my guess. The colt's diet is too rich for him. His hooves look like they've been struggling with laminitis.'

The owner looked as if he were about to argue with Aurora. Crispin bent swiftly and examined the front hoof. Setting the hoof down, he brushed his hands off on his trousers and met the man's gaze with an even stare. 'The lady's right. That's my assessment as well.'

'Well, he did have a bout of it this winter. The new stable boy overfed him,' the owner offered as an excuse. Crispin nodded congenially, his point having been made. With a hand at Aurora's back, he ushered her on to the next stall.

'He wasn't going to admit it,' she fumed under her breath.

'All's well that ends well, Princess,' Crispin murmured in her ear. 'There's other horses. We both know you were right and he knew it, too, even if he didn't want to acknowledge it.'

He spied a stand selling sweets and steered them towards the booth. 'What do you like?' Crispin asked, gesturing to the vendor that he'd take a bag of peppermints.

'You should guess.' Aurora tossed her head.

'Hmm. Toffee?' Crispin guessed.

'Too sticky.'

'If practicality is your consideration, I'd say licorice drops,' Crispin guessed confidently. 'A most practical sweet if ever there was one; good for the digestion, freshens the breath and not sticky.'

'You're teasing me.' Aurora pretended to be offended.

'Just guessing, but I'm right.' He grinned triumphantly. 'I'll take a bag of licorice and some toffees…' he turned to Aurora with a wink '…for the twins.'

She made a face of mock disapproval. 'Very sticky business. I don't think Tessa will approve.'

Crispin shrugged carelessly and laughed. 'I'm their uncle. It's my job to spoil them with treats their mother doesn't allow.'

He paid out the coins for the treats and they strolled away to find a place to indulge in the sweets. 'How did you get to be such an expert on uncles who spoil nephews?'

'My father's sister, Aunt Lily, had a very nice husband who did his best to look out for us.' Crispin led them over to a wide-trunked tree, away from the crowd. He opened one of the bags and offered it to her, watching her enjoy the treat. He helped himself to a peppermint.

'I can't remember the last time I had sweets.' Aurora giggled and then covered her mouth with her hand self-consciously.

'Nor me,' Crispin admitted. 'Sweets weren't a priority in the places I've been lately.'

'Being home has its luxuries,' Aurora said.

Crispin let his eyes linger on her lips. 'It certainly does. You're not still mad at me?' His voice was little more than a whisper.

'No, not really. Why?' she breathed softly in anticipation.

'So I can kiss you.' Crispin feathered a kiss against the column of her neck, feeling her pulse ignite with desire.

'Do you think my favours can be bought for licorice drops?' she flirted in hushed tones.

'Can they?' He subtly backed her around the tree trunk.

Aurora's eyes fired at the tantalising banter. 'Kiss me and find out.'

This time his kiss took her lips, his tongue tangling slowly with hers, savouring the heat of her mouth, the sweet licorice on her breath. His hand slid behind her neck, cupping her head, the pad of his thumb stroking the curve of her jaw. His need for her spiked. He'd give anything for a bed to lay her down on and relieve them both of their heightened desire. Had it only been three days? It felt like an eternity since he'd bedded her. His body ached with deprived passion.

She moaned beneath his mouth, as frustrated as he by the futility of their situation. The tree might hide a stolen kiss, but Crispin knew better than to risk anything more, although all his instincts clamoured for him to pull up her skirts and take her.

Her hands were at his trousers. He covered them with his own. 'We must not risk it. Besides, we haven't found you a horse yet,' he joked in husky tones that indicated the solution was as unsatisfying to him as it was to her.

'I'll never get my reward at this rate,' Aurora grumbled good naturedly a few hours later. She'd found only one horse worthy of her academy by the middle of the afternoon, a sleek Hanoverian warmblood perfect for intermediate riders, but as they came up on the last roped-off section on the outskirts of the grounds Crispin heard Aurora suck in her breath and exclaim, 'That's the one!'

He followed her gaze to the knot of horses in the section and immediately knew the horse to which she referred. A chestnut stallion stood out from the rest, his mane braided tightly to show off his long neck. Even at a distance, the presence of thoroughbred blood was obvious in his lean body.

Aurora wasn't the only one drawn by the horse. A small group of people had gathered around. A few were asking questions about the other mares, all nice-looking horses with an air of above-average quality. Most were interested in the stallion.

Aurora broke from his side and shouldered her way to the front of the decidedly male crowd. Crispin uttered an oath under his breath and made his way forwards to Aurora's side in time to hear the owner say, 'Perhaps one of my mares would suit a lady such as yourself better. This stallion is a man's horse.'

Crispin stifled a groan. Aurora would not stand for that. True to form, Aurora's dark head shot up from her examination of the chestnut stallion. 'I assure you I'm man enough for the horse,' she said coldly.

'He's not for sale,' the owner said pointedly.

'Not for sale to me? Or to anyone?' Aurora queried, unwilling to be denied and far too savvy to be dismissed with such a comment. 'I rather doubt we're all assembled here to stare at a horse that is unavailable.'

Crispin fought the urge to intervene, but he'd learned the hard way what Aurora thought about chivalry. He might still have to step in, but not yet.

'Not to you. I don't sell to women,' the man said bluntly, turning towards another interested customer. 'His dam is from a thoroughbred line and his sire is a Cleveland Bay. He's six years old, a good jumper.'

Not to be ignored, Aurora moved around to the horse's mouth and pulled back the horse's lips to see the teeth. 'Six, you say? More like eight,' she interjected into the conversation from which she'd been excluded.

The man whirled on her. 'Are you calling me a liar?' A hush fell over the gathered group.

'I'm merely calling you mistaken,' Aurora retorted boldly. 'It makes me wonder what else you have mistaken.'

Crispin put a warning hand on her arm. 'Aurora, please, have a care,' he murmured.

Someone moved towards them, parting the crowd, drawing Aurora's gaze. For a moment, Crispin thought he felt Aurora step closer to him.

'Miss Calhoun. Of course it is you causing this flurry of conflict.' The speaker who'd emerged from the crowd was a tall, slender man with fading brown hair and cold grey eyes that assessed Aurora with unswerving scrutiny.

'Windham,' Aurora said curtly.

'You must be Crispin Ramsden.' The man turned his attention to Crispin. 'I've heard a lot about you.'

'I cannot say the same for you.' Crispin met the man's icy glare evenly. Whoever this man was, he made Aurora uncomfortable.

'My daughter rides at Miss Calhoun's academy. Surely you're not thinking of purchasing this animal for your students to ride?' Disapproval was evident in his voice, his gaze returning to Aurora again with something akin to disdain. 'I must inform you that the horse is not for sale because I have already purchased it. I am merely here to pick the beast up.'

'How much was the horse?' Crispin asked the owner, who reluctantly named the price Windham had paid.

'I'll give you triple,' Crispin said confidently.

The crowd gasped.

Windham interrupted. 'The horse is sold, Lord Ramsden.'

But the owner was greedy and Windham had already lost. 'I'm sorry, sir, the price has just gone up.'

The little knot of people murmured over the exchange and began to drift away, sensing the excitement was over. Windham fixed his anger on Aurora. 'I hope my daughter is not being treated to unladylike displays during lessons such as the one I witnessed back there.'

The man's eyes could freeze hell, Crispin thought wryly, treating Windham to an assessment of his own and finding him lacking in any personal warmth. Beside him, Aurora did not back down to the none-too-subtle scolding. 'I assure you, Mr Windham, your daughter is not being "treated" to anything unfit for her,' Aurora answered squarely, but Crispin had to stifle a chuckle. He was quite sure Aurora spoke the truth and even more certain that Mr Windham and Aurora would absolutely disagree on what exactly constituted 'unfit' for Eleanor.

Her sharp answer earned a flicker of surprise in Windham's grey eyes. 'Well, I should hope so.' It sounded as if he held little hope at all of that being the case.

Crispin made arrangements with the horse trader and turned to go. Windham still lingered, his hand reaching out to grab Crispin's arm as he passed. Crispin tensed and shot the man a pointed look. 'Take your hand off me,' he growled.

'Pretty expensive ride you bought yourself. Hope it's worth it,' Windham spat derisively, his gaze flicking to Aurora. Not even the most forgiving of gentlemen could overlook his intended meaning. Crispin bristled, his fist tensing. If this hadn't been England, he would have gone for his knife already.

Peyton materialised beside him, a restraining hand on his shoulder. 'You forget yourself, Windham,' Peyton said with the steel command of a man long used to being obeyed. 'Cris, we need to go. Tessa and the others are waiting at the carriage.'

Gregory Windham clenched his fists in frustrated silence. How dare the earl intervene! How dare Dursley choose to champion the no-account Aurora Calhoun over a fellow gentleman. There they'd stood arrayed against him, Aurora between the two all-mighty lords with that haughty tilt of her chin, saying nothing while Dursley's rakehell brother simply outbid him on the horse.

Windham understood now there was a glaring oversight in his original plan. Provoking the villagers against Aurora Calhoun wasn't enough. Today's demonstration proved it. She didn't need the villagers to provide her with services. Anything she lacked, Ramsden would see that she had it. If he was to succeed, he needed to go directly to the parents of her students. He needed to ruin the riding academy by removing the students. Ramsden could do nothing about that.

Windham grimaced. When he was done with Aurora, he might go after Ramsden too and pay him back for his shabby treatment of a fellow gentleman today. This was far from over.

Chapter Eight

'You can't punch them all.' Aurora flopped down into one of her worn chairs, fixing Crispin with a stare. Dusk approached outside. Crispin had stayed after they returned to help her feed the horses for the evening and to make room for the big hunter to be delivered tomorrow.

He pulled off his boots and took the other chair. 'What is Windham to you, Aurora?'

'That's a cheap strategy, answering a question with a question,' Aurora commented, trying to divert the conversation.

'So is evasion,' Crispin replied. 'The man's dislike of you is palpable. I'm not convinced people randomly hate at that level of intensity without reason.'

Aurora drew a deep breath. The subject was deeply uncomfortable. 'He thought he fancied me. He asked me to be his mistress.' Gregory Windham was a man of intense extremes. Many people described his tendencies as merely puritanical. She'd go much further and describe them as cruel.

'You rejected him and he didn't take the notice well,' Crispin surmised grimly. 'Could he be behind the occurrences in the stables?'

Aurora bit her lip. 'I hope not,' she said quietly. It was her greatest fear that the culprit was Windham. He was a formidable enemy, secretive and dangerous. There was no limit to the lengths he would go and she wasn't certain she could fight him under those circumstances. She suppressed a shudder.

'I didn't mean to bring up any unpleasantness,' Crispin said.

Aurora shrugged, wishing she could just as easily shrug off Gregory Windham's threatening presence. 'Thank you for what you did today. I will pay you for the horse.' It galled her that business had to be done that way, a man's way, but it had almost been worth it to see Crispin tread on Windham's arrogance.

Crispin grinned. 'Who says I'm giving him to you?'

'I do.' Aurora smiled, dispelling the gloom of the prior conversation.

Crispin held her gaze for a moment and Aurora could feel desire flickering to life in her core. It was positively unnerving to think he could stir her passion so thoroughly with a single look.

To her surprise he rose. 'I should be going. I'll be down in the morning. I confess to being eager to see what the big horse can do.'

Ah. The horse. Her surprise was replaced with understanding. He could not initiate love-making tonight without worrying that it might be seen as claiming his dues for payment on the hunter. The gallantry of his choice touched her unexpectedly.

Aurora stood and went to him. 'Don't you dare look at me like that, Crispin Ramsden, and think you can leave.' He couldn't initiate love-making, but she certainly could.

She ran a hand along his chest, watching his eyes darken with anticipation. 'Why don't you stay so you can be here when the horse arrives?'

She could see him struggle to hold on to his restraint and she enjoyed having the upper hand at the moment. She had no illusions about that lasting. 'Aurora, I didn't come here expecting to stay. I would not want you to think I had made such presumptions.' They both knew precisely which presumptions he meant.

'No expectations,' Aurora whispered huskily. 'This is not about owing, Crispin. This is about wanting.' She slipped her hand to his trousers, cupping him boldly through the cloth.

'No expectations,' Crispin repeated, his voice hoarse with mounting desire, although it was clear to both of them his body had plenty of those at the moment.

'No obligations.' She pressed her body against his, her hands grabbing his cravat and pulling him towards her.

'Surely we need one or two rules?' Crispin queried, his hands resting on her hips, his need to demonstrate a modicum of restraint satisfied and discarded now that they had reached an understanding.

She gave a seductive smile. 'You have to learn, Crispin Ramsden, when you're dealing with me, there are no rules.'

Crispin gave a throaty chuckle. 'Princess, what's the fun of that? Without rules there's nothing to break.'

Crispin woke in the night, instantly alert. Beside him, Aurora slept peacefully unaware, but years of military training taught him such a response could only mean one thing—an intruder. In immediate reaction, his hand crept over the edge of the bed to his boot. He deftly withdrew the thin blade from its hidden sheathe inside the leg of the boot and listened to the night sounds of the stable: the horses shifting in their sleep, hay rustling with their movements.

Perhaps the sound had been nothing more than a restless horse. Crispin strained to listen through the usual sounds of a stable at rest. Then he heard it: booted footsteps. Someone was in the stables.

The audacious bastard.

Crispin rolled out of bed in a fluid motion, blade at the ready, navigating the dark room from memory. He gained the corridor joining the stables to the apartments, flexed his hand around the hilt of his knife and advanced. Crispin entered the stables and made out the outline of a figure. 'Halt where you are and drop any weapon,' Crispin demanded in commanding tones.

The man took one look at Crispin in the dim light and bolted for the turn that lay between them and his freedom.

Crispin ran towards the intruder, racing to the only exit, but his speed was hindered by his bare feet. Still, at the turn, Crispin made a valiant effort and launched his body at the man. They both went down, but Crispin's hold was tenuous on the ankle he'd managed to grab. The intruder wiggled and scrambled like a man possessed, screaming at the top of his lungs in his attempt to wrest free of Crispin's hold. Fear can be a powerful ally at times and it gave the man an extra dose of strength. Crispin's hold on his foot slipped, the man yanked and scrabbled to his feet, running and stumbling the length of the stable, yelling all the while.

Crispin gave chase, but at the door he had to desist. Bare feet would be no match for the shod intruder over outdoor terrain. 'Dammit,' he swore, leaning against the door frame to catch his breath.

Lantern light fell over Crispin and he turned to find Aurora standing in the middle of the aisle, a dressing robe hastily thrown on, her dark hair loose and tousled about her. 'Whoever that was, he was screaming like an Irish banshee.'

In spite of the circumstances, Aurora put a hand over her mouth and started to laugh, then raised her eyebrows. 'Oh, my, now I can see why.'

Crispin drew his brows together in consternation. Laughter seemed a highly inappropriate reaction to his efforts. He'd tried to stop an intruder for her after all.

Then he followed Aurora's gaze down his torso and realised what the intruder had seen. The hilarity of the situation was not lost on him. Crispin lowered his knife, relaxing his hand. 'Considering the circumstances, I'd scream too.' He grinned at Aurora. He was completely stark naked.

'He was nude! He had a knife and he was nude!' Ernie repeated for the countless time, shifting nervously from foot to foot, relating his horrific encounter with Crispin Ramsden the night before.

'So you've said.' Gregory Windham drummed his fingers anxiously on the scarred dining table in the private parlour he'd reserved at the village's Bull and Boar tavern. He listened impatiently to Ernie's garbled accounting of the bungled outing, keeping one eye on the clock. He was expecting important guests at three. Ernie needed to leave before they arrived.

Ernie was patently incompetent, but Mackey had declined to be involved in any further episodes at the Calhoun stables after Ramsden's arrival, citing some damnable ethics about breaking and entering. Ernie didn't suffer from any such malady, but Ernie was a fool.

'If you'd been caught, you could have jeopardised all our plans. You must be more careful next time.' He slid two coins across the table to Ernie, who took them reluctantly.

'We agreed on more,' Ernie stammered.

Windham fixed Ernie with an unpleasant stare. 'I pay for success. Now go. I have other business to attend to.'

Ernie would still have his uses. Ernie would be the perfect scapegoat if anything went wrong. A slovenly man whom most villagers generally viewed as lazy, people would have no trouble believing the worst of him. It would be a simple matter to lay all the trouble at his doorstep if the need arose. Until then, Windham needed better henchmen.

It was just as well that he was about to marshal new troops to his cause this afternoon. These respected citizens would be henchmen and not even know he was using them for his personal gain.

The men arrived at three o'clock sharp, eager to fill their plates with Windham's largesse. A full buffet lay spread before them in the private parlour, bottles of wine neatly decanted at their tables. Windham had spared nothing in return for their attention.

Before today, these men knew each other by name only and only because they lived in the same area. After today, Windham would give them something more upon which to further their acquaintance. Their daughters and wives rode at Aurora Calhoun's riding academy for women. He wanted to put a stop to that. If he told these men what he knew, what he suspected and what he'd seen at the horse fair, Gregory Windham felt certain he'd achieve his goal. They would conclude as he had: a woman like Aurora Calhoun was dangerous and must be stopped.

'Gentleman,' he began once they'd helped themselves liberally to the wine, 'thank you for meeting with me. We do not know each other well, but we all have something in common. Our women ride at Miss Calhoun's stables and I think there are some concerns you need to know about if the women we care for are to continue associating with Miss Calhoun in that venue.' He watched the men exchange looks. One or two heads nodded. Gratified, he continued. 'There are rumours that the women wear trousers to ride, and that they practise riding astride.

'Now, I am not one to put too much credence into fantastical gossip, but neither am I one to overlook reality when it slaps me in the face. Miss Calhoun makes a regular practice of wearing trousers herself. She rides astride in public places. Based on these displays, it is difficult to believe there isn't any truth to those rumours.' There was an outbreak of murmured agreement and vigorous head nodding. Gregory Windham put up a hand to forestall comment just yet. He had more he wanted to say.

'I might not even be worried about such riding practices if they were limited to the stables,' he said with a feigned amount of magnanimity. 'What worries me most is how these behaviours are spilling over into other practices that extend beyond the stables.' He went on to recount Aurora's confrontation with the horse trader. 'I do not think this occurrence is an isolated incident. I think Aurora Calhoun not only acts like a man, I think she incites the girls at the riding academy to do likewise. My Eleanor, a quite biddable girl most of the time, has actually voiced her resistance to the match

I've arranged with Baron Sedgwick. She's become uncontrollable these days and I can only attribute such behaviour to Miss Calhoun.'

Mr Twillinger, an older man in his fifties, spoke up. 'I've recently re-married—a man must have his heir, you know. I'm not getting any younger and I want a son to leave the business to, but my wife has other ideas. She wants to travel and spend time in London. She's young and I expect a little flightiness from her until she learns her place, but egads, she wants to look at my ledgers and help with the finances! I have to draw the line somewhere.'

Gregory Windham nodded his sympathies. Alfred Sykes and Latimer Osborne spoke up, voicing similar thoughts about their daughters.

'I do not think we're alone, gentlemen,' Gregory put in when the men had a chance to share their own misgivings, adding fuel to his carefully stoked fire. 'I've discovered there are tradesmen in town, like Mackey the blacksmith, who are uncomfortable doing business with Miss Calhoun.'

'What shall we do?' Alfred Sykes asked.

'It's very simple. We pull our daughters and wives out of the riding academy. Miss Calhoun cannot spread her poorly conceived ideas about women's entitlement if there's no one to listen.'

There was a thoughtful pause and Gregory held his breath. Then Mr Twillinger, the businessman of the group, nodded his agreement.

'I like it. Straightforward, but effective. Although, for it to work, we've all got to do it. It's got to be like an embargo. It won't work if only a few drop out.'

'We've got to be subtle,' Mr Sykes put in. 'We should pull out gradually so that it's not obvious. We need to avoid offending Dursley.'

'If we're successful, we might not only shut down the academy, we might even run her out of business.' Mr Twillinger rubbed his hands together.

'And good riddance that will be.' Windham nodded with puritanical solemnity. He'd worked diligently over the years to secure the family wealth. His credo had always been 'do it to them before they do it to you', and that was precisely what he intended to do to Aurora Calhoun.

He'd worked too hard arranging a marriage for his daughter that finally catapulted him into the ranks of the peerage. An upstart female with odd notions of feminine propriety would not ruin his plans now. The strategies he and the men devised tonight would be the next step. He thought about the inquiries he'd sent off after Mackey's run in with Ramsden's fist and a thin smile spread across his usually dour face. Soon, he'd know all Miss Calhoun's secrets.

Chapter Nine

It was happening again. Aurora set aside the tack she was repairing and sank down on the hard wooden bench in the tack room, her mind still on the break-in. Nothing had been taken or damaged as far as she could tell, but her sixth sense suggested something had happened. She just didn't know what. Something, somewhere in the stable, had been jeopardised.

All for the sake of getting to her. Aurora put her head in her hands. The last two days had been quite taxing. She and Crispin had spent the day after the break-in sorting through the tack and saddles looking for potentially damaged pieces. Nothing had turned up so far. Crispin must have caught him almost immediately.

That raised another concern. Crispin had awakened, but she hadn't, not until the intruder had started his unholy caterwauling. It galled Aurora to think she would have slept through all of it. If she'd been alone, would she have awakened in time or would she have discovered the treachery only after it was too late? If she'd been alone, would she have had the strength to subdue the attacker?

She liked to think she'd slept so deeply because of the rather vigorous 'activities' she and Crispin had engaged in beforehand, but even that road wasn't safe to travel. If that was the reason, then Crispin was definitely becoming a distraction she could ill afford, especially if it put the very safety of her horses and students in question.

The only bright spot during the last two days was the arrival of the two new horses. She and Crispin had put them through their paces in the arena and managed to take them out on a cross country ride. The big Cleveland Bay and the Hanoverian warmblood had proven to be worthy additions. Even now, she smiled at the memory of the wind in their faces, racing across the fields, jumping stone fences and tumbled-down portions of walls. The impromptu steeplechase and what had followed afterwards beneath a wide-spreading oak tree had both been exhilarating.

She and Crispin. That phrase had cropped up in her thinking quite often since his arrival. She really needed to do better. There was no such thing as she and Crispin. She did herself no great service in pretending there was. It would be too easy to think she could lay her burdens on his broad shoulders. He'd been there when the intruder struck purely by luck. She could not assume he'd be around for ever. Indeed, he'd made it clear he did not intend to be around more than a few months, let alone for ever. He would go and she would be left on her own to fight her own battles alone. Again. *The way she liked it.*

Aurora set aside the broken bridle pieces. She'd fought this battle before on her own. This would not be the last time. It would happen again and again until men were no longer threatened by a woman's abilities, but this time it would be different. This time, they wouldn't run her out. She had her own land now, her own stables. True, Dursley held the lease, but there was protection in that. This time she wasn't an itinerant instructor relying on others' land and horses for her lessons. This time, men might forbid their daughters from practising with her, but she had other outlets now. She could breed horses, sell horses, train horses. Oh, yes, this time, thanks to the backing of Tessa and Peyton, it would be different. No one would be able to push her out, to erase her presence. They would have to acknowledge her existence and her ideas. This time, she simply wasn't going to go away.

Aurora clung to that bittersweet thought and headed to her apartment. It was time to get cleaned up for dinner. Tessa had invited her to Dursley Park for a quiet family evening. Of course, it wouldn't truly be quiet, not with the twins around. None the less, the thought of being surrounded by Tessa's family brought a smile to her face and a flutter to her belly. Crispin was part of Tessa's family and Aurora had no reason to believe he wouldn't be there.

Aurora poured cold water into a basin and splashed her face, hoping to drive some common sense into her head. She had to stay focused where Crispin was concerned. He'd turned out to be far more dangerous than she'd imagined. Beneath his rugged exterior and his reputation as an adventurer, there'd been a gentleman. Not the kind of gentleman one was used to seeing, the kind that dressed up in fancy clothes and emasculated themselves with stiflingly proper manners, but a gentleman all the same. He'd stood up for her. At the horse fair, he'd treated her with all the respect due a lady and yet had left her breathless with the evidence of his desire in ways a gentleman seldom dared.

Aurora shivered, not so much from the cold washing water, but from the memory of his touch. At the horse fair, his light touches at her back, on her arm, his low voice murmuring at her ear, had all been intoxicating. In some ways, those caresses had been more provocative than the intimacies they'd already shared, recalling to her the possibilities of what could be.

What *could* there be? She strode to the trunk at the base of the bed and pulled out the gown of plum merino wool she saved for visits to Dursley Park. She dressed quickly, letting the pragmatic side of her mind cool her passions. Beyond the passions they'd already shared in bed, there was little else that could come of being Crispin Ramsden's lover. She'd known from the beginning there was nothing to expect other than mutual physical pleasure. What more did she think there was?

Aurora did up the tiny buttons that secured the high neck of the gown. It was easier to think there wasn't anything else when he'd merely been an adventurer, the type of man who loved and left when hearts were broken. She could understand that man. She didn't understand the man he'd revealed to her by accident or intention, the man who was both rogue and gentleman. Rogues didn't have expectations, but gentlemen did and that was far more hazardous than any trouble she could have foreseen the day he'd ridden into her life. In that regard, she could only disappoint him.

Crispin Ramsden did not disappoint, Aurora thought, sliding into the shadows of the hallway outside the Dursley nursery to watch the enchanting scene unfold. Inside the warm yellow room, Tessa's two little boys clung to the back of their 'pony', squealing loudly and often while Crispin 'cantered' about the nursery. Aurora put a hand to her mouth to stifle the laughter that bubbled up within her. Not laughter *at* Crispin, but a laughter that wanted to burst forth and join in the fun, a laugh of pure joy. However, she knew her presence would break the spell so she remained in the hall, watching.

'You're a better pony than Daddy,' Alexander exclaimed, tugging on a handful of Crispin's long hair. 'You have a mane.'

'Again! Again!' Nicholas yelled.

'I told you to cut that hair, Cris. Consider it penance,' Peyton ribbed from the rocker where he held the littlest Ramsden with the consummate ease of a loving father.

Crispin shot Peyton a long-suffering look and took off around the rug for another circuit, the boys yelling gleefully on his back. 'Who would have thought two year olds could wear one out so completely in such a short matter of time,' he complained playfully. It was clear to Aurora that he didn't begrudge the boys a minute of his time. He adored the little scamps and when they got older, she didn't doubt their uncle would show them a trick or two. *If he was around,* she silently amended. Peyton and Tessa had waited years for him to come home. Who knew how long he'd stay? Crispin had been plain spoken about the fact that he had yet to make up his mind about the property or how permanent his situation here would be.

Crispin collapsed on the floor and rolled the boys off him. 'The pony's tired. The pony needs to rest.'

'And boys need their supper if they want to grow up strong.' The nurse bustled forwards to gather up the boys.

This was the perfect time to announce her presence. Aurora moved from her dark alcove, but Crispin's words stopped her and she slid back into hiding.

'I envy them, Peyton. They've got a great father in you.' Crispin stretched out on the floor, trying not to lie on top of soldiers and blocks.

'They've got two good uncles in you and Paine,' Peyton replied, shifting the baby to his other arm.

'That's amazing considering we didn't have much of a father to model ourselves after.' There was a mournful sarcasm to Crispin's tone.

Peyton gazed down at the baby boy in his arms. 'Tess says that loving isn't something you learn. She says it's something you feel. The longer I know her, the more I think she's right.'

Aurora shifted uncomfortably in her hiding place. The conversation was intensely private. She felt like a spy with her inadvertent eavesdropping. Crispin was such a complete man in and of himself that she had not stopped to ponder about his family beyond Peyton and Tessa. To hear him speak of his parents was deeply personal and, she sensed, quite rare. She should announce her presence, but her curiosity over what Crispin might reveal next kept her rooted in the hall. There would be no more disclosures.

At that moment the twins broke back into the room. 'Get up, horsey!' they yelled, mobbing Crispin on the floor. He promptly seized them and began a loud tickle-wrestling match that drowned out Tessa's arrival in the hall.

Aurora jumped at Tessa's light touch on her arm.

'I didn't mean to startle you,' Tessa said, following Aurora's gaze. 'Ah, that explains what you're doing out here.' She gave a low laugh. 'It always moves me to see Peyton with the children. It's a side of him no one gets to see but me.'

Light from the nursery illuminated Tessa's face. The love encased in that expression for Peyton was humbling. Aurora could not fathom the depth of trust, of respect that must flow between them for that much love to flourish. To open oneself up to such a possibility was to open oneself up to incredible risk, a risk she'd only taken once and for which she'd suffered greatly.

'Crispin is good with the boys,' Tessa continued. 'He's a natural father, only I suspect he doesn't know it yet. I hope time with the twins will help him recognise that side of his life while he's here. Peyton's greatest wish is for Crispin to take on Woodbrook and build a family there.'

It had been on the tip of Aurora's tongue to ask if that was also Crispin's wish, but the boys' squeals escalated and Tessa gathered up her skirts and waded into the fray.

'Oh, dear, boys, let your uncle come downstairs.'

Crispin looked up through the mess of hair hanging in his face. 'All right, you heard your mother.' Crispin sat back on his heels and set Alexander on his feet, smoothing down the boy's wrinkled smock. Aurora's throat knotted at the kindly gesture. She thought of Tessa's remarks. Crispin as a father? Why had she not seen it before? Of course Tessa was right. Crispin's patience with the horses, the way he doted on Sheikh, taking great pains to personally see to Sheikh's care, all spoke to the amount of devotion Crispin possessed—an amount of devotion he went to great lengths to hide. Aurora rather doubted overt devotion worked well in his occupation.

She felt his eyes move past Tessa and catch her staring. She blushed furiously, glad that the high neck of her gown served to hide a bit of the flush.

'Good evening, Aurora. You're just in time for the fun.' Crispin rose from the floor, his hands going to his hair in a hasty attempt to retie the leather thong that had come loose. He was dressed casually in a shirt, dark-blue waistcoat and breeches, having made no attempt to dress for dinner although Peyton had. Against Peyton's subtly polished veneer, Crispin was wildly handsome. Even Crispin's sensuality was bold. No one could look at him and doubt this man enjoyed bed sport or that he could deliver everything his wicked eyes blatantly promised, just as they were doing now at the sight of her.

Aurora's blush heated. Did he not have a care for others in the room? No one but Crispin would even contemplate seducing a dinner guest in the nursery beneath the watchful eyes of his brother. She shot him a look of censure for what little good it did. His hot, roaming gaze was giving notice, making her feel as if her wool gown was of the thinnest gauze. He wanted her and he intended to have her before the night was out.

Dinner was no better. Aurora tried to keep her mind on the excellent meal laid before her, but apparently no venue was sacred to Crispin when he had seduction on his mind. There was the usual assortment at the table—Petra and Thomas, Annie and Cousin Beth, Tessa and Peyton—but Crispin was heedless of their presence, or perhaps they were all incredibly naïve. Or perhaps she was incredibly randy.

'Aurora, is your mare in season?' Crispin asked from across the table where he was treating her to the spectacle of his hand absently caressing the stem of his wine glass.

Aurora choked on her wine. Why wasn't anyone else choking? She scanned the table, half-expecting Peyton to raise a scolding eyebrow. No one appeared the least bit shocked. Did no one see what he was really asking? 'I expect two of them to be in season soon.' Aurora held his gaze, determined to play his game to its fullest.

'There's only one I'm interested in,' Crispin replied easily, his foot suddenly rubbing against her ankle. Aurora stifled a jump. How would she explain to everyone why she'd suddenly leapt up from the table?

Petra innocently entered the conversation. 'Aurora's got a quarterhorse mare that would be excellent with Sheikh.'

Petra's comments were the perfect distraction. Aurora shot Crispin a wry grin. She could not sit there and let him get away with this one-sided game of his. Besides, games were more fun when shared. It was time to go on the offensive. Hands were off limits since they were across the table, but she had her feet and her mouth.

She caught Crispin's eye and took a bite of the succulent game hen, making sure to flick her tongue across her lips. During the fish course, she kicked off her slipper under the table and gave him a dose of his own medicine that turned his eyes to blue flame. While they waited for the fruit platter, she decided using hands wasn't a foregone conclusion after all. She just couldn't use them on him. She coyly toyed with the high buttons at the neck of her gown, absently unbuttoning and re-buttoning them. When the fruit platter came at the end of the meal, she bit into a huge strawberry and let the juice stain her lips before she licked it off.

As soon as it was decently permissible, Crispin pushed back his chair. 'If we're not standing on formality tonight, I'd like to take Aurora to the portrait gallery and show her a few of the ancestors.'

Even Aurora shot him an incredulous look. Had she really reduced him to such levels? Who would ever believe Crispin had suddenly developed a love of art? But Peyton merely nodded. 'I don't think you've ever seen the family paintings in all the time you've been here, Aurora. Be sure to see the one of our great-uncle and his stallion. You may have heard of him, he won a few races in his day.'

Crispin came around to her side of the table to escort her and Aurora had enough wit left to say, 'The stallion, Count Dashing? I do know him. He's the stuff of local legend.'

Crispin marched her out of the room, his hand on her back warm and firm, his voice taut with desire at her ear. 'You are a minx of the highest order.'

'Developed a penchant for portraits?' she teased sotto voce.

'Where else were we to go? I could hardly say I wanted to show you my bedroom. As for my penchants, my only penchant right now is getting you out of that dress and all those damned buttons.'

'Will that be before or after the portrait viewing?' Aurora was all coolness in response to his heated replies, sweeping into the darkened gallery ahead of him, enjoying his aroused discomfort for the moment.

'Shut up and kiss me,' Crispin growled, his mouth seizing hers with hungry force, his efforts backing her to the nearest wall. The wall was hard and unyielding against her back, much like the planes of Crispin's body pressed against her front. She welcomed the roughness of the moment, the claiming and spending of all the pent-up frustrations and desires. Had it only been two days since he'd been in her bed? It seemed an eternity. The games were finished. There was only the blunt honesty of their mutual need, hot and physical.

Crispin had her skirts up, his hand at the juncture of her thighs, searching, finding entrance. She bucked hard against his hand, instantly alight at his intimate touch, her need for him something wild and primal, threatening to rage out of control like some uncontainable fire. 'Don't make me wait, Crispin,' she sobbed, her hands frantically fumbling with the fastenings of his breeches. She wanted him hard and fast, deep inside her, but Crispin had other ideas.

He swept her up in his arms and carried her to the wide viewing bench set in front of a series of portraits. Skirts went up, trousers came down and he covered her completely with his length. She welcomed the heat and weight of him, all muscle and strength as she settled him between her legs. Aurora supposed the velvet of the bench cushions allowed a modicum of comfort, but in truth the feel of the fabric against her bared skin served to heighten her desire to a fever pitch. Crispin surged into her and she cried out, becoming living flame beneath him.

Such ecstasy should be illegal. She shut her eyes tight, attempting to find an anchor against the onslaught of his passion, suddenly aware that his passion could easily consume her, suddenly fearful that she would let it.

'Open your eyes, Aurora. There is nothing to fear here,' Crispin coaxed in husky tones, reading her mind far too easily for her sense of security. Then again he seemed to make a habit of it. 'I want to see your satisfaction in your eyes. Don't cheat me, Aurora.'

He thrust hard and her hips instinctively reared up to fully sheathe him. At the last moment, her eyes flew open, her body deciding against the wisdom coached by her mind as Crispin filled her with seed and pleasure.

In the aftermath of their passion, Crispin whispered temptingly, 'It is not enough to have you clandestinely in the dark, Aurora. Stay tonight.'

'Someone has to watch the stables,' she protested.

'I'll send men to watch the stables,' he countered easily. 'Stay. I'll come to you, love you properly in a bed as you deserve and we can talk. We need to talk.' He kissed her deeply, his body moving against hers, an intoxicating form of persuasion. But there was no question of accepting.

How easy it would be to fall for the allure of his power. The world was his to command. If she let him, he could fix even the more complex issues that plagued her. As potent as the implicit offer was, Aurora knew she could not set aside her principles, not even for a night. Her answer was simple and immediate and difficult. 'No, Crispin.'

'You're stubborn,' Crispin growled, his body not ready to take no for an answer.

Aurora gently pushed at his chest and began to wriggle out from under him before she lost her resolve. 'It's not just the stables. I can't ask Tessa to countenance the nature of our relationship beneath her roof. She is a respectable woman, Crispin. After all she and the earl have done for me, I would not shame them.'

Crispin sat up on his knees, pushing his hair back from his face with a grin full of mischief. 'If you insist on us being respectable, you leave me no choice. I'll have to escort you home.'

Aurora tossed him a coy smile in return. 'I guess you will. You're quite the gentleman.' But she knew without words there'd be nothing 'respectable' about Crispin's idea of an 'escort' home.

Hours later, her gentlemanly escort lay beside her, breathing evenly in his sleep, an arm draped lightly about her hips, apparently not as disturbed by what transpired between them this evening as she was. They'd not got to the talking. She'd seen to that, sensing the impending hazards that surrounded such a conversation, but her strategy had not succeeded entirely.

She did not understand what had happened; only that something had changed. She'd understood the passion in the gallery when it began. It had been straightforward and honest; two people hungry for the pleasure the other's body could provide, but it hadn't ended that way.

Crispin had demanded a more personal connection right at the end, a look into her eyes, a look into her soul—albeit only a glimpse, but a look none the less. She feared relinquishing even the barest of peeps, dreading that it would become a slippery slope into revealing far more than she intended, far more than what was necessary between two people who were interested only in a short affair based on physical pleasure.

That was it.

She had her answer. In the morning she'd remind Crispin this, whatever *this* was between them, was only about sex. For reasons he need not be apprised of, that was all it could ever be. She had to say it first before he could talk about whatever it was he'd wanted to talk about last night.

Crispin's hand flexed gently around the curve of her hip and Aurora's hard-won contentment with her solution faded in the wake of another thought. What if she was wrong? What if there could be more? But she knew better, didn't she?

The temptation she'd felt in the gallery to give in to Crispin's strength and lay her problems on his shoulders surfaced again. Dangerous optimism rose in her mind...*maybe this time it would be different.* There was no reason to believe Crispin was another Jonathon, but he was a man and at their core weren't all men the same? She'd do better to stay her course and stand her principles than to go risking them on a man like Crispin Ramsden who'd been clear from the start that he was going to leave.

Chapter Ten

Aurora did everything she could the next morning to ensure that she maintained the advantage. She woke first and dressed quickly to avoid any temptation of a morning bedding. She busied herself with morning chores in the stable, forking hay for breakfast and organising the tack room.

All her planning was for naught. Crispin found her anyway, mucking out a stall. He grabbed a shovel and joined in, making it clear he would not be ignored. Good lord, the man was redoubtable. He stopped at nothing when he was on a mission. And he clearly was now.

'You left before we could talk.' Crispin tossed a shovelful of dirty straw into a big bucket set in the aisle.

'I didn't want to wake you.'

'Of course not. If you woke me, you'd have to talk to me,' Crispin snapped, flinging another shovelful with extreme vigour, confirming her earlier instincts. Crispin was turning out to be far more the gentleman than she'd counted on.

Aurora leaned on her shovel. She needed a get-away until his chivalric ardour cooled. 'I need to see to the horses. If you could finish here, I'll move on to Kildare's stall.'

'You're not leaving this stall until we talk,' Crispin said hotly, his frustration with her attempts at evasion obvious. But his demand sat poorly with her.

Aurora squared her shoulders and faced Crispin. 'Why are you doing this?'

'Doing what?' Crispin drawled.

Good lord, he was actually going to make her say it. 'Acting like a gentleman who has compromised a lady.' She blew out an exasperated sigh. 'It was just sex. I thought you understood that.'

Just sex? That was usually *his* line. Crispin took a moment to let the novelty of having his own words flung back at him wash over his brain. What a fine bit of irony this was: to finally meet a woman who wanted no claim on him and to discover that the arrangement was not wholly satisfying in that regard.

'Well, we've been having a lot of "just sex".' Crispin set aside his shovel and leaned against the stall wall, arms crossed, looking hard at Aurora. The interesting parallel between mucking out stalls and the nature of this conversation to 'muck out' their relationship was not lost on him.

'Very nice sex too,' Aurora said in clipped tones, implying that she felt it should stay that way too.

'That's not the point. The point is that we've not been taking any precautions.' He'd mentioned it before after the first time and had let it go with her hasty assurance that there'd be no risk, but that had been just the once. Odds were they were safe on that account. Since then, it had been significantly more than once. He was running out of fingers and toes.

'Ah, so you've turned out to be more like Peyton than I suspected,' Aurora said with a hint of sadness. Was that regret he saw momentarily in her eyes? It was there for a brief moment. Regret that he was like Peyton? Or something else?

He bristled a bit about the Peyton remark. Perhaps that's what she'd been angling for, something to start a fight with, to distract him from his purpose. 'There's no shame in being like Peyton. My brother is a very noble man,' Crispin said, but there was no fighting force to his statement. He would not quarrel over her supposed barb. He was certain now the comment was meant as a red herring. The regret he'd glimpsed was intended for something else.

Crispin redirected the conversation once again. 'We must face facts, Aurora. We have risked a child on more than one occasion.'

There was that soft sadness again in her tone when she answered. 'And if we have? What do you propose we do? Should we marry and make each other miserable for thirty or forty years, pretending we're something we're not?' She smiled gently at him to dull the underlying sharpness of her words. There was a quiet serenity to her beauty in that moment, a marked contrast to the Aurora he knew in trousers, who commanded every moment with her overt strength and tenacity. But this serenity had power too, the power of a woman who knew her level and was comfortable with it.

If worse came to worst, perhaps that would be enough for him. He shifted his stance against the wall, trying to fight the rising anxiety her words conjured in his mind.

'I can see it already.' Aurora picked up on the slight shift. 'Just the thought of marriage makes you edgy. You've got your back to the wall, figuratively and literally.' He couldn't deny there was a note of smugness when she spoke.

He'd conveniently pushed such thoughts away while he'd grappled with his duty. He'd always been so careful in the past, vowing to himself that a child would never suffer for his momentary pleasures. In that regard, he'd never be like his parents. But with Aurora he'd been careless, not once, but numerous times. He would not doom a child of his to bastard status no matter what it cost him.

Aurora began pacing slowly in the aisle. She shook her head. 'No, I will not let you torment yourself, Crispin. There is no need for concern. There won't be a child. Ever.' Her eyes were fixed on his face. He knew she was looking for his reaction, perhaps waiting for him to smile with unabashed relief.

Indeed, he should be *vastly* relieved. He waited for relief to surge through his body with its sudden burst of adrenalin. He'd escaped the parson's mousetrap, but he felt an inexplicable sadness far removed from what he'd expected to feel.

'Why?' he asked numbly, watching Aurora's pale face, noting how she fiddled idly with a halter left hanging on a peg outside the stall. Whatever she was going to tell him seemed to cost her greatly.

'I took a bad fall jumping several years ago.'

A terribly bad fall, Crispin thought, if it had left her insides so ruined.

'I'm sorry,' Crispin said simply. He'd seen bad falls, horrible riding accidents. He didn't need details to know all the nuances she referred to.

She shrugged, her gaze seemingly intent on the buckles of the halter. 'I'm not. It was a blessing in other ways. It showed me my worth and I saw the world for what it really is. Without the accident, I might never have understood my true strength.'

'So you left Ireland and came here?' Crispin risked, probing further.

'Yes, there was nothing left for me there. That's why it can only be just sex between us. Surely, some day you'll want sons of your own and a wife who can give them to you.'

Crispin chuckled. 'What would I want sons for? Peyton and Paine have supplied me with enough little boys to keep me more than busy.'

Aurora gave him a strong look. 'Men have a way of changing their minds about those things.'

'Has a man changed his mind about you?' Crispin said boldly. 'Is that where this concern comes from? Did a suitor jilt you?'

'Not a suitor, Crispin. A husband.' Aurora let the truth out.

Perhaps such a truth was the only way to make him understand. 'Crispin, I'm divorced.

'Jonathon was the son of an Irish baron. He needed heirs.' She sat on the hay bale, Crispin hanging on every word.

'How does a groom's daughter come to marry a baron's son?'

'My mother was the daughter of an earl and, bastard or not, I could outride everyone in the county.' Aurora shrugged. 'I might have aimed higher than a baron if I'd been born on the right side of the blanket. Even so, Jonathon had dreams of building a renowned stud line from Darby.'

'So your horse became your dowry?'

'In a manner of speaking. My grandfather's connections and Darby's potential recommended me to Jonathon. His father hedged a bit in the beginning. He wanted something better for his heir. But Jonathon professed it was a love-match and practical too, once it was known my grandfather approved of the match. The two of us didn't care what anyone thought. We were quite blind to the realities surrounding us. We were in love.'

'You sound as if you doubt that.'

'We were young. He had turned twenty-two the spring we married. I was nineteen. We knew about passion. We sneaked off on our own every chance we got, but what did we know about love? Turns out we didn't know very much. I fell six months after the wedding and we were divorced six months after that. True love didn't last the year. Now, if you don't mind, I really must get busy. I've got lessons later today and I want to put Dandy through the jumping course again before they arrive.'

Crispin would not allow her to dismiss him. He did not want her to think she'd succeeded in scaring him off. There was no reason to be put off by her disclosure. He'd meant it when he said he did not plan on wanting a family of his own. 'I'd like to watch. Dandy is dragging his left leg over the jumps. He's bound to knock a pole off if we don't get his hind legs cleaned up,' Crispin said, knowing

Aurora in all her astuteness would understand the implied message: he would not be frightened off that easily.

Some of the tension visibly went out of Aurora. It was a small note of satisfaction that she'd wanted him to stay in spite of her verbal efforts to the contrary.

She stepped towards him and kissed him on the cheek. 'We understand each other, then? Just sex?'

'Just sex,' Crispin affirmed.

'Promise?'

I promise.' *For now*, he amended silently, seized with the childish urge to cross his fingers behind his back. There was more he wanted to ask, but he settled for the knowledge he learned today. He let her move on to another stall. He was beginning to understand what drove her to create limitations to their growing relationship. He wished he'd learned as much about himself.

He'd broached their discussion, hoping to be relieved of a burden he'd thought he wasn't ready to assume, only to discover he was disappointed to be relieved of it. Now he had no excuse to pursue something of a more permanent nature with Aurora. If he wanted something permanent, he had to own up to it himself. Is that what he wanted? He'd only known her a short time, but he could not imagine riding away from Dursley Park and leaving her behind not knowing when he'd return.

Would she go with him? She had her own place, her own business. She'd worked too hard to achieve those goals to simply throw them away and wander the globe. Could he stay for her? The property at Woodbrook seemed to offer a perfect solution. They could move her venue there. At Woodbrook they might stand a chance of being themselves. Goodness knew he was stuck with the place. The blasted entail was proving impossible to break.

Crispin laughed out loud in the empty stall. What was the matter with him? He was usually so decisive. What did he want? More importantly, could he trust himself with it if he reached out and grabbed it with both hands? He had not come home looking to fall in love, but he recognised the signs. Good God, if this was what falling in love did to a man, it was no wonder men fought it to the last. And yet, if a woman like Aurora Calhoun waited on the other side, it might be a fight worth losing.

Aurora reached out and seized the fence railing with both hands, fighting back her anger and frustration. She didn't dare give vent to it out here in the stable yard where everyone could see. Stoically, she watched Catherine Sykes's pony trap rumble down the road, carrying a tearful Catherine away from the riding lessons that had given the shy girl so much confidence.

Catherine had come early before the other girls arrived, accompanied by her father, and told Aurora she'd be discontinuing her lessons. It was time to go to London and prepare for her début. Her parents wanted to go in advance of the rush and see her well settled before the true competition for husbands began.

The girl had trembled and valiantly fought her tears. Aurora had given her what encouragement she could with the girl's father standing there. She'd given Catherine's father the name of a riding instructor in London and told them they must call on the earl's aunt and Eva during the Season. Catherine must tell Eva she was a friend of Petra's. If anyone could get the lovely, but shy, Catherine Sykes to blossom, it would be Eva.

Aurora had said all the right things and meant them all sincerely. She'd known this moment would come. It had been Catherine's parents' plan all along to see their daughter launched in London. Catherine was of course very lucky to have parents with enough wealth to manage a London début for their daughter, but she hadn't expected it to come so soon. Aurora thought she'd have Catherine for another month, maybe two. She'd never guessed they'd want to go early. From the looks of Catherine, pale and teary, Catherine had not guessed it either.

Something was afoot. Aurora watched Petra and Eleanor stop in the drive and exchange a few words with Catherine. They'd driven over together in Peyton's old gig. They pulled into the stable yard. Eleanor went immediately to change while Petra jumped down and came to stand by her.

'Rory, Catherine says she's leaving for London,' Petra said quietly.

Aurora nodded.

'I was surprised they were going up so much earlier than planned,' Petra pressed. 'What do you make of it?'

Aurora just shook her head, not wanting to burden Petra. 'Her parents have her best interests in mind.' But silently she thought with a sinking feeling, 'I wonder who I will lose next?'

It was a good thing the St Albans steeplechase was only a few weeks away, the first part of March. Then it would be spring and she could turn her attentions to breeding one of her mares. Maybe Crispin could be coaxed to letting her use Sheikh for that purpose. Maybe it was even a good thing the students were starting to leave. She had no illusions that Catherine's departure was an isolated incident. Someone was encouraging the girls to withdraw. It had happened before too. First they left with legitimate-sounding excuses, then the excuses became more vague and far-fetched. If there were no students, perhaps the subtle and not-so-subtle attempts at sabotage would stop. The students would be beyond her abilities to influence. She could be left on her own with her horses.

Aurora tried to see the situation positively, but throughout lessons, she couldn't help but wonder who had betrayed the academy's secrets? Was Crispin right? Had it been one of the girls who unwittingly exposed the secrets?

She eliminated Petra immediately. Catherine Sykes was also an unlikely candidate for the dubious position. Letitia Osborne was a born gossip. It was possible the girl could have said too much at a church circle, but she doubted Letitia's gossip would have spurred anyone to the vandalism and damage that had taken place. Whoever was responsible for leaking the secrets had told someone who would have been appalled at the disclosure; *and* had the ability to organise this revenge.

She kept coming back to Eleanor Windham. She watched Eleanor take a clean jump over the modified brick wall in the arena. The girl had betrayed her not on purpose, she was sure, but it was likely the girl had been forced to it by her father, even threatened. Eleanor was being forced to marry Baron Sedgwick. It was not impossible that she'd been forced to spill the academy's few secrets. Who was there to help her? She and her father were the only ones beside staff who lived in the big manor house. Aurora was certain the staff were either blindly loyal to Windham or sufficiently cowed not to risk their positions by aiding Eleanor in any way. No, when Eleanor wasn't here at the stables, she was most assuredly on her own. Betrayer or not, Aurora's heart went out to her. Who knew what else the girl had been forced to endure?

'I will not endure silence from you, girl,' Gregory Windham fairly shouted down the long dinner table. The candlelight on his face made him look like a long-faced ghoul.

'My apologies,' Eleanor said stoically, keeping her features blank. She'd learned long ago hiding any emotion was the best way to avoid trouble with her father. She didn't need trouble now. She needed to convince him of her abject obedience. She needed to have the freedom to roam the estate if her plan was to succeed. Being confined to her room was not a setback she could afford. There were three months until the wedding, but she could not wait until the last minute.

'I just told you that lessons would have to cease at Miss Calhoun's,' her father repeated.

'Yes.'

'Don't you have an objection to that?' he baited dangerously.

Oh, she had objections all right, but to voice them would be folly. 'If you believe it to be best for me to leave the academy, then I will.'

'Would you like to know why?' he pressed and then went on, not waiting for an answer. 'I've received word today that she's Irish, half-Irish.' He spat the words with all the disdain he used for those who weren't English. 'And a divorcée, cast off by her husband as an unsuitable wife! No wonder, when she's carrying on with Crispin Ramsden without so much as a blush for her behaviour.'

It had been on the tip of Eleanor's tongue to say that Aurora believed a woman's prerogative was the same as a man's. And truly, who was she to blame? Crispin Ramsden was about the handsomest man Eleanor had ever seen. If he'd looked at her even once, she'd have been carrying on with him too. But all thoughts died and she answered her father evenly, 'That's despicable. Such licentious behaviour is not to be tolerated,' because that's exactly what her father wanted to hear.

Her father gave a cold smile. 'Always remember, my dear, that it's never too late to repent. Aurora Calhoun could be saved with the right discipline to show her the way.'

Eleanor shivered. She wondered if the community even guessed at the depths of her father's discipline. He might be the biggest supporter of the church. His money might have bought the bell, the new elegantly carved pulpit and the silver communion chalice, but she doubted the community would be so welcoming if they understood his perception of Christian justice.

She regretted ever telling him about the situation at the stables, although it had been inevitable. She was not so foolish as to lie to her father and to think she'd escape punishment. If Aurora ever found out, Eleanor prayed she'd understand. Aurora was strong and she had the Ramsdens in her corner. Eleanor hoped it would be enough to protect her.

Eleanor knew what she had to do for herself, to save herself from marriage to the corrupt Baron Sedgwick. She was not naïve enough to think the choice she made had consequences for herself alone. Aurora would bear the consequences too. Once she was gone, Aurora's stables would be the first place her father would go and there would be hell to pay.

Chapter Eleven

Dandy refused the jump for the fourth time. Aurora reined him sharply in a circle and turned him to try the approach again. It had been a terrible week. First Catherine Sykes had left. Then there'd been a letter waiting for her from Letitia Osborne's father, informing her that Letitia had been called away to nurse an ailing cousin. Now, Dandy balked at the simplest of jumps.

Crispin crossed the arena, taking Dandy's bridle in his hand. 'Easy, boy, what's going on this morning?' He ran a soothing hand down the horse's long face. 'He's definitely out of sorts.' Crispin had made it part of his morning habit to stay and watch her work out the new hunter after taking care of Sheikh. He knew Dandy as well as she did.

Crispin checked the horse's eyes and nose for any discharge. Finding none, he bent his ear to Dandy's belly, listening for any telltale signs of stomach trouble.

'Well?' Aurora asked, sharp in her impatience.

Crispin shook his head and moved to the horse's hindquarters. He ran an experienced hand down Dandy's left leg. Then the right and back to the left. 'Slide down, I think I have found something.'

Aurora didn't like the sound of that. She swiftly dismounted and bent down with Crispin. 'The left leg feels hot to me,' Crispin said. 'I'd bet he's got a bit of inflammation.'

Aurora felt the left leg and had to concur. The leg was warm to the touch. 'I checked him out this morning in the stable. There was no sign of this.'

Crispin nodded. 'It could be that the trotting and the warm up aggravated it. Let's get him back to the stables and get a poultice on it. Chances are a week of rest will clear this up.'

Aurora would normally agree. Horses got sore legs. It was not unusual. There were several common reasons for it: rocks in shoes, sharp debris in pastures, an overly strenuous workout. But none of those seemed to apply in Dandy's case. He'd only been out in the pasture for a few hours yesterday and she checked the pasture daily for any unwanted rubbish or potential danger.

They headed back to the stables. Crispin gathered liniment and bandages from the tack-room shelves. Aurora cross-tied Dandy in the aisle and took a moment to investigate Dandy's stall. Too many things had happened lately for her to dismiss Dandy's injury as a normal occurrence.

With a shovel, she sifted through the hay. She hadn't removed the old hay yet from yesterday. She'd planned to do it after Dandy's morning workout while he ate.

Something glinted in the straw. Aurora bent down to examine it. 'Crispin!'

'What is it?' He materialised almost instantly in the stall, kneeling down beside her.

'Glass. There was a sliver of glass in the hay.'

'Any idea how it got there? A broken lantern, perhaps?' Crispin suggested, but they both knew Aurora ran a strict, clean stable. It was unlikely a shard of glass would accidentally find its way into one of her stalls.

'Whoever did this did it when I left for dinner,' Aurora supplied, the next realisation following immediately on its heels. 'That means the stables are being watched.' Someone knew her comings and goings.

Aurora rose and left the stall. 'Let's get Dandy taken care of.' She drew a deep breath, fighting the tears that threatened. Doing something would help. If she could just concentrate on the task at hand, she could push away the horrors that threatened to overwhelm her. It was all suddenly too much—the effort to set the village against her, the students leaving, the attempt to hurt Dandy and possibly her. If they hadn't caught the injury when they had, she could have been thrown during practice.

Someone desperately wanted to strike out at her and they were willing to put horses and people in jeopardy to do it. If only she could prove that it was Windham! But evidence of his involvement had proven elusive.

Aurora held Dandy's halter while Crispin swabbed the back leg with liniment.

'Ah, I see it now. Here it is, come have a look, Aurora,' Crispin called. 'The lighting in the arena wasn't bright enough for me to see. There's a thin cut on the inside of the leg.'

Aurora moved to Crispin's side and examined the slender line nearly obscured by the hair on the leg until one really looked. She stood and sighed, returning to her position. 'It's never been this bad before.' Her voice was far shakier than she'd anticipated.

'What's never been this bad?' Crispin looked up briefly.

'Attempts to run me off.'

'Oh?' Crispin reached for a roll of bandages.

'Students have left before, a few townspeople have made it socially difficult for me to do business, which resulted in me not being able to offer lessons, but no one has ever struck out so maliciously with attempts.' She tried a little humour. 'Usually the vicar visits and politely explains things to me long before it gets this far.'

Crispin didn't laugh. He held her gaze with his steady blue eyes, his mouth set in a grim line. 'Students have left here? I didn't know.' He firmly tied off the bandage and stood. 'Why didn't you tell me?'

'What would you have done? Some of them were bound to leave

at the end of spring. They simply left earlier than expected.' Aurora set to shovelling clean hay, safe hay, into Dandy's empty stall. 'No one will admit it's for any other reason.'

'I would have liked to have known.'

'It's not your problem. It's mine. I'll be here long after you leave.'

'Who says I'm leaving?' Crispin took the shovel from her. 'Here, let me do that.'

'Are you staying? I had not heard.' An irrational bit of hope leapt in her. Had she misjudged that about him too? The adventurer had turned out to be a gentleman. What else might she have been wrong about? Was it too much to hope that he might be enough like Peyton to give up his wandering ways?

'I haven't decided. I just don't like others making my decision for me,' Crispin said tersely, shovelling the last of the hay into the stall.

If his words dashed her hopes, it was no more than she deserved, Aurora scolded herself. She knew better than to hope for such a thing. Staying would complicate things immensely.

For starters, it would violate the whole temporary premise of their relationship. He would be expected to marry and start a family regardless of what he attested to today. Even as a second son, he would need to look far beyond the likes of her as a suitable wife. She was another man's cast-off, an untitled Irish woman whose only recommendation in life was that she could sit a horse like no other.

She was certain it would be far worse to watch him move on to another woman under her very nose than it would be to kiss him goodbye and watch him ride out of her life, out of England off on another adventure. At least then she could console herself with her memories of their brief affair.

She cleared her throat, struggling to maintain her self-control. 'We'll need to watch for fever and signs of further infection.' She attempted to sound matter of fact.

She was usually not so maudlin. The morning had been full of unpleasant surprises, that was the only reason her thoughts were wandering so far afield.

'He'll be fine, Aurora. I think we caught it as soon as we could. This time next week, he'll be taking those jumps again,' Crispin reassured her. He looked past her towards the apartments. 'I could use some tea and toast and I think you could too. Breakfast seems to have passed us by.'

Perhaps breakfast was only Crispin's effort to keep her busy and her mind distracted from unpleasantness, but Aurora set to her task of heating water in the kettle and slicing bread, grateful for the activity. She could hear Crispin putting the medical supplies away in the tack room and fought against the comfort such an image invoked and the impossibility.

Crispin came in time to set out the plates and they assumed their usual positions across from each other at the little plank table. 'I'll set up a cot in the groom's room,' he said after a few bites.

'Why?' Aurora was entirely caught off guard. Admittedly, her brain wasn't functioning as it should this morning, but she couldn't work out why he'd do that.

'I'll sleep down here until the situation is resolved,' Crispin offered offhandedly.

'That's not necessary,' Aurora replied coolly. It was becoming too easy to rely on him, to take his presence for granted. It would be all that more difficult to give him up when the time came. 'Dandy will be fine, as you've said. I've nursed more than one horse through a sore leg.'

'That's not the situation I'm talking about, Aurora.' Crispin's tone was stern, his blue gaze steady and serious over the chipped mug of tea.

She tried a coy smile. 'I thought we'd resolved that situation earlier this morning.'

Crispin shook his head slowly. 'We did. I'm talking about the threats being made to your stables. I do not want you down here by yourself. You've deduced the stables are being watched. Perhaps my presence will prevent any further invasions.'

'I am capable of protecting my horses. Now that I know they're in jeopardy, I can be on better watch. You needn't go to such lengths,' Aurora argued. Having him underfoot every night would create an illusion of permanence on temporary conditions, a very potent and unrealistic combination.

Crispin laughed. 'You're the most stubborn woman I've ever met.'

'I prefer independent,' Aurora countered, a smile working its way to her lips against her will.

'Fine. Independent,' Crispin acceded. 'Independent or stubborn, either way, you're blind to the real concern. I am more concerned about your safety than the horses. Whoever is behind these attacks might try to harm you next once it's obvious that their efforts to run you off have failed.'

'I know how to use a gun.'

'Then that will make two of us in a fight,' Crispin said. 'Hopefully it won't come to that.' He set down his mug and rose. 'I have business of my own this afternoon, but I'll see you tonight.'

Aurora humphed. That was one way to win an argument—simply leave. She couldn't argue against an adversary who wasn't there, but in truth, she would be foolish to refuse his assistance. It had crossed her mind that the attacks were following a pattern of escalation, growing steadily more perilous. The organiser of these assaults was apparently not willing to stop until he attained his goal. If lesser methods of intimidation did not work, the signs seemed clear he would take greater measures. Today it had been Dandy, the horse Windham had lost at the fair. Tomorrow it could be Kildare. Windham meant to do well at St Albans and he understood Kildare posed a threat to that success. He also saw her as part of that threat.

If the ringleader was Gregory Windham, it was almost assured something more drastic would occur than Dandy's sore leg. Aurora shuddered to think what that might be. If she had to choose between facing Gregory Windham's perversities alone or suffering through the temptations presented by Crispin Ramsden's brand of chivalry, the choice was obvious.

'Windham is the obvious choice.' Crispin walked with Peyton in the long portrait gallery of Dursley Hall's main wing.

'So you know about Aurora and Windham?' Peyton asked casually, stopping to take in the portrait of a young Lily Ramsden, his father's sister.

'She told me after the episode at the horse fair.' Crispin smiled at the portrait. 'Do you think Aunt Lily and Eva are doing well in London?'

'I'm certain they are, if Eva hasn't driven her batty yet with fittings at the dressmakers. I've never seen a girl love fabric like Eva.' Peyton chuckled. 'Tessa assures me it's quite natural though. Perhaps you'll look in on them while you're at St Albans? Tessa and I won't be going up to town until May for Eva's official début on account of the new baby.'

'Why would I be going to St Albans? As for London, May is too soon for my tastes. I was hoping to delay an appearance until the races started in earnest.' Even then, he'd hoped to get no closer to the Mayfair mansions than Newmarket.

Peyton gave him a quizzical glance. 'Forgive me, I assumed you'd be going to St Albans with Aurora in a couple of weeks for the steeplechase.'

'Why ever is she going up for that?' Crispin didn't bother to pretend he knew anything about it. What else had the minx elected to keep from him?

They kept moving down the line of pictures marking in paint the stamp of the Ramsdens in Cotswold history. 'I think she means to compete from what Tessa tells me.'

'She can't. Only men can enter,' Crispin shot back without thinking.

Peyton held his gaze. 'I don't believe that small distinction has ever stopped Aurora Calhoun in the past.'

Crispin recalled the intense workouts he'd witnessed on the big hunter, Kildare, whom only she rode. He highly doubted Aurora would let anyone else ride that horse. He was starting to see their first encounter in a new light. She'd been out practising cross country the day she'd nearly slammed into Sheikh on the Dursley Road.

They stopped again, this time in front of the portrait featuring Count Dashing. 'Did you show her this one?' Peyton inquired obliquely.

'Ahem. No,' Crispin said sharply, wondering how his brother had managed to get the conversation so far from his original intent. 'As I was saying earlier, Windham is the most likely culprit behind the attacks.'

'You're most likely right,' Peyton averred. 'I am sure you know by now that he'd asked Aurora to be his mistress. He was distraught to say the least when Aurora jilted him. The man went a little crazy in my estimation. A distasteful business all around.'

'That's what bothers me,' Crispin replied. 'Windham doesn't seem like a man who'd ever seek out a woman of Aurora's background. She's—well, to put it bluntly, she's too wild. Not his type at all.'

Peyton faced the portrait of Count Dashing. 'Windham likes to tame wild things. You should visit his stables some time and see how it is. I suspect the very characteristic you mentioned is the reason he was attracted to Aurora.'

Crispin read a wealth of meaning behind Peyton's careful words and bland expression. He'd known men like Windham before—

cruel, with a hidden sadistic streak that ran deep, thoroughly corrupting those it came in contact with.

'It occurs to me that I should pay Windham a call,' Crispin said at length.

'That might be a good idea. He'll be going to St Albans at any rate. He and Baron Sedgwick have plans to make a name for themselves. They have a silent share in one of the horses racing. The Flyer, I think the horse is called. He's owned by a Mr Weston. A strong goer, from what I hear, but not the favourite. Still, I think Windham believes the horse could finish in the top three or better.'

'Aurora's Irish jumper would put that notion at risk,' Crispin said slowly, a variety of scenarios suggesting themselves all at once in his mind. 'This puts an entirely different construction on Windham's motives.' Crispin had seen Aurora's carefully trained horse and he'd seen Aurora's unique skill. Woman or not, he had no doubts that she would be a top-level competitor. Windham had more reasons to see her out of the way than merely being a wounded suitor.

It explained the dangerous levels he was willing to go to and it confirmed that those dangers had not yet reached their zenith. More importantly, it confirmed he'd been right in his supposition that Aurora would be the next target.

'I'm going to see Windham this afternoon.' Crispin did not want to hesitate now that he saw the game in its full scope.

Peyton nodded. 'Do me a favour, the gypsies have arrived. They're camped on the western corner of the land. Stop in and welcome them. I haven't been able to get out and do it myself.'

Crispin smiled. For seventeen years, ever since Peyton had taken over the title, gypsies had been welcome on Dursley land, their presence livening up the drab end of winter. 'I'd be glad to.'

'And one more thing, Cris—don't punch Windham. At least not yet.'

Chapter Twelve

Crispin had long recognised that horses spoke to you in their own language if you took time to listen. He'd also learned that how a man took care of his horses was a fair measure of his merit. Both of those items were in abundant evidence at Gregory's Windham's stables.

The stables were immaculate with an aura of almost unbelievable sterility, but that did not make the stables a horse-friendly place. The head groom was a strict, dour man who ruled everyone and everything with the power of a whip, which he was wielding with great liberty in the paddock upon Crispin's arrival. Sheikh threw up his head, immediately sensing the underlying evil of the place.

'Shh, boy,' Crispin crooned, recognising the necessity of getting Sheikh away from the setting. He caught a young stable boy by the arm. 'Watch my horse. Take him out into that quiet pasture over there and let him graze.' He flipped the boy a gold coin that widened the boy's eyes considerably. 'I'll explain to your master what I instructed you to do.'

With Sheikh taken care of, Crispin headed back to the paddock where the grey stallion was still getting the better of the head groom and his lunge whip, but not for much longer. This had been a protracted fight from the look of the stallion. Foam flecked at his mouth and spotted his coat. There was a welt or two from the sharp-tipped whip and Crispin felt his anger rise at the obvious mistreatment of such a fine animal.

If it hadn't been for his promise to Peyton, he'd have stepped into the paddock and given the man a taste of his own medicine. It was a quick experiment to learn exactly how a lunge whip felt and the results were usually lasting. As it was, Crispin opted merely to voice his opinion. 'You might do better to coax him with an apple.'

The head groom turned to face him at the paddock railing, sniffing his disapproval of the stranger. 'An apple will teach him he's the master.'

'It will teach him that this is to be a partnership between horse and rider.' Crispin climbed the paddock railing without invitation and lightly vaulted to the ground. He reached into his pocket for the apple he always carried for Sheikh. 'Step back, please,' Crispin instructed.

He approached slowly, holding the apple out in front of him, talking softly and low the whole while. The stallion backed away instinctively, but Crispin stayed his course and continued to advance. When the stallion had nowhere else to retreat, he laid back his ears. Crispin kept up his low toned patter.

The horse began to trust him. Crispin nodded his head in encouragement when the ears relaxed. The horse's neck inched forwards towards the apple. Crispin took the last step and offered it in the flat of his palm. The horse lipped at the fruit cautiously. With his other hand Crispin stroked the horse's long neck, working his way to the horse's back. 'That's right, boy, don't be afraid. I won't hurt you,' he crooned. To the head groom's dismay, a few of the stable hands who'd stopped to watch gave a smattering of applause.

'It don't take much to bribe a horse with food. That's a cheap trick and a short fix,' the man growled from his post on the paddock fence.

Crispin shot the man a baleful look. He checked the bridle, dismayed by the damage the bit was doing to the horse's mouth. If that kept up, the horse would be ruined in short order and a ruined horse was often a mean horse, forced out of necessity to defend themselves. He checked the legs for other damage. Finding none, Crispin swung up gently on the horse's bare back.

At his weight, the stallion fought, but Crispin stayed him with the pressure of his thighs. After a few rambunctious circles, the stallion took his weight and presence. The stable master spat on the ground as Crispin rode the horse by in a steady trot. The others applauded again at the horsemanship on display.

'Hey, mister, need a job?' an onlooker called out in appreciation.

'You can have old Stanley's,' another called out to the chagrin of the head groom, who was apparently 'old Stanley'.

'He doesn't need a job,' a new voice called out. Crispin spied Gregory Windham hailing the group, crossing the yard in wide strides. 'That's Lord Crispin Ramsden,' he said casually, coming to lean on the fence. The man was very good at dissembling. If he didn't know better, Crispin would have thought the man was looking forward to this unexpected visit from a local friend. 'No doubt he's here to make a nuisance of himself in our stables.'

Crispin trotted the stallion over to Windham and slid off the big grey's back. 'This could be an excellent horse if Stanley over there doesn't ruin his mouth first. You'd do better to use a snaffle bit on him for a while at least. I might tell him to lay off the whip a bit too.' He didn't expect his advice to make any difference. Still, for the horse's sake, he'd make the effort.

'Come to see the competition? Flyer doesn't board here,' Windham said in low tones, leading the way to the stables, away from the others at the paddock. Out of earshot of any unwanted listeners, all trace of friendship vanished. 'Miss Calhoun still thinks she can enter that hunter of hers in St Albans?'

'Still? You mean after your underhanded methods of seeing her bow out?'

'Now, see here, Ramsden, I haven't an inkling of what you're talking about.' Windham made a show of chagrin at the charges.

'No need to dissemble, Windham, I know all about you. The glass placed in Dandy's stall, the night-time visits to destroy bridles, the attempts to create an accident at Aurora's stables.'

Windham took a different tack. 'So she's duped you too.' Windham stopped and gave a pitying shake of his head. 'She wants to turn you against me because she doesn't want me to compete against her in London. Don't feel bad, she's quite a temptress. I was taken in once by her as well.' The man was a consummate liar. Another, less-experienced, soul might be taken in by his commiserating bonhomie, but Crispin had seen Windham's cold disregard at the horse fair and he could feel the man's vindictiveness permeate the stables. These horses lived under a reign of fear. Aurora had not misled him about Windham's true nature and what he required in his employees.

'Man to man, I must say she can be quite, ah, "compelling", if you know what I mean and I rather think you do.' Windham had the audacity to wink conspiratorially.

Crispin's rage boiled. How dare Windham stand there and suggest he'd shared intimacies with Aurora of which he'd never had a glimpse.

'All that dark hair of hers, those bedroom eyes begging for it. I don't think I've ever seen eyes so green before, green like the Irish land she comes from. I imagine…'

Windham didn't get to finish. Crispin shoved the man against the stable wall and held him there. 'I know what you really are. You're a piece of filth dressed up in fine gentleman's clothes and a criminal to boot. If anything goes wrong at the stables again, I'll personally come looking for you.'

'You can't prove it was me, Ramsden.' Windham's cold eyes blazed with naked hostility.

Crispin roughly released him, thoroughly regretting his promise to Peyton. 'I can try. Your minions will talk and in their eagerness to purchase their own freedom, they'll be more than happy to turn you in.'

'Perhaps you'll be happy to buy your own freedom with your silence when I'm done with you,' Windham snarled.

'Are you threatening me?' If this had been one of his 'diplomatic' missions in the uncharted areas of Macedonia, he'd have drawn his knife by now.

'Absolutely,' Windham snarled.

Crispin nodded his head. 'Then have a good day. I'll find my own way out.'

Crispin's mood improved greatly once he had swung up on Sheikh and headed to the gypsy camp where he was greeted warmly with kisses from the old women who had known him in his younger days when they'd first come to Dursley land.

'We will have music and dancing tonight,' the caravan leader, Tomaso, said. 'You must come.'

Crispin grinned. It struck him quite suddenly that he knew exactly what he and Aurora would do tonight. Gypsy fiddles would be just the thing to take her mind off her recent troubles. It also struck him that the gypsies might know of her. Surely she'd accompanied Peyton and Tessa to the gypsy camp in the last three years?

'Aurora Calhoun? The Irish girl with the horses?' Tomaso gave a wide smile. 'Do we know her? We brought her. She and the big horse of hers travelled with us for a spell before the countess decided to convince her to stay.'

That settled it. He would bring Aurora and they would dance under the stars and they would forget about Gregory Windham for a bit.

'The gypsies are here?' Aurora exclaimed over his news, a huge smile wreathing her face. 'That's better than anything I've heard today.'

Crispin would have thought he'd brought her a diamond brace-let. He couldn't imagine any woman in London reacting with such pleasure over a visit to a gypsy camp.

'Give me some time to wash up and change.' Aurora was suddenly a whirlwind of activity, slipping into the bedroom and shutting the partitioning curtain between them, but not before Crispin caught sight of the rather fancy green gown laid out on the bed.

'What's that thing on the bed?' he called. It looked very unlike anything Aurora would possess.

'Oh, that…' Aurora groaned from beyond the curtain. 'Tessa brought it down. It's for their ball.'

Crispin managed a groan of his own. He'd forgotten about it. 'That's not until later this spring, isn't it?' He remembered now Tessa mentioning something about a ball for Petra and Thomas.

'Yes, it's the first of April and I'll need time to alter the gown.' Aurora's voice was muffled in the cloth of her shirt. Crispin imagined her shirt sliding over her head, her slim torso, and the curve of her waist slowly coming into view as the shirt worked its way upward. His body stirred at such imaginings.

He'd slake those needs later. For now, he needed to subdue them. 'I'm going to check on Dandy one more time before we go and make sure the Dursley men are in place for the night,' he improvised swiftly, giving his body something else to do besides thinking of Aurora Calhoun naked behind the thin barrier of the curtain.

Aurora was waiting for him when he returned, clad in a multi-coloured gypsy skirt and open-necked white blouse favoured by the Romany women. Her dark hair was loose down her back, falling in long inky waves. A bright green silk scarf was tied about her waist. The relief he'd acquired from checking on Dandy was short lived. God, she was beautiful. No London débutante could have looked finer in her silk gowns and jewels than Aurora did in her gypsy garb.

'My very own gypsy princess.' Crispin grinned appreciatively at her. 'The gypsies told me you travelled with them for a spell.'

She nodded. 'Safety in numbers.' She gave a wry smile. 'They were camped near the village I was working in at the time when it became apparent that the village felt they would be better off without me. The gypsies were kind enough to take me up with them. It was the fourth place in four years I'd been forced out of.'

Crispin shook his head. 'There will be none of that talk tonight. Tonight is for fun.' He waggled his dark brows playfully and was rewarded with Aurora's laugh.

'So it is,' she said, slipping her hand into his, looking up at him with dancing green eyes that tempted him beyond measure. She winked at him and he knew all thoughts of silk gowns and impending balls had fled her mind.

'What are we waiting for? Come on, let's go to a *real* party.'

They travelled in simple style, bareback on one of Aurora's sturdy geldings. The horse was strong and well trained, taking them both up for the short trip to the gypsy encampment. Aurora rode behind him, arms about his waist, her body pressed warm against his back, and he felt like a king with all the riches of the world laid at his feet. What more did a man need than a good horse, a beautiful woman and a knife in his boot just in case?

Dinner and darkness were in progress when they arrived, the bonfire sparking in the oncoming dusk with its orange flames. A great cheer went up and they were immediately surrounded by those happy to see them. Over the heads of the others, Crispin briefly caught sight of Aurora being bustled off to the women, exchanging kisses and hugs after a year apart. Tomaso swept Crispin into the group of men who were already busy talking and drinking, clucking disapprovingly over his attire. 'I have things that will fit. You cannot wear an Englishman's clothes tonight.'

Crispin easily slipped into the loose trousers and shirt worn by other men in camp, feeling a certain freedom come over him. He'd worn a variety of costumes during his time abroad; the flowing robes of the Bedouin in North Africa and the loose clothes of the Macedonians. It helped him understand the people he worked with better. He became them. Tonight was no different.

He tightened the wide sash at his waist and felt his gypsy soul awake, the part of him that begged release from the strictures of the English world. He had not realised how much he'd suppressed this feeling since his return home. It had been a simple matter to subdue it amid all the daily business of the Woodbrook entailment, the horses at the stables and, of course, Aurora.

Someone shoved a tankard of ale into his hand and he drank deeply, pushing the thoughts away. He didn't want to think that this was how it started—losing one's true self in the mundane worries of everyday living until one forgot who one's true self was altogether. Eventually there would be nothing to remember.

Dinner was ready to be served and they joined the women. His change of attire was met with hearty approval. 'Aurora, come feed your man,' one of them called out.

Aurora swayed through the crowd with a bowl of stew and a loaf of bread on a tray, fitting in effortlessly with the life of camp. How many women did he know that could do that? Would want to do that? Even the courageous Tessa, who'd lived most of her life in St Petersburg, Russia, had succumbed to the allure of a house of her own, a family and all the consequence Peyton's title afforded her. Of course, he knew Tessa loved his brother without question. Her marriage hadn't been driven by convenience, but still, Peyton hadn't asked her to travel the length of the globe with him, offering her no promise of stability.

Aurora found a blanket for them to settle on and eat. 'Everyone is doing well this year,' she said excitedly, sharing with him news of the friends they'd only just discovered they shared. She dribbled a bit of stew on her chin and Crispin reached to wipe it off with a faded cloth.

'Gypsy camp agrees with you.' He grinned at her obvious happiness.

Aurora tossed her head back and looked up at the night sky where early stars twinkled. 'What more does anyone need? If we could all leave each other alone to live our own lives, we could live simply.'

'You'd need your stables, surely,' Crispin probed delicately. His body tensed, waiting for her response, not realising until that moment how many hopes he'd hypothetically pinned on her answer.

Her gaze was still riveted on the spangled sky. 'I need my horses. They're portable,' she corrected.

'And the stable? What function does that serve?' Crispin dared, encouraged by her answer.

'It's my protection from the rules, from society. That's what I tell myself anyway. It makes me feel better, makes me believe in my own independence, but in truth, I know Peyton and Tessa are my protection. I only dared setting up the stables because Tessa could guarantee me some longevity. I understand my situation right now is unique in that respect. I do not expect to encounter it again should I ever leave here.'

'So you're here for the duration, then?' Crispin's spirits sank a bit.

'I don't think of anything in terms of for ever, Crispin.' She turned her eyes from the sky and met his gaze sharply. 'It's too hazardous to one's well being to think that way. It only leads to disappointment.'

'And yet you want to be acknowledged as a horse breeder. Don't you need a stable to do that?' Crispin carefully dropped the information he'd learned from Peyton that afternoon. 'It's why you're going to St Albans, isn't it?'

That startled her. 'I only need my horses to be a breeder. It would be possible to hire on to someone's string without owning a stable.' She studied him. 'How did you know about St Albans?'

'Peyton mentioned it this afternoon,' Crispin said. He discreetly opted to keep his thoughts on her breeding ambitions to himself. Not many men would elect to hire a woman on their horse string, no matter what her breeding record was like, but perhaps he could help her with that. There were some men of power, rare as they were, who would make exception for a woman of skill, especially if she had the backing of an influential man. It was possible he could help her take the next precarious step in her dreams at St Albans, but first he had to convince her to let him come too.

'Peyton tells me you plan to enter the steeplechase at St Albans as a rider.'

'Yes. I want to show everyone the kind of horse I am capable of training. I'm the best rider to do that.' There was a hint of defiance to her tone.

If Peyton had hoped he would dissuade Aurora from that course of action, his brother would be disappointed. After his unsatisfying 'discussion' with Windham, Crispin could not in good conscience argue against her going. He would not unwittingly assist Windham in achieving his goal of having Aurora out of the way.

'When do we leave?'

Surprise registered on her lovely face. She'd been expecting a fight. 'We?'

'That's right—we. I am going too. I need to check in on Eva and Aunt Lily,' he glibly borrowed from Peyton.

'Then I suppose 'we' will leave the last week of February.' Aurora smiled. She stood and shook out her skirts. 'Now, "we" will dance.' She reached for his hand and pulled him up, leading him to a circle of dancers. The fiddles had started up and a round dance was underway, women dancing in a circle inside the ring of men.

Usually Crispin abhorred dancing, but this kind of dancing was different. It wasn't done in a ballroom to the synchronised organisation of an orchestra with expected patterns and rules. This kind of dancing was what man was born to do, wild and free under the sky and stars. This kind of dancing took his soul and loosed it. He gripped the shoulders of the men on either side of him as they executed something akin to a Cossack step.

Aurora was before him, her hips swaying, her feet moving in a rapid step, a tambourine someone had given her in her hand. The circles broke apart and she danced for him alone now, her eyes locked on his, her body proclaiming the lush promise of her passion in the undulating of her hips. She reminded him of the veiled houris he'd seen in the pasha's courts in Constantinople.

Then it was his turn, time for the men to dance for their women. How he danced; a sinuous masculine yet provocative set of moves he'd learned in the severe, stark regions of Macedonia, a dance the young men did to impress the village girls at the spring festivals. He'd originally learned it to please the villagers, but tonight, he felt the real message of the dance, of the wild turns and jumps designed to impress a woman with his strength and his prowess. Tonight, he was a man who wanted to prove himself to his woman.

His woman. Crispin spun with the other men, the phrase pulsing through him with strength and power. His woman. Aurora had become his woman. He was going to St Albans to protect her, to assist her in her dreams. Not just ownership, but partnership. Windham would not lay a hand on her as long as he was capable of preventing it because she was his.

The realisation was as stunning as it was true. When had it happened? When had they moved from lonely strangers with separate plans merely looking for a temporary respite from their usual solitude to *this*? Perhaps this was what he'd been thinking this morning, only then he'd tried to couch his need in terms of responsibility. It hadn't worked because it hadn't made sense. But this made sense.

He collapsed, breathless from his efforts, at Aurora's feet.

'Your man dances well.' A woman laughed nearby Aurora. 'He must be a stallion in bed to dance so well.'

In the firelight, he saw Aurora blush becomingly.

His woman.

Her man.

Did Aurora recognise it too? The one thing that they'd not ex-pected to happen had. No matter how much she protested it was all 'just sex', it wasn't, not any more—perhaps it never had been. They just hadn't seen it. If he had any reservations about whether or not he was falling in love, the evening seemed to have settled them. He was in love with Aurora Calhoun. Now, he needed to work out what to do about it. Until then, he could not declare his feelings without scaring her off.

Chapter Thirteen

Crispin's head lay in her lap, the firelight playing across the sharp planes of his face, his eyes laughing up at her while she ran her hands through his dark hair, ink black against the flames. 'I haven't danced like that for at least a year.'

'Tessa told me you abhorred dancing.' She had pulled most of his hair free in her stroking and it lay loose now, framing his face, adding to the wild handsomeness that defined him.

'It's true. I abhor *ballroom* dancing,' Crispin amended easily. 'But not this kind of dancing. This dancing is real, a true expression of feelings. It *means* something.'

What would he say if she pushed him? If she asked him what his dancing tonight meant? Would he be forced to mouth words he didn't mean or sentiments he didn't feel?

She opted to savour the moment for what it was and said nothing. What did she want to hear anyway? A lie? A promise that could not be kept? And for what purpose?

The dancing gave way to quieter entertainment. A fiddle played a slow ballad and somewhere around the campfire a woman's voice took up the words of the song, a tune about young, unrequited love. The song was followed by another, wrapping the night in tranquil peace, lulling the audience towards sleep. Aurora felt herself start to drop off, her head falling forwards.

'Come on, sleepyhead, time for bed.' Crispin sat up and drew her to her feet. 'Tomaso says we can sleep in his *vardo* tonight.'

Tomaso's *vardo* held very little beyond a big box-framed bed and a large trunk for clothing, but the bed was all that mattered to Aurora. She undressed quickly, eager to be under the covers, more than a little self-conscious over the fact that she had nothing to sleep in and more than aware of Crispin's keen gaze following her every move.

It was silly really to feel such shyness now. They'd been naked together before, they'd explored each other's bodies in the dark, but never had it been so blatant. Now, the lamp was still lit and the heat of the moment had yet to come.

'You're staring,' Aurora commented, folding her skirt and laying it on top of Tomaso's scarred trunk.

'Do you mind?' Crispin was still clothed, having only managed to take off the soft shoes Tomaso had loaned him. He came up behind her, enveloping her completely with his body. His arms wrapped around her, gently cupping her breasts, his lips warm against her neck. 'You're beautiful and it struck me while you were undressing that I've yet to make a complete study of your body.'

The bed was behind them. He turned her towards it and smoothly lowered her. He followed her down, making no move to undress himself. Aurora watched him intently, waiting to see what he proposed, all her sleepiness evaporating in the wake of this new, slow seduction of his.

He started at her breasts, a warm hand on the flat of her stomach while his mouth suckled. She felt her need rise, her core running hot, but it would be a while yet before he gave her satisfaction. His mouth traced a path of kisses to her belly, his hands splayed on either side of her hips, kneading lightly. One of his hands stopped suddenly. His thumb retraced its path and she knew what he felt. He looked up at her, lifting his face from her stomach. 'The accident?' he asked quietly.

She nodded. The scar was eight years old and had faded considerably. It could still be felt from a certain angle and perhaps even seen with the right light, but she hadn't looked at it for years, hadn't consciously felt for it. In its time, the scar had been ugly, surrounded by puckered skin and swollen bruises. It had been repulsive. Once, she'd believed it would never heal. She hadn't been the only one who felt that way.

Crispin shifted his position, trying to make the scar out in the minimal light of the *vardo*.

'Don't, Crispin, it's of no account.' Aurora tensed, fighting the old sense of embarrassment. The scar was repugnant, it made her flawed. Jonathon had not been able to stand the sight of it.

'I've seen far uglier wounds,' Crispin cajoled, still fascinated with studying the area.

'I assure you it has taken a long time to get it looking this good.' Aurora rolled to the side, attempting to dislodge Crispin. This time he acceded.

He crawled back up to the pillow and stretched out beside her, drawing her against him, buttocks to chest, a safe harbour in the night. 'Tell me about the accident.'

'I told you already. I fell off a horse,' Aurora prevaricated.

'I want all the details.' He tenderly pushed aside a strand of her hair and nibbled idly at her ear.

'You don't want to know.'

'I do. I am tired of other people knowing more about you than your lover does.' His hand closed possessive and warm about her waist. Her lover. The words were delicious and perhaps this was one secret she didn't need to keep, at least not from him. In the dying light, she decided to take a chance.

'It was at a fall hunt, towards the end of the day. There were five of us who were feeling reckless and wanting to give our horses their heads. I was unduly proud of my horse, a big chestnut hunter named Darby.' She stopped here to gather her thoughts. As a rule, she didn't think of Darby if she could help it. She'd loved Darby. Together they'd been invincible. Everyone in the county admired Darby and it had been a point of pride to her and her father that she sat the mount so well.

'We decided to have an impromptu race on the way home, our own rough steeplechase. The first one home got to claim a forfeit from any of us.'

'For whatever reason, I was determined to win. Like a true steeplechase, there was no set course, only the goal of arriving at the finish first. I'd ridden these lands since I was old enough to take a pony out. I set out at a full gallop, cutting straight across country even though the direct path I'd chosen was littered with stone fences and country stiles. Most of the fences had low spots and I easily jumped them. Only one in our party dared to pursue my route. The others took their chances on easier ground. I led him a merry chase, but as we neared the end, I thought to pull away and I dared a high fence I knew his horse would not take. Darby had yet to be bested by any fence and I was confident all would be fine.

'Well, it wasn't.' Aurora shifted against Crispin, trying to subdue her rising emotions. 'Unbeknownst to me, the ground was grossly uneven on the other side. There was no way to plan for that landing. Darby cleared the fence barely, but he could not get his feet firmly on the ground. We went down and he rolled heavily on top of me.'

'You must have been terrified.' Crispin drew her tight against him, offering her the comfort of his body.

'I was unconscious. I'd hit my head upon landing. It was perhaps a blessing. The rider with me pulled me out from under Darby and got me home. The doctors say I was lucky my lungs weren't crushed or that a broken rib didn't puncture a lung or that I didn't suffer a hoof to the head. There were so many things that could have gone wrong if Darby had landed differently.' She paused and drew a deep breath. 'My da long thought it was Darby's last gift to me that he landed as he did, almost like he'd done his best to protect me.'

'When I could be moved, a month later, my da took me home to our place, but it didn't take me long to work out nothing was going to be the same again.'

Crispin's hands were absently moving in gentle circles on her abdomen. 'You're alive. You're riding. That in itself is an accomplishment. You didn't give up. I know plenty of men who wouldn't ride again after such an episode.' He paused. 'Is this why you want to ride at St Albans? To prove something to yourself?'

'I ride for the stables, to show people I can breed a champion,' she said staunchly, not wanting to admit that Crispin had hit the nail dangerously close to the head.

They lay quietly together. She could feel the rise and fall of Crispin's breathing against her back. 'You know, Aurora, I have a scar too. Do you want to see it?'

She felt the warmth leave her back, felt the mattress ease as Crispin stood up, leaving her deprived of his presence. If anything could distract her from the maudlin thoughts her recollection had roused, it would be the sight of Crispin Ramsden taking off his clothes. She rolled over to face him, determined to take advantage of the light as he had.

Crispin drew the shirt over his head, revealing the muscled planes of his chest, the tapering waist with its sculpted abdomen, the dark arrow of hair tempting the eye to follow it down where it merged into the hidden confines of his trousers. He knew she was watching and he smiled wickedly, working the loose trousers with deliberate slowness.

'Where exactly is this scar at?' Aurora teased.

'You'll see.' He stepped out of the trousers and let them fall to the floor.

'No underwear?'

'No point in it. Just slows me down.' Crispin gave a throaty chuckle.

'Now about that scar?' Aurora said.

'Here, on my thigh.' Crispin presented her with an excellent side view of his well-sculpted buttocks.

She'd half-expected not to find anything, but he'd not teased her. A thin white line ran from his buttock around to his hip. 'That's a convenient scar to show the ladies,' she joked, reaching a hand out to trace it with a finger.

'Getting it wasn't convenient, I assure you. That's courtesy of a Turkish blade and being outnumbered three to one up in a mountain village near the old town of Negush.'

'I've never heard of it.' Aurora reached for his hands and drew him back down to the mattress.

'It doesn't matter.' Crispin came willingly. 'The point is, it's only a scar and I lived to tell about it. Just like you.'

It was on the tip of her tongue to say too bad everyone hadn't felt that way, but such a remark would invite more questions, questions she didn't want to answer, questions that would make no difference in the end except perhaps to ensure that there was an end to her and Crispin. Frankly, she'd rather forestall the inevitable for as long as she could.

'We've shown each other our scars, what should we do next?' She boldly wrapped her hand around his shaft, thumbing the sensitive head in a languorous caress that won her a growl of approval from Crispin.

With the morning came reality. The magic of the night spent under gypsy stars was gone. Crispin was dressed again in his regular clothes and she was anxious to get back to the stables. Dursley men had watched the premises while they'd been away, but she had horses to exercise and it was time to get ready for the trip to

London. They said their goodbyes to the gypsies, thanked Tomaso for his *vardo* and set off on the gelding for home.

At the stable, Crispin busied himself with tasks for the horses, leading them out to the pasture, mucking out stalls.

'Do you mean to stay all day?' Aurora commented when it became apparent he had no intention of leaving.

Crispin leaned on a mucking shovel. 'I suppose I do. Sheikh needs a good ride. Perhaps you'd like to saddle up Kildare and join me.' He gestured towards the hunter she meant to take to St Albans.

The ride was a good idea, but she sensed he had something more than a workout for the horses in mind. Her suspicions were borne out halfway through the ride when they drew up to the top of a hill, stopping to let the horses rest and take in the view.

'We should talk about St Albans,' he said without preamble.

'You don't have to come. You spoke in haste last night,' Aurora offered quickly.

'I mean to come. That's not what we need to talk about,' Crispin countered. 'You're mad to ride in the steeplechase. It's a gentlemen-only event. Even if you win you can't claim the prize. If you're discovered, you'll be disqualified.'

'I'll ride under an assumed name. I'll pass myself off as male. I'm tall enough and weight can be added to the saddle. I've done it before.'

Crispin shot her a quelling look before returning his gaze out over the rolling Cotswold hills. 'Why am I not surprised? Are there any rules you haven't broken?'

'I suppose there aren't. I'll be fine.' Aurora knew she had to tread carefully here. Crispin was getting possessive. She'd sensed last night that something had changed for him in their relationship in spite of his promises to the contrary.

Crispin shook his head. 'A local steeplechase or race day at a fair is one thing. Something as prominent as St Albans is very different. For one, Gregory Windham will be watching you. Surely he suspects you don't have a rider.'

'Perhaps I intend to hire one once we arrive,' she answered easily. 'There will be a lot of jockeys hoping for work.'

Crispin looked dubious. 'Windham's not stupid. He'll suspect something; to say nothing of the danger you are placing yourself in. What's to stop Windham from committing some nefarious act during the race? You can't really believe he'll play fairly once the race starts?'

No, she didn't believe that. Steeplechases were notorious for their 'anything goes' atmosphere. Most steeplechases didn't have any places set aside for spectator viewing except for the finish line. As a result there were plenty of places a rider would be unobserved. 'I'll be prepared. I can handle a gun if need be.'

'It's far too perilous of an undertaking, Aurora. Let me ride for you. Kildare's big enough to take my weight and there's still time for him and me to train together.'

Aurora studied the broad-shouldered man beside her. He refused to meet her eyes, keeping his gaze focused on the landscape before them. It was an impossible offer, but no less touching for its improbability.

'I'll consider it.' What else could she say?

Crispin gave her a brief nod that suggested he understood such an answer was the best he'd get for now.

'There, I think that's all of it.' Tessa folded the last garment and laid it in the full travelling trunk. She stepped back from their packing labours and smiled at Aurora. 'I envy you your adventure a little. I wish Peyton and I were going with you.'

'No you don't, Tess. You're not ready to leave the baby.' Aurora smiled at her friend's half truth.

Aurora looked around Tessa's rooms. The rooms were hers only nominally. Everyone knew she and Peyton shared a chamber. But the rooms had served as an excellent staging area for packing Aurora up for St Albans and they'd spent the last two days fitting an unbelievable amount of clothing into two travelling trunks.

'I still don't think I need all of this,' Aurora protested. She'd planned to take one small trunk with her riding clothes and equipment, but Tessa had been appalled. She had insisted on loading up a trunk with several carriage dresses, riding habits, afternoon gowns and even a ball gown.

'I hope it's enough.' Tessa studied the array of gowns carefully stowed in the trunk.

Aurora thought she must be joking. They'd only be gone two weeks total, but when she turned to tease her friend it was obvious Tessa was quite serious.

'I don't intend for this trip to get out of hand,' Aurora said solemnly. Even as she said the words, Aurora knew it was already so far out of her hands, out of her control and it had been since the moment Crispin declared he was going with her.

Now, instead of going alone with her anonymous horse, Aurora would be arriving amid what amounted to fanfare. She was travelling with all the prestige and comfort the Dursley name could marshal. She would arrive in the earl's big travelling coach with Lord Crispin Ramsden as her escort and Cousin Beth as her nominal chaperon (Peyton insisted on an outward show of propriety). Instead of wearing her old worn gowns and trousers, she'd be dressed in the height of fashion in Tessa's altered dresses. Instead of staying in one of the cheap coaching inns in St Albans, she'd be lodging at Coleman's Turf Hotel, sponsor of the steeplechase.

In the end, she'd acquiesced to their plans. How could she fight them all? There was only one decision left to make and she would put it off until the very last.

'Have you thought more about letting Crispin ride Kildare?'

Tessa asked, straightening up the odds and ends left strewn about the room.

'It's my race. I can't let the Ramsden clan shoulder my entire burden.' Aurora tried to side-step a direct answer.

'They're a managing sort. When they aren't managing someone else, they're trying to manage each other,' Tessa said fondly.

Aurora didn't share Tessa's easy nature on the subject. 'I will not be managed. I cannot afford to be.'

Tessa stopped sorting the stockings they'd discarded earlier and faced Aurora with a stern look of authority. 'You're not going to want to hear this, but please listen to me. I know what you want. You want a world where women can be equal. I do too. The world is not a fair place. We're changing it for our daughters and their daughters to come, but, Rory, the world won't be changed by next week. You are practical about most things, so be practical about this. If you race and are discovered, you will not gain the acclaim you seek for your stables. You will get the exact opposite—scandal—and that scandal could ruin your chances permanently.' Tessa shook her head. 'You have a capable champion in Crispin. I don't understand why you hesitate. Set aside your stubborn pride, Aurora.'

'I've come too far to stumble now.'

'That's exactly my point,' Tessa said sharply. 'Letting Crispin ride doesn't detract from all you've accomplished. Let him be your partner in this.' She softened her tone. 'You don't have to decide tonight. Come, it's time for us to go to bed. You'll want a good sleep to start the journey tomorrow and Peyton and I want to be up to see you all off.'

Four days to St Albans, counting the one night in London. She would make her decision by the time they arrived, Aurora promised herself as she got ready for bed in a guest room at Dursley Park. She had four days to decide if she could trust another man with another of her most precious dreams.

Chapter Fourteen

Four days later, after an overnight stop in London to carry out Crispin's supposed duty to Eva and Aunt Lily, Aurora, Crispin and Cousin Beth approached the medieval marketing town of St Albans.

The town was a direct stop on the London Road and their journey had been punctuated by an increased amount of coach traffic. 'The town is all inns!' Aurora exclaimed, straining to take in the sights as their carriage passed through town.

'I've heard it mentioned that the town averages about sixty travelling coaches a day. When I made arrangements for rooms, I was told the town could accommodate up to one thousand lodgers,' Crispin supplied, taking a glance out his own window.

'Looks like they'll need all the rooms they can get. The streets are full.' She could hardly keep the excitement from her voice. St Albans was not an old race. It was only five years old, but the race had gained steadily in prestige as organised steeplechases gained popularity as a legitimate sport. Now, she was here, ready to prove herself and her horse. Kildare would have his chance to race in the most prestigious steeplechase currently run on English soil. Soon everyone would see the kind of horse she could train. Soon everyone would see what a woman was capable of doing. Soon, if all went well, the ghost of Darby and the accident that had irrevocably changed her life would be laid to rest.

The going through town was slow, the streets choked with pedestrians and other coaches, some passing through, but most of them arriving for the big event four days away. If it was this busy now, Aurora could imagine how congested it would be as the day of the race neared and was glad they'd arrived early.

Their coach passed the abbey church and the four-hundred-year-old clock tower, making its way to the other side of town and Coleman's Turf Hotel. The Turf Hotel was located on the far edge of town close to the heath known as Nomansland where much of the steeplechase would take place. The hotel itself was a large, imposing, plain-fronted brick building that ran the length of a town street. Much of its size came from the result of its proprietor, Thomas Coleman, purchasing an adjacent house and turning it into stabling that held up to thirty horses.

The hotel was especially designed to cater to the horseman's needs. Not only was there stabling, there was an exercise yard for the horses as well. Dandy and Kildare and the carriage horses would be well taken care of during their stay. She could see why Crispin and Peyton insisted upon staying here instead of taking rooms at a smaller inn. The quality of care the animals would receive far surpassed anything a crowded coaching inn could offer.

Still, mixed with her excitement was a healthy amount of trepidation. Staying at the Turf Hotel meant staying in the centre of activity. She would be visible, doubly so since she'd be on Crispin's arm. He was not a man to be overlooked in a crowd.

Aurora scolded herself. These megrims were unworthy of her. She was being silly. She'd come here to be noticed, perhaps not as the woman on Crispin's arm, but none the less she'd not come to fade into obscurity. Being with Crispin would get her the notice she desired and the acceptance she might have struggled to gain otherwise.

Of course that acceptance would not be automatic. It hinged on two factors. First, Kildare had to place well. Second, the decision of a rider. She was no closer to that decision than she had been when she took her leave of Peyton and Tessa. Fortunately, Crispin had not pressed her for an answer. He'd been content to avoid that subject during the long hours of their journey.

The carriage pulled to a halt, waiting in line with other arrivals to unload new guests at the hotel. Aurora was glad for the last bit of respite the delay afforded her, one last chance to marshal her courage. She was not oblivious to the orchestrations going on around her. The campaign being waged on her behalf was becoming clear little by little. The fine address, the fine carriage, the fine clothes packed in her trunk—all attested to the fact that the Ramsdens had decided to promote her cause.

She shot a covert glance across the carriage where Crispin sat reading, oblivious to the thoughts running through her mind. This campaign was not Peyton's idea. He'd always been a quiet champion, counselling caution. She knew he supported Tessa and thus her indirectly, but he would not choose to proactively launch her in this manner. Left to his devices, Peyton would choose to be more minimal in his approach, starting small, confident of local success before laying siege to St Albans in such a public venue. No, this campaign on her behalf was being waged by Crispin.

'Why are you doing this?' Aurora queried.

Crispin looked over the pages of his book. 'Doing what? Reading? Most people read to pass the time on a long journey.'

Aurora kicked him playfully, earning a smile from Cousin Beth, who discreetly kept her eyes on her knitting. 'Don't be obtuse. I mean coming to St Albans and throwing your lot in with me.'

Crispin grinned. 'Because I like a challenge.' He shut his book with a resounding snap. 'It looks like we're here.' The carriage lurched forwards to a vacant spot in front of the hotel.

He jumped out the moment the carriage came to a halt and reached in to hand her down. 'Come on, Princess, let us take this town by storm.'

* * *

'By storm' was a gross understatement, Aurora decided as the days before the steeplechase slid by in a vibrant kaleidoscope of experiences. The hotel was finer than any she'd seen. The proprietor's reputation for fine organisation was quite accurate and extended beyond the stables. Each room had hot-and-cold water and the dining room served excellent meals with equally good wine. For the men there was a billiards parlour. For the ladies, the hotel provided maids to help with gowns and dressing.

Aurora protested that she didn't need the extravagance of a maid, but Crispin insisted, saying that such a luxury would be expected of a woman travelling under the Dursley aegis. The trunk full of gowns barely filled the dressing room assigned to her, but there they hung pretty and pressed under the care of a pert lady's maid named Polly, who turned her and Beth out to best advantage for the lavish meals served in the dining room.

Crispin had the room next to theirs, but Aurora already anticipated she'd be spending more time in his room. To her credit, Cousin Beth understood both her public and private role as chaperon and said nothing about the implicit arrangement. From the looks of the populace in town for the race, they wouldn't be the only ones reinventing the rules of propriety in the privacy of their own arrangement. It was clear that there were a wide variety of women and relationships present. Some men had brought wives, many had brought mistresses. This was a small town, after all, and the strictures of London did not apply for the duration of the event, but Crispin had smiled patiently at her and then gone about the arrangements in a manner that pleased him. That meant two rooms.

As for Crispin, he was proving to be at ease in their surroundings. They'd no sooner been seated in the hotel dining room for dinner the first night when they were approached by two old acquaintances of his.

'Ramsden, is that you?' Two gentlemen stopped at the table to shake hands with Crispin. 'How are you, Captain?'

Crispin stood up to greet them. 'Baring, Captain Fairlie, it's good to see you.'

Fairlie? The name caught Aurora's attention. One of the first things she'd done was to request a roster of the registered horses as soon as she'd unpacked. Captain Fairlie owned one of the horses who'd be racing, a mare named Norma.

'Allow me to introduce Miss Aurora Calhoun and Miss Beth Ramsden, my cousin.' Crispin gestured towards them both.

'Ah, you must be associated with the Calhoun stables,' Mr Baring said. 'I saw your horse in the stalls, Pride of Kildare, is that right? Looks to be an excellent jumper, very powerful shoulders,' he complimented.

'Thank you. We are hoping he'll do well,' Aurora replied before turning her attention to Captain Fairlie. 'Your horse, Norma, is entered, I see. Are you riding her yourself?'

'No, I've managed to convince Captain Becher to ride her for me.'

'That will even the odds quicker than anything.' Crispin whistled in appreciation at the mention of the renowned steeplechaser. 'Becher is an outstanding rider.' He glanced over at Aurora. 'Fairlie here has his hackles up with the odds setters. He thinks Norma should be the favourite, but they've all decided Poet should have that honour on account of having won last year.'

'Well, we'll see what Poet can do this year. Jem Mason's not riding him this time.' Fairlie rubbed his hands together in anticipation. 'It's good to see you again, Ramsden, you've been gone a while. I'm sure we'll see you around the stables these next few days. We'll have a pint and catch up.' Fairlie and Baring nodded towards her. 'It's a pleasure to meet you, Miss Calhoun. Best of luck to your horse.'

They were the first of many guests to stop by their table. By the end of the evening, all of the entered racers had put in a brief appearance; John Elmore, the owner of Grimaldi, Mr Frith, Mr Weston, the major owner of The Flyer, Mr Bevans, Mr Parker, even Mr Anderson, The Poet's owner, passed by the table to number among the growing list of their acquaintances.

'*Captain* Ramsden, is it?' Aurora quizzed him when the tide of gentlemen seemed to have ebbed later in the evening. There was always a rash of "captains" at a steeplechase. Military men usually proved to be exceptional riders in the sport. But with Crispin, she suspected the title was more literal than figurative as it was in the case of Martin Becher. Becher's 'captaincy' came from heading up a local group of yeoman.

Crispin shrugged. 'Captain Lord Crispin Ramsden, technically, but that was ages ago, practically another lifetime. I was in the cavalry, I think I've told you that before. I was very young then.'

Aurora tossed him a small smile over her wine glass. 'Of course you were in the cavalry. The way you ride, I expect you could have routed the French all on your own.'

Crispin met her eyes steadily. 'I thank you for the compliment. It is the perfect segue to talk of other things. Dare I ask if you'll permit me to ride Kildare on your behalf?' His voice was low, not wanting to risk being overhead by nearby diners.

Aurora looked down at her plate, her hand idly playing with the stem of her glass. 'I have not decided.'

Crispin might have said more, but at that moment another old friend stopped by the table to greet him. The reprieve wouldn't last for ever.

Aurora watched Crispin talking with the newcomer and wondered why she prevaricated. If she rode, she risked everything if she was discovered. She didn't need to ride to accomplish her goal. She wanted the stables recognised, not be a topic of scandal. It had not escaped her attention that when Crispin had introduced her, the men had assumed she was perhaps a female relation attached to the stables. No one had assumed she owned the stables. They'd find out eventually. The vagueness would work for now, but how long did Crispin think they could keep up this ruse?

They finished the excellent meal of jugged hare and Crispin offered to walk outside with her after Cousin Beth returned to their rooms. Together, they strolled to the stables. The stalls were much quieter now. Only stable boys and grooms were about, settling the last of the horses for the evening. They found Dandy and Kildare housed next to each other and doing well in the new surroundings. Kildare nuzzled Aurora, looking for an apple. She rubbed his long face, gently stroking his white blaze.

'How long do you think we can fool them?' Aurora said quietly.

'Fool?' Crispin reached out to stroke Dandy's neck.

'I noticed at dinner that your introduction of me was rather vague.' She added quickly, 'I didn't mind. I understood the necessity for it, but if we're successful and they come to the stables for training, or for stud, they'll figure it out quickly enough.'

Crispin sighed beside her. 'There's ways to prolong it. Have you ever thought of creating a fictional head of the stables? Someone who's abroad and has left the stables in your capable hands?'

Aurora shook her head at that. 'I won't front a lie.'

'Perhaps there could be a real person who could stand as nominal head and who wouldn't interfere with your daily running of the whole enterprise,' Crispin continued, undaunted by her refusal.

'I don't know who that would be. I can't ask Peyton to do it.'

'No, not Peyton. He doesn't have the right sort of connections that would do you any good. You need a man with connections to the horse world.'

What she needed was a man like him. It had become apparent in numerous ways over the past four days that she needed him, not just as a presence in her bed, but as a presence in her life. He managed to succeed where no other man in her life had. He was her partner, not her guardian, not her protector.

He did not seek to take away her autonomy, but to assist her. Life with Crispin was easier than life had been alone. He did not ask her to lay her burden down, he merely asked her to share it. Did he recognise how potent his actions were? Was he aware of the temptation he created? Did such choices mean he'd decided to stay?

'Penny for your thoughts,' Crispin said. 'I can see your mind is whirling with plans.'

'Are you suggesting you might be the man to head the stables?' Aurora ventured, knowing he wouldn't guess the depth of courage it took to ask the simple question.

'I might be. What would you say to that?'

Could she ask him to stay without feeling that such a request was tantamount to trapping him? Until she had those answers, she could not be sure of her answer.

'You don't have to be alone any more.' Crispin reached for her, cupping her cheek with his hand. 'I'm here now.' He kissed her softly.

Yes, you're here now, she thought, giving herself over to the warmth of his kiss. And now would have to be enough.

They spent the next two days exercising the horses, taking turns riding Kildare over the heath in Nomansland in the early morning, studying the steeplechase. In reaction to the outcry the previous year over the lack of challenge in the jumps, this year's hurdles were much more challenging, too challenging in Aurora's opinion.

Her biggest concern was at the start, which featured a wide brook near the bridge at Colney Heath. 'Coleman should start on the other side,' Aurora said their second morning after Kildare had struggled with the brook, only truly clearing it after he'd been warm and in full stride.

'He means to start from the London-facing side.' Crispin shook his head. 'Perhaps if we look for a different approach,' he suggested.

'We've looked. The other riders have looked,' Aurora argued as two riders drew near to them. She recognised the horses as Mr Baring's Caliph and Mr Elmore's renowned grey, Grimaldi.

'Are you discussing that improbable brook?' Caliph's rider, a Mr Christian, said with obvious frustration.

'Yes, it's no good,' Crispin concurred. 'It's possible if we came at it from the other side, but the horses won't be warm enough to master the brook so early in the race with the way the course is laid out.'

'Well, come with us this afternoon and lend your voice,' Christian said. 'We're meeting with Coleman to go over final details. Perhaps if we're all of one mind, we'll be able to sway him.'

The afternoon meeting resulted in a successful verdict. Aurora felt an enormous relief when Crispin reported that Coleman finally relented and changed the direction of the start.

'I'm sorry you couldn't be there,' Crispin said after sharing his news. He was busy stripping off his cravat and shirt in preparation for a hot bath. 'I did nothing more than spout your wisdom.'

'Thank you.' The compliment mitigated her disappointment. It had galled her beyond the pale that she should be so completely shut out of a discussion that affected her so greatly. Instead of arguing on behalf of her horse's safety, she'd been relegated to a hotel room where she'd had to sit and chew her nails for two hours while men deliberated.

She had put the two hours to good use, however. She didn't lack for anything to think about. There was Crispin's tentative proposal about the stables, and the decision about Kildare to consider. Aurora raised the lace panel of the curtains gilding Crispin's front and centre hotel room that overlooked the busy street below. He had not failed her.

'While you were gone, I had time to think. I decided I would withdraw Kildare if the start was not changed,' she said quietly from the window.

'You wouldn't have been alone. I think Elmore might have withdrawn Grimaldi. The horse is getting too old to take chances,' Crispin affirmed, his voice coming in muffled tones from the bathing room.

Aurora could hear the running water splashing in the tub. The hot water had turned out to be an incredible luxury and a most-needed one after long hard hours in the saddle.

Aurora turned from the window in time to catch Crispin's return to the bedchamber unabashedly naked. 'Forgot my towel.' He held up the thick white towelling.

Good lord, he was a gorgeous man, so perfectly put together. She could hardly be blamed for staring. With those long legs and powerful thighs, he was Adonis and David all rolled into one.

'There's room for two in the tub.' Crispin grinned, divining her thoughts. 'Come on, I'll help you with your buttons.'

His hands were slow and warm at her back, taking their own time with each of the tiny buttons that ran the length of the bodice on her borrowed dove-grey afternoon gown, performing a little seduction of their own as Crispin went about his task.

'Why did you decide you'd pull Kildare out of the race?' Crispin whispered against her neck, another button falling loose.

'I've already lost one horse to foolishness. It seemed the height of folly to repeat such an error, especially when I could prevent it by simply pulling out.' She was nearly lost to his touch, but she couldn't give in yet. There were things that needed saying.

'You were thinking about Darby?' Crispin coaxed, pushing the gown from her shoulders, the buttons undone.

'It's hard not to think about Darby. Kildare is his brother,' she said, breathlessly. It was one of her last secrets. 'Kildare is younger, of course, but they share the same sire. He was two when I left Ireland with him.'

* * *

No wonder she was so damn determined to ride, Crispin thought, his hands ceasing their caress at the news. She might not admit it, but he could see how this was some kind of penance for failing in the past, some kind of catharsis. He understood what it cost her to consider withdrawing Kildare from the competition.

Aurora stepped out of her gown and shed her undergarments. 'The water's getting cold.'

They were getting pretty good at this particular dance, the one where someone said too much and they backed off by returning to practical conversation. He slid in first and helped her into the big tub, sitting her between his legs.

She leaned her head against his chest and moaned her delight at the hot water.

Crispin picked up a washcloth he'd dropped into the tub earlier. 'Shall I help you with your bath, madam?' he crooned against her ear.

'That promises to be very wicked.' She laughed, a low intimate chuckle for him alone. He felt his member rise and knew she felt it too.

'Perhaps after you help me with my bath, I'll help you with something else.'

Crispin ran the cloth over her breasts in a gentle, kneading caress and then lower between her legs, massaging her core decadently until she arched against him, finding her pleasure. He revelled in her pleasure. Never had a woman's pleasure been as satisfying to him as it was to watch Aurora and know he'd been the one to bring her such bliss. He loved her passion, he loved her body, how it ignited at his touch, how his ignited at her merest suggestion. Most of all, he feared he loved her.

Aurora rolled in his arms, splashing water over the sides of the tub. 'Your turn.' Her eyes were green fire, promising all nature of pleasurable wickedness.

'Hold on to the sides of the tub, I don't want you to drown,' she instructed, managing to straddle him in the confines of the bath.

He did as he was told. He needed his hands for balance against the slippery surface of the tub, but the inability to use his hands to touch Aurora, to palm those breasts that she boldly presented to him at eye level was an exquisite torture that heightened his already intense desire. She bore down upon him, sliding on to his shaft, using the water to ease her way.

He could not recall ever being taken in a tub before. Or, for that matter, ever really being taken, not fully, not completely in the way Aurora took him now, moving her hips in soft tormenting circles while he surged inside her. God, if men knew what riding astride could do for their love-making, they would ban habits and side-saddles immediately. Crispin arched into her. She slid her hands up his chest, thumbing his nipples with her nails until he groaned his ecstasy.

He wouldn't last much longer. She sensed his impending need to climax closing in on them. He would not be alone; her need was close too. At the last minute she leaned over him, taking his mouth in a bruising kiss while his desire claimed them both.

He was hard pressed to get out of the tub, let alone to get dressed for the formal dinner and dancing that would take place downstairs that evening in celebration of the race tomorrow. But he would be expected and most definitely missed.

Crispin managed to struggle into his clothes alone. Aurora had removed to her rooms. He could hear Polly, the maid, singing next door. He'd like to send Polly away and help Aurora with her *toilette* himself, but only a husband could claim such a position. A husband or a man of certain rights. Since Aurora was neither wife nor mistress, he could claim neither. It was unlikely to change. Neither of them were the marrying type and he would not demean her by asking her to be the latter. She was far too independent to be any man's mistress.

But their situation did not change the fact that he cared for her, deeply. Their arrangement had long since stopped being about 'just sex', no matter what she told herself. He finished dressing in black evening wear and went next door to fetch Aurora. It was time to go downstairs and endure the evening's festivities.

He was not ready for the woman who met him at the door. Aurora was stunning in a ball gown of pale rose satin, her dark hair piled high on her head and looped with pearls. She might have been gracing the finest London ballrooms.

She put out a hand and drew him inside. 'Come in for a minute.'

She fussed with his cravat, making unnecessary adjustments. 'I have something to say before we go down. I told you earlier that I'd decided to pull Kildare if the start wasn't changed.'

He nodded encouragingly, sensing how difficult this conversation was for her, but uncertain where she meant to go with it.

'I decided something else as well while you were gone this afternoon. I decided you should ride Kildare tomorrow.'

Chapter Fifteen

Did no one guess at the fiction Crispin Ramsden played out before them nightly? Gregory Windham scoffed in the shadows of the Turf Hotel ballroom. He watched Aurora waltz past in Ramsden's arms, Ramsden smiling down at her, laughing, totally enchanted with the whore in his arms. Admittedly, she was a fetching bit of temptation tonight in pale rose silk trimmed with dainty cream lace and matching silk ribbons. The temptation lay in the vision of happiness and innocence she presented. None of it was true, of course. He had the papers to prove it just waiting to be revealed. Whatever Ramsden had talked himself into believing regarding Aurora Calhoun's virtue, he would soon be disabused of it as publicly as Windham could manage.

As for Aurora, she'd get no better than she deserved. Unable to arrive until today himself, Windham had set his men to watching her progress from afar this week, watching her glide through society on Ramsden's arm, letting the magic of his name open doors for her. It was disgusting.

He saw the way Ramsden's coterie of friends, men of some influence in the horse community, made exceptions for her, treated her as something of an equal. His men's reports were full of examples of her excellent riding in the practices and the remarks others had made about her sound horsemanship.

It galled Windham to think that while Ramsden's name had opened doors for her, she'd actually proven worthy of the respect accorded to her—or so those bloody sots thought. Windham doubted they'd feel so inclined once her plan to ride Kildare was exposed.

Unfortunately, there had been no signs that she intended to ride that big hunter of hers herself. He'd been certain she'd attempt some foolish disguise. That was when he'd planned to make his move. He'd uncover her deception and more, but so far, she was foiling his plans. However, she'd made no overtures to hire a jockey and now with the race scheduled for tomorrow, it was virtually too late. Did she mean to let Ramsden ride? Ramsden was in his element, surrounded by former acquaintances from his military days and his skill on horseback was commendable, on par with the renowned Captain Martin Becher himself.

Windham didn't want Crispin Ramsden to ride. Not only did his presence in the race diminish Flyer's chances to place well, but it took away an opportunity to place Aurora Calhoun in the eye of a reputation-ruining scandal. There was absolutely nothing illegal about Ramsden riding. He could hardly raise a hue and cry about a legally qualified rider. Men were supposed to ride in steeple-chases. He couldn't bear the thought of Aurora coming out of this unscathed. With Ramsden aboard, her horse could likely win and he'd have no way to protest against such a legitimate win. Ramsden had to be removed and he would be, shortly.

The thought brought a cruel smile to Windham's lips.

An accident was already arranged. He was just waiting for Ramsden to spring the trap. An accident would serve both short-term goals and long-term. It would get Ramsden out of the race and it would suggest to Aurora that the man she cared about was not untouchable. What might Aurora pay to keep Ramsden safe? What might she do?

He felt the familiar tightening of his body in anticipation, his mind filling with images of a penitent Aurora on her knees, begging him as she should have begged him before. She should have been glad of his notice—jubilant, in fact. She was of no rank and Irish to boot. She was far beneath the notice of a man like him, a man with breeding and wealth, able to give her all she could want, all she could expect in return for the simple act of being his.

'I thought you didn't like ballroom dancing.' Aurora laughed up at Crispin, who gallantly navigated them through a lively gallop. She was thoroughly enjoying herself tonight. Now that the decision had been made, she felt an enormous burden removed from her shoulders.

Crispin grinned gamely. 'I don't like it, but that doesn't mean I'm not good at it.'

The night had a festive air to it. The lobby of the Turf Hotel had been transformed into a ballroom, the furniture pushed back for dancing and the dance floor was crowded with all those who'd come to St Albans for the races. The music ended and Crispin escorted her over to a group of people, acquaintances of his who'd now become acquaintances of hers over the days in town. Other women might dream of silk dresses and London balls, but this was all she'd ever dreamed of since she had left Ireland; acceptance among other horse enthusiasts. Crispin had given her that. Never mind that her presence at Crispin's side had ensured much of that acceptance. He'd paved the way most assuredly, but he'd done so in a manner that allowed her to speak her mind among his group of friends and his friends had not rejected that input.

Whether he knew it or not, he was slowly eroding her reasons for keeping her emotional distance from him. The biggest reason of all was simply that she refused to give a man control of her life. But clearly, Crispin had demonstrated he didn't want to dictate terms. The one time he'd tried to do so had merely been out of a sense of obligation. He wanted to be her partner in this venture.

The very thought was as intoxicating as it was novel. She didn't want to contemplate how long that would last. She'd meant it at the gypsy camp when she'd told him she didn't believe in for ever.

Crispin leaned close to her ear. 'I'm going out to check on the horses. I'll be back in time for the next waltz.'

Aurora nodded and watched him go before turning her attention to a discussion of tomorrow's field of horses and whether or not last year's victor, The Poet, would be as competitive this year.

That discussion passed, the next dance passed. Crispin hadn't returned. Maybe he'd stopped to talk with a groom at the stables. Or worse. Maybe one of the horses had come down with something. That started the first wave of worries. Maybe something had happened to him. True, they'd not caught a glimpse of Gregory Windham all week, but he could have arrived undetected this afternoon or he could have been here all along and chosen to keep to himself, although she could hardly imagine Windham choosing such an option. The man was too status hungry to remain a wallflower.

'Miss Calhoun, is everything all right?' one of the young men with John Elmore's entourage inquired.

'I'm worried that Lord Ramsden hasn't come back.' She started moving towards the door before she'd even completed the sentence. The young man—Jeremy, she thought his name was—followed close behind, stopping to say a few words resulting in a small parade of men gathering behind her.

The stable area was empty, the stable boys and grooms having gone to their beds earlier in anticipation of the long day tomorrow. Aurora's concern rose. There was no one about whom Crispin might stop and talk with. If no one was about, it would be far easier to perpetrate a crime.

'Crispin!' Aurora called out into the stable at large. There was no immediate answer. She turned down the aisle where Kildare and Dandy were housed. She lifted up her skirts and barely refrained from breaking into a run. 'Crispin!' she called again. Did she imagine she heard a moan? Good lord, surely it wasn't coming from inside the stall where he could get kicked or stepped on by a thousand pounds of horseflesh?

Careless of the ball gown she wore, Aurora opened the stall door and stepped inside, slippers crackling on straw.

Her eyes adjusted to the darker interior and she found him at once propped against a wall, obviously injured. Kildare pranced nervously, keeping his distance from the faces that crowded the door of his stall.

'What happened?' Aurora knelt beside him, hands immediately searching his body for injury. She quickly undid his shirt, noting with quiet horror the bruising around his ribs. Out of the corner of her eye she noted Captain Becher had slid into the stall to quiet Kildare.

Crispin grasped her hands and managed hoarsely, 'Windham is here.'

'Did he do this to you?'

'Seven of his men did this.' Crispin winced as her hands ran over his ribs.

'I don't think anything's broken.' Aurora breathed a sigh of tentative relief. Bruised ribs were bad enough, but a broken rib could endanger a lung.

One of the men who'd followed Jeremy squatted down beside her and affirmed her assessment. 'He's bruised badly, though. He'll need to get those ribs wrapped.'

'How are your legs?' Aurora asked, fearing the men had tried to cripple his knees.

'My knees are all right.' Crispin grunted, struggling to rise. 'I'll be fine.' He was already chafing at being treated like an invalid, but he was clearly not fine. Two men helped him outside the stall. If he'd been fine, he would have dragged himself back to the ballroom. Aurora could see that he was pale, that it cost him a great effort to speak and that the blows to his ribs were causing him not only discomfort, but pain too.

'The horse is fine. I smelled his food, it's fine, too,' Becher said, stepping out behind them and dusting off his hands. 'Do we know who might be responsible for this?'

Crispin sank down on to a hay bale in the aisle. 'We have a good idea, but he owns a share in one of the horses racing and I hesitate to name names out of courtesy to the owner. I don't want a scandal to implicate the innocent.'

'Shh, don't talk so much,' Aurora admonished.

'I doubt he'll be a part-owner much longer,' someone said gruffly. 'This is not the behaviour of a gentleman. We'll handle it discreetly, non-violently, if you give us a name.'

Aurora could see Crispin thinking it over. After a moment he said, 'No. This is a personal affair and I'll handle it in a personal manner.'

'Are you certain? This attack cannot go unaddressed. This impedes Kildare's chances tomorrow,' Becher put in. 'Ramsden can't ride. It's out of the question with his ribs in this condition.'

Crispin protested. 'If they're wrapped tightly enough, I can do it.'

Becher turned a disbelieving gaze on him and shook his head. 'You're tough, but there is no way you can take those jumps safely. The impact of the landing alone would be enough to cause severe pain, to say nothing of the jarring speed of a canter over several miles.'

Crispin tried to rise. 'Miss Calhoun's horse deserves to race.'

'Race, yes, Ramsden, but not to risk serious injury. That's precisely what that horse will be risking with you on his back. You won't have all your abilities to guide him safely through the course,' Frith put in.

'There's no time to get another rider,' Crispin argued, his gaze flicking meaningfully towards her. Aurora read the message hidden there for her. This was her chance. She took the opening, praying that the entrée Crispin had helped her carve out this week would be enough.

'I'll ride,' she said firmly. 'It's my horse, after all.'

That silenced the group momentarily. A few exchanged looks. 'Well, I dare say Miss Calhoun could ride,' Captain Fairlie suggested in a hesitant drawl. 'We've all seen her during the workouts. She's as capable as you are on that horse, Ramsden.'

Aurora shot a sharp look at Crispin. He was nodding, the others were nodding as the suggestion took root. 'There's none better,' Crispin endorsed.

'Except for the obvious factor. She's a woman. It is distinctly illegal,' Frith pointed out.

'She'll have to ride as a man,' Baring said. 'We might all privately agree that she's capable, but the public won't understand.'

Frith spoke up again. 'Remember, the man who did this knows Crispin is hurt. He expects Kildare will be forced to withdraw. Will he expect Miss Calhoun is riding if the horse stays entered?'

Crispin shook his head. 'Whoever is behind this could not expose her without great expense to himself. He won't dare risk it. I'll make sure of it.'

It was all settled when the group finally managed to carry Crispin up to his rooms and wrap his ribs. Aurora would ride and Crispin's friends would see to all the necessary arrangements that would keep her and their little secret safe.

Aurora gingerly slid into bed next to Crispin, careful not to disturb his injuries. 'Why didn't you tell them it was Windham?' She asked the question that had been in the forefront of her mind since she'd found Crispin in the stall. She'd been entirely surprised when he'd chosen not to disclose the name.

'Lots of reasons.' Crispin shrugged in the darkness. 'For one, I didn't want to expose The Flyer. It's not their fault. Windham is acting entirely of his own accord and I didn't want them lumped in with his shenanigans. They're hurting for money; if they lose Windham's share right now, they'll be hard pressed to keep their stables. They shouldn't be punished for Windham's transgression. More importantly, I wanted to keep you safe, at least as safe as I can. If word got out tomorrow morning that Windham had attacked me or harmed Kildare, who knows what he might do in an attempt to save face. He would most certainly challenge the identity of Kildare's rider and if he were successful in his petition, we'd look as dishonourable as he does.'

'You were thinking fast. I would have blurted it out without a second thought.' What Crispin said made sense and she was grateful for his cool head.

'I had more time to filter the situation than you did,' Crispin remarked wryly. 'There's not much else to do in a stall with your ribs crushed. Between how to manage the attack and all the things I'd like to do to Windham when I get my hands on him, I was pretty busy.'

The last part got her attention. 'Crispin, what are you planning?' Caution infused her voice.

'Don't worry. I simply intend to extend some neighbourly goodwill towards Windham tomorrow. He'll have an excellent view of your victory tomorrow, sitting right next to me. I'll be keeping my friends close and my enemies closer and only he and I will know the difference between the two.'

'How do you think you'll manage that? You are hurt. You have to recognise you have some limitations right now. You can't go charging after Windham with your fists.'

'I have something better than fists in this case. I have information.'

Aurora sighed. The man was impossible, but he had her trust. If he said he could manage Windham long enough for her to ride, she believed him. 'I didn't want my dream to come true this way. I wouldn't have seen you hurt.'

'I'll be fine. Tomorrow, you'll be fine. You'll have to add weights to your saddle to make the twelve stones, but you'll be fine.' He laughed a little, remembering too late that it would hurt.

Aurora didn't laugh. Tomorrow she'd be fine. Flyer's rider had no interest in seeing her hurt on the course and, in fact, was not even aware that it was his mount Windham owned a share in. She didn't have to worry about foul play in that regard. 'I'm not worried about the race. I'm more concerned about after the race.' Thwarting Windham tomorrow would not curtail the private vendetta Windham waged against her. In fact, she was sure it would only serve to inflame him further.

'The cares of tomorrow can wait until then, Aurora. Rest assured, whatever they are, we'll meet them together,' Crispin murmured.

And for once, Aurora let herself believe it.

The race wouldn't start until noon. That left him plenty of time to effect his plans with regard to Windham. Crispin had woken sore, but in good spirits. Aurora had helped him dress. Then she and Beth had gone down to breakfast and out to the stables with one of John Elmore's crew for a race-day inspection. Crispin thought it a good idea that as many people as possible see Aurora as the genteel Miss Calhoun in her skirts walking through the stables to squelch any potential speculation.

He wouldn't see her again until after the race. He wished he could be there to boost her up on to Kildare and give her all sorts of last-minute advice she didn't need, but he had a job to do. Crispin turned on his heel once Aurora and Beth were out of sight and walked back into the dining room, intent on hunting down his quarry.

Windham was eating eggs and ham. Best of all, he was eating with a group of people, gentlemen who'd come to watch and wager on the race. A crowd served Crispin's purposes perfectly. The snake was trapped.

Windham was pompously listing Flyer's attributes when Crispin approached the table. 'Good morning, Windham,' he said loudly with an enormous amount of bonhomie. He slapped the man hard on the back for good measure. 'Thought I'd find you here.'

Windham's genuine look of surprise to see him up and walking was hugely gratifying. 'Ramsden…' he managed to splutter, his face visibly paling. The table was staring at Windham now, waiting expectantly for introductions.

Crispin elected to help him out. The more people who saw them as 'acquaintances', the tighter the corner he could back Windham into. 'I'm Crispin Ramsden from Dursley,' he introduced himself to the group at large. 'Windham and I are practically neighbours. We bid on the same horse a few weeks back.' He was all jovial friendliness. He could tell many of the people at the table were impressed with Windham's connection.

'I've come to ask your help on a matter, Windham, and to extend an invitation to sit in my box at the grandstand. I've reserved excellent seats at the finish line. We'll be able to see the winner the moment a hoof crosses the line.' The group was looking at Windham with envy now. To be invited to sit with Ramsden and to have such prime seats was an entirely desirable proposition.

As Crispin anticipated, Windham had no choice but to accept. Only a fool would publicly reject the generous offer. Crispin put an arm about the man's shoulder in an ostensible show of friendship, but his grip was iron as he sought out a quiet corner for their 'discussion'.

'What is the meaning of this farce?' Windham dared some bravado once they were alone.

'Men you hired attacked me last night. I have warned you on prior occasions I would not tolerate any harm being done to me or to those under my protection,' Crispin growled, careful to reveal the tip of a knife beneath his sleeve. 'Don't think sore ribs will stop me from using this. You will listen to what I have to say.'

'You cannot prove it. You'll never find those men. They're long gone from here.' Windham paled further, swallowing hard at the sight of Crispin's blade. He summoned his last trump. 'Why all the effort, Ramsden? I've already succeeded in winning. You're out of commission. Kildare cannot enter the race unless you mean for your Irish whore to ride. I will expose her to the race committee and you'll be unable to do anything about it.'

Crispin gave a glacial smile. 'I believe you have a stake in Flyer and a daughter about to marry a baron. I doubt either of those parties would like to know the shenanigans of which you are capable. Baron Sedgwick cannot withstand such a scandal. There are other rich girls for him to marry whose fathers are hungry for a title.'

Cold calculation spread across Windham's frightened features. 'You bastard. How dare you threaten my daughter's wedding.'

'That ploy won't work with me. From what I've heard, she'd welcome the scandal if it saved her.' Crispin was all icy politeness. 'I believe we have an accord. For the sake of your reputation, you will sit with me in my box, surrounded by my friends. They don't know what you've done, not yet anyway. That will be for you to decide. You will say nothing in regards to Kildare's rider. With luck, you'll toast to Kildare's victory at the end of the day. In return, I'll let you run back to Dursley with your tail between your legs just like the cur you are.' Crispin smiled wolfishly. 'Come, my dear friend from Dursley. The race awaits.'

Waiting had never been her strong suit. Today, her patience had disappeared altogether. Aurora paced the confines of her room, checking the clock hands again and again only to be disappointed in their progress.

At ten-thirty she allowed herself to dress. She'd dismissed Beth and the maid, wanting privacy as she gathered her thoughts, to say nothing of her anonymity. She wanted to dress as a man alone. She bound her breasts tightly with strips of white cloth until they were flattened enough to pass scrutiny. She buttoned her shirt and turned from side to side in the mirror to survey the effect. It would pass. No one would know. *Unless she fell and was carried off the field unconscious and some well-meaning soul searched for injuries.*

Aurora closed her eyes tight against the memories of Darby, of the day she'd fallen so terribly. She could not afford the distraction. Hastily, angry with herself, she reached for her riding trousers and pulled them on. Of its own volition her hand skimmed the scar below her waist, a lasting reminder of her folly. The gambler's hope rose in her mind. *This time it would be different.*

She tucked her hair firmly up underneath a knit fisherman's cap and placed her riding cap over it, her confidence returning. Darby would not want her distracted with the past. If her da were here he'd be telling her to clear her mind of nothing but the course. This was not a case of history repeating itself. Aurora tugged at her jacket. She was Aurora Calhoun, a woman who had succeeded under extraordinary odds. She'd survived an accident that could have rightfully claimed her life. She'd survived a husband who'd cast her off and put her outside acceptable society. She was strong. She would not fail now.

Aurora shot a glance at the clock. At last it was time, time to make her appearance in disguise and lead Kildare through the throng gathered outside the Turf Hotel to the starting line at Colney Heath. She was surrounded by Crispin's friends and quietly assured in cryptic comments from a stable boy who didn't understand what he was relating that Crispin's plan was going according to schedule. But, in spite of Crispin's thoughtful assurances, she still expected to hear Windham's voice ring out with some charge of fraud as she passed through the streets on Kildare.

There were no such charges and she reached the starting line without any fuss. She shielded her eyes against the bright sun and scanned the grandstand for Crispin's box. A little smile played on her lips as she located it. Crispin sat there, surrounded by his racing comrades and a tense Windham sitting on his right. So that's what he'd meant about keeping his friends close and his enemies closer. She'd have to get the details out of him later. Crispin would prevent Windham from exposing her and in turn Crispin's friends wouldn't let Windham hurt Crispin. Windham could hardly do anything to Crispin with so many of Crispin's loyal friends present. It was good to have one less thing to worry about.

Beside her at the start, Captain Becher flashed a quick wink, his humour much improved over Norma's five-to-one odds. Beneath her, Kildare pranced in excitement. Kildare knew with a competitor's intuition that he was about to race.

Aurora leaned down to pat the stallion's neck, a million thoughts jostling through her mind. Today was both for the past and the future. Today was for putting the ghosts of yesterday to rest and reaching for the bright promise of tomorrow. If her father knew, he'd be proud; proud of Kildare and proud of her. A bugle trumpeted, calling the horses to readiness. Aurora turned her thoughts to the course, seeing each jump, each turn in her mind. There was no room for thoughts of anything else now.

The bugle trumpeted again, blowing the notes that heralded the start. Aurora tensed, gathering the reins to her. Kildare bunched his muscles beneath her and they were off.

Chapter Sixteen

The whole field surged as one, horses jostling, riders looking for space to make their own. Becher pushed Norma to the front, a lead pack containing Parasol, Norma and Grimaldi separated from the others. Aurora felt Kildare fight the bit, wanting to catch the leaders. She held him back, preferring to run strong with the middle horses. A few fell back, wary of the early first jump.

Aurora flew over the first jump, feeling Kildare take the difficult leap over the brook easily. She gave Kildare his head, wanting now to catch the leaders as the pack thinned and Kildare settled into his natural stride. Anything could happen in a steeplechase. It was one of the fundamental underpinnings of the very nature of the race. Her father had taught her at his knee how very quickly the race could change.

This steeplechase was no different. Little over a mile from the starting line, Parasol led with John Elmore's prized Grimaldi in second when the first accident hit. Aurora was riding in fourth, three lengths behind the leaders, and saw it all clearly. To her horror, Grimaldi stumbled after the fence and fell, effectively scratched from the race. With a quick glance, she saw Grimaldi's rider, Billy Bean, rise, shaking intensely from the impact and trying to dust himself off. Grimaldi was already struggling to his feet and limping. They would not rejoin the chase.

There was naught she could do for them and she focused her attention on the next fence, a hedge of sorts with a sloped landing on the other side. Parasol held the lead alone and two horses lay between her and Parasol; Becher on Norma and Mr Weston's Flyer, the same horse who had the dubious pleasure of being partly owned by Gregory Windham.

Aurora risked a backward glance under her arm. Plenty of strong horses lay behind her: Shamrock, Bittern, Captain Bob, Caliph and Laurestina ran in the last big group; closer still by only a few lengths were Poet and Cumberton. They were surging, making their move. The withdrawal of Grimaldi had inspired them to greater lengths. With Grimaldi and Billy Bean out, there was hope to overcome the favourites. It was tempting to urge Kildare to faster speeds to put a larger distance between her and the upcoming riders, but she cautioned herself against it. If they caught her, so be it. There was still two miles to go. She would wait. She would want that speed closer to the end.

The accident with Grimaldi was not to be the only incident that day. With two-thirds of the race completed and Poet pounding furiously behind her, Aurora took a fence and heard the horrific scream of a horse in pain. She threw a backward glance to see The Poet staked on the jump at a queer angle that chilled her blood. Her glance was enough to tell her the horse would not recover. Bile rose in her throat at the thought of the beautiful champion being destroyed.

It was almost her undoing. Memories of Darby, of her own fall, threatened to break loose. Tears stung in her eyes, blurring her sight. A fence was almost upon her and she blinked furiously to clear her vision. She searched her memory for the jump. It was a particularly tricky one, higher than it looked. To clear it safely, she had to start the jump earlier than might seem wise. She and Crispin had talked this fence over extensively. She thought of Crispin, waiting at the finish line, of how he believed in her. She could not fail now on grounds of sentimentality. She gathered her courage and Kildare soared.

They cleared the jump, but she knew it was due to her horsemanship more than Kildare's size and speed. She could feel the big hunter tiring beneath her. He'd needed her coaching, her careful timing, to make the leap. The natural talent of the horse would not be enough on a leap like this.

Such circumstances were to be expected with under a mile to go. This part of the race was designed to show off a rider's capabilities more than the horse's. Her strategy was paying off. She was glad she'd held Kildare back from surging after Grimaldi's stumble.

Norma, Flyer and Parasol still remained ahead of her, but the gap was closing. Parasol and Flyer battled each other for the lead, trading places several times. That could work to her advantage. They would tire each other out and leave an opening for Kildare. The last quarter-mile would tell all.

Aurora had a large stretch of flat plain ahead of her and she speeded up slightly, closing the distance between Kildare and Norma. Close up, Norma was sweat-flecked, but still running strong. Aurora wondered how the horse's jumping muscles felt. Did the mare have the strength for the last jump, a high water fence? The mare didn't have the deep chest Kildare had inherited from his Irish draughthorse ancestors.

The finish line loomed in the far-off distance, Coleman's grandstand filled with spectators came into view. Aurora assessed her choices for the last half-mile when two things happened. Slightly ahead of her, Norma stumbled on the flat, losing her footing, and the renowned Becher fell, rolling away from the oncoming racers. It wasn't a harmful fall, and, while it might buy her a few extra seconds, Aurora knew Becher would be horsed in minutes and following in her wake.

She urged Kildare onwards, making the most of the opportunity the brief mishap had afforded her. Norma would have to work hard to catch Kildare. Aurora was two lengths behind the duelling Flyer and Parasol. Parasol was running a spectacular race, having led since the first mile except for Flyer's off-and-on challenge for the lead.

Aurora was close enough to see the two horses now, Parasol sweating vigorously from the efforts. The last jump approached. That's when the second item happened; the amazing Parasol refused the jump. Flyer took the jump and Aurora took it immediately afterwards while Parasol's rider wheeled the snorting horse around for a second try.

The race was all about speed now and whatever the rider had saved for the finish. Aurora lifted her rear from the saddle, hoping to spare Kildare the extra weight, her thighs pressed tight to his sides asking for all his reserves, her body off the saddle and leaning low over Kildare's neck.

Competition fuelled her. Her kind feelings for Mr Weston aside, Aurora wanted to beat Flyer. She didn't want to lose to any horse, let alone one the despicable Windham had sponsored. Ahead of her, Flyer began to slow; the big horse was built more for power than speed and had spent his reserves competing with Parasol. Elation fired her blood. Kildare had enough left. It was only a matter of mathematical inevitability and they would overtake the fatigued Flyer.

Behind her, Parasol vied with the return of Norma. They were both strong horses with smart riders. She passed Flyer as early cheers went up from the grandstand. She heard the hooves of Parasol and Norma overtake Flyer. For a moment it was a three-way sprint, but Parasol had already run her race. Parasol fell off and Kildare sprinted hard, matching Norma stride for stride.

Adrenalin thundered through Aurora's veins. Her arms were damned tired, her legs ached from the strain, she could hear Kildare's breathing coming heavy and fast. A smile took her face from the pure joy of the race. She was flying, she was living her dream. Beside her, she heard Becher let out a whoop as they cornered the last flag. Aurora went to the right of it, Becher to the left. Did she imagine a slight cut of the corner on his part? It was too close to tell.

The yells intensified from the grandstand. Five lengths to go! Aurora kept her eyes fixed on the finish, perfectly sighted between the ears of her hunter. She fought the temptation to look over at Becher. Did she have a nose? She wouldn't win by much more than that, but neither would he. Try as she could, Norma could give him nothing more.

They crossed, so close together the victor wasn't clear to Aurora. Four lengths behind them Parasol finished, and then Flyer crossed the line another several lengths behind Parasol. Aurora pulled Kildare to a walk and let the valiant stallion cool off. Becher was swamped with admirers and a jubilant Captain Fairlie. Up in the starter's box, Thomas Coleman and the other race officials conferred over the results. She was careful to stay apart from the interested crowds, although the feat was difficult since she and Kildare were involved in the astonishing finish.

Becher seemed to understand her apprehension. It wouldn't do now to be discovered. Becher edged Norma towards Kildare and while it brought the crowds, it also brought Becher close enough to act as spokesperson for both of them. Over the heads of the crowd gathered about them, she finally saw the only spectator she cared about seeing. Crispin made his way through masses, shouldering over to her and taking Kildare's reins. A quick glance at his grandstand box told her Windham had been effectively trapped there by conversation. She was safe for the moment.

'Captain, why don't we get these horses to the stables where we can wipe them down and take care of them,' Crispin called up to Becher.

Glad for any reason to be away, Becher nodded and they led the horses to the safety of Coleman's stalls. The walk to the barns was sheer torture for Aurora. Still filled with the exhilaration of the race, she wanted to throw her arms around Crispin and celebrate, but her disguise made such a display impossible.

The crowds stayed at the grandstand, wanting to hear the results of the close race. They had the stables to themselves. The instant Aurora had Kildare at his stall, she slid off into Crispin's arms and kissed him soundly, letting all her enthusiasm claim the moment. 'We did it!'

Crispin's arms were tight around her, without regard for his bruised ribs. 'You were magnificent.' He grinned broadly, his enthusiasm equalling hers. 'I wish I could have seen the whole race. I saw you coming over the last jump, though, and you looked great. I knew you had it then.'

She nodded her head vigorously. 'I knew it too.' The words came out in an excited rush. 'It was only a matter of time before I took Flyer.'

Crispin laughed. 'Then I saw how close Norma was and I started to worry. Parasol came out of nowhere, not even a favourite, but I could see even at a distance she was too tired.'

They talked over the last bit of the race in each other's arms, springing apart only when they heard rapid footsteps approaching the stall. 'Milord, news from the grandstand!' an eager stable boy called.

Crispin stepped outside the stall. 'What is it?'

The boy was breathless, having run across town with the message. 'The race has been contested.'

Aurora felt a moment's trepidation. After all that had happened, had she been found out? Had someone not kept the secret?

'It's Becher!' the boy said. 'Someone contested his last turn. He cut the flag. He went left when he should have gone right. He strayed off the path. If it's true, he'll be disqualified. That means your horse will win, milord.'

The boy turned around and ran into the chest of Captain Martin

Becher. 'Is that so?' He seemed unbothered by the claims, slapping his riding gloves against his palm.

The boy blushed and stammered, 'That's what they're saying down at the course.'

Becher flipped him a coin. 'Get along with you, son.' The boy ran off and Becher looked past Crispin's shoulders to find her in the interior of the stall. 'I think it would be best if that disqualification didn't happen,' he said quietly.

Aurora nodded. If she was the sole victor, there would be a lot of attention sent her way and questions about the unknown rider who'd substituted for Crispin Ramsden the morning of the race. There would be enough attention as it was, but if the famous Becher won, much of that attention would be deflected.

Aurora changed quickly into a dress, ready to assume her role as the representative for the Calhoun Stables, and the threesome headed back to the grandstand. The race site was still abuzz with activity. They made their way to the starter's box where Coleman and the officials still agonised over the final standings. 'We have news to help your deliberations,' Crispin called out in jovial tones.

Coleman climbed down. 'What do you know?'

Aurora squared her shoulders and said authoritatively, 'The Calhoun rider says Becher didn't cut the flag. He stayed on the path.'

Coleman nodded. 'We're leaning that way ourselves. Several other observers say they saw no proof of taking the flag improperly.' He thanked them and climbed back up to the box. Moments later the bugle blew to signal for silence.

'We have the results of the race,' Coleman's voice boomed out over the quiet crowd. 'In third place, The Flyer, owned by Mr Weston.' Polite applause and congratulations met the announcement. Weston gave the crowd a wave. Aurora shot Crispin a confused look. Flyer should have been fourth. 'In second place, Parasol, owned by Donald Seffert.' The applause increased for the magnificent horse. 'In first place, for the first time since the running of the St Albans steeplechase, we have a tie. Seeing that there was no violation of the course, the officials cannot determine a clear victor. With great pleasure, we award first place to Norma, owned by Captain Fairlie, and first place as well to The Pride of Kildare, owned by the Calhoun Stables.'

The crowd applauded and yelled wildly, caught up in the excitement of the tie. Captain Fairlie helped Aurora up to the blocks set up as a stage for the presentation of the cup and wreath of roses.

Aurora thought it was quite ridiculous that it was all right for a woman to claim the award, but not be able to actually earn it. However, she smiled brilliantly to the crowd, who thought her only a pretty representative of what must surely be her father's or brother's enterprising stables.

'We didn't anticipate such a finish,' Coleman began, speaking out over the crowd. 'Coleman's Turf Hotel will of course provide a second cup in due time. Congratulations to our victors. We'll celebrate with a post-race champagne supper at the hotel this evening at eight o'clock.' This announcement was also met with applause, everyone knowing that Coleman kept an excellent hotel cellar.

'Congratulations, Miss Calhoun,' Captain Fairlie escorted her back to Crispin's waiting arm. 'Your horse ran an exceptional race and is certainly a credit to the rider's abilities as well as the Calhoun Stables. We'll have a lot to talk about at dinner.'

'Perhaps I could impose on you, Captain Fairlie,' Crispin jumped in. 'Could you see Miss Calhoun back to the hotel? I have to see someone off. His carriage is waiting to take him back to his home.' Crispin winked at Aurora. 'Windham sends his congratulations. He regrets he won't be able to join us tonight for the celebrations.' She could imagine Crispin bundling Windham into a carriage and sending it off, ridding them of the man's odious presence for a little while.

* * *

Dinner was a lavish affair complete with white linen tablecloths and champagne flutes. 'The place is utterly transformed.' Becher laughed, taking his seat at the large round table where Crispin and Aurora sat surrounded by the other winners. He winked at Aurora. 'Miss Calhoun, in the course of an ordinary day this place is usually just a watering hole for all of us ex-military men. We shoot billiards, talk horses, and drink Coleman's excellent wines and ales. But tonight, ah, tonight, it is revealed in its full glory. Perhaps it is your beauty that makes the transformation so utterly complete,' he complimented gallantly.

Aurora blushed prettily at the comment. 'You do me a great honour, Captain.' She was doing her best not to feel self-conscious in the gown Tessa had sent. It was a lovely confection of pale cream silk trimmed in celery-coloured ribbons and lace. The neckline was a bit of a plunge, showing off far more of her cleavage than she could ever remember Tessa showing, but Crispin had taken one look at her upstairs and convinced her it was perfect for her victory dinner, chivalrously offering to help her out of the gown later.

Aurora reached for her champagne flute and sipped, covering up the little smile that played about her lips, a smile she wouldn't be able to explain to anyone at the table without extreme embarrassment. Dressing for dinner had proved quite the experience. Between Crispin's sore ribs, her achy muscles from riding and the complexity of Tessa's gown, neither one of them had been able to dress themselves, which had resulted in some creative manoeuvres.

Her smile threatened again at the mental of image of Crispin, unable to bend over and put on his own trousers, lying prone on the bed while she slipped his dark evening trousers up his legs, his buttocks flexing while she slid the fabric up over his hips, her hands stopping to sightsee as she worked the fastenings.

Of course, he'd got his revenge the moment she stepped into Tessa's cream gown and realised she couldn't possibly do it up on her own. She giggled and put a hand over her mouth, trying to re-focus her attentions on the conversation at the table. She looked up to catch Crispin's eyes on her, hot and bold, and knew she hadn't fooled him. He knew precisely what she was thinking.

'What do you think it is about the Irish? Irish-bred hunters seem to outperform English stock on a regular basis,' John Elmore mused aloud to the table.

Everyone shook their heads. 'It's a mystery,' Becher said jovi-ally. 'It's probably the water,' he joked.

'Oh, no, it's not the water.' Aurora gave full vent to her smile, glad to have an excuse for it. 'It's the grass. There's more lime content in it,' she said matter of factly.

'You are not jesting?' Weston leaned forwards, intrigued.

'Seriously.'

Becher slapped his hand on his knee and whooped. 'She's a keeper, Ramsden. I'd give anything to find a woman who knew as much about horses as Miss Calhoun.' He reached for his own flute and raised it. 'A toast, everyone, to the beautiful, knowledgeable, incomparable Miss Calhoun.'

With good grace Aurora accepted the toast, savouring the moment. She'd never be an incomparable on the stage of the London *ton*, might never be openly acknowledged for her horse training beyond this table, but this moment was enough. She'd raced and she'd won on her own merits and these men recognised her talent for what it was.

The evening was the stuff of dreams. On her right, Captain Fairlie talked about breeding a stallion of his with one of her mares. On her left, Mr Weston talked about training techniques and sending a few two year olds to her who had not shown promise in flat racing, but showed signs of being jumpers. Across the table, Crispin was engaged in his own conversations, but his gaze was never far from her, his desire unveiled, promising all the pleasure he could deliver later back in their rooms, sore ribs notwithstanding. If she knew Crispin, they'd manage well enough. God, how she loved him.

Her mind tripped at the realisation, losing track momentarily of her conversation with Captain Fairlie. *She loved Crispin Ramsden.* For better or for worse, she'd come to love the arrogant man who'd kissed a stranger in the Dursley Road, who'd danced with the gypsies, who championed her right down to every last unconventional eccentricity she possessed. Her heart was in dangerous territory, but not tonight.

Tonight, she could not ask for more. If history conveniently forgot to list Becher's win on Norma as a tie, if her newfound love foundered against the tides of reality, so be it. Tonight, she had her victory. Her horses had been recognised for their quality, she had her reputation established, and she had a man she loved for however long it lasted.

Chapter Seventeen

The next day was a market day and like many of the race participants, she and Crispin elected to stay the extra day to rest the horses before travelling home. She was determined to savour every minute of it. Time was suspended and Aurora refused think of the realities that lay outside the cocoon of St Albans.

What choice did she have? she reflected as she dressed in another of Tessa's lovely walking dresses. The revelation of the night prior would be for her alone. She could no more tell Crispin Ramsden she loved him than she could hold back the tides. She shot a look at the bed and found him awake, hands behind his head, watching her intently as she moved through her morning *toilette*.

'Are you going to dress me next?' he drawled.

'Still too sore to put your own pants on?' She smiled and moved to the bed, hips deliberately swaying.

'Still too hard,' he parried wickedly, reaching for her.

'You're a lusty man, Ramsden.' She laughed as he hauled her down, his hands already under her skirts. How did a woman tame a stallion such as this man? Was such a thing even possible? What would she do with a tamed Crispin? She wasn't even sure that was what she wanted.

Dressing Crispin took rather longer than it needed to, but it was clear from his vigorous antics that his ribs, while still tender, were bothering him less. Aurora sat astride his now trousered legs and finished tying his cravat.

'I would never have guessed you'd do so well as a valet.' Crispin's blue eyes twinkled. He sat up and let her help him into a paisley-patterned blue-on-blue waistcoat. He swung his legs over the bed, grunting a bit at the effort, and reached for her hands. He gave her a look of boyish expectation. 'Now, Aurora, what shall we do today?'

'Let's be tourists.' She smiled impishly, catching his enthusiasm. Today would be their own private holiday, a day off from horses, a day off from Windham, a day off from the future.

There was breakfast in the hotel dining room, featuring plates piled high with rashers of bacon and eggs. People stopped by their table. There were invitations to impromptu events planned by those who were staying the extra day. With a quick glance at Aurora and a knowing smile, Crispin politely declined them all.

After breakfast, they walked the streets of St Albans, taking in the quaint sights, Crispin proving to be a veritable font of local knowledge. 'I've been here a time or two over the years.' He shrugged it off easily when she queried him.

'All right, if you're so smart then, tell me about the clock tower.' Aurora tugged at his hand and pulled him down the street to the medieval monument.

They stood in front of it, Crispin assuming the mocking stance of a guide like the type visitors might hire in London. 'This was built in the fourteen hundreds once St Albans became an established town in the medieval times, but by no means was the medieval town the first civilisation in this area. Romans settled here ages before.'

'I'm impressed.' Aurora slipped her hand back into his, revelling in the luxury of being able to do so without social concern. No one knew them. For all anyone knew they were a husband and a wife in town for the markets. While their clothes were well made, their outfits didn't particularly mark them as nobility—well, Crispin at least as nobility. Today they could be anonymous and hold hands if they wanted. And she wanted.

'If you'd like to be truly impressed, I know some far more interesting facts about St Albans than the bell tower,' Crispin whispered close to her ear, conspiratorially.

They moved on down the narrow streets, Crispin keeping up a chatter of trivia. 'There's Ye Olde Fighting Cocks, the inn where Sir Walter Raleigh stayed.'

Aurora looked around. 'I'm amazed how anyone makes a profit with so many inns competing for business.'

Crispin chuckled. 'It's on the main road to London, there's plenty of traffic. If you ask a resident, they'll tell you St Albans has the most public houses of any town in the country.'

Aurora threw Crispin a saucy look. 'Is it true?'

'Well, from personal experience I would say so. I have taken a pint in at least all of the pubs on one occasion or another,' Crispin admitted with a wry grin.

'Bashing around town with Becher?' Aurora probed.

'Not Becher. I've not known him that long, but some of the others. We'd come out during the Season when London got too boring, which it often did.'

Aurora tilted her head up and studied the man beside her. 'I'm trying to picture you as a young buck on the town.'

'Having some difficulty?'

'Difficulty in picturing you being happy about it,' Aurora confessed. Outwardly, she could easily see Crispin dressed in a lord's clothes, commanding the attention of every young lady in the ballroom, tall and handsome and possessed of a wildness no tailor could disguise behind fashion. He'd proven to be quite a chameleon. A costume could change him utterly; he could even manage the behaviours that went with the costume. She'd seen it at the gypsy camp, at her stables, at Peyton's dinner table, here at the races among his military acquaintances. No wonder he was so valuable to the government.

But inwardly she could not imagine him being happy amid the games of London. The more she knew about Crispin Ramsden, the more she found it easy to believe he'd come looking for a place like St Albans, a bustling market town full of middle-class citizens and a transient population that didn't look twice, didn't ask questions, didn't hold expectations.

'Well, you'd be right. I preferred the military to the ballrooms of London.'

Crispin led them around a corner. 'Ah, there it is, just as I remember, the Peter's Square Market.' It was one of two markets in town, full of people shopping from food stalls. In early March there wasn't much to choose from in the way of fresh fruit, but Crispin bought a basket from a basket weaver and set to work with a wink, saying only, 'I've got an idea.'

They wove through the stalls, collecting the makings of a picnic. She laughingly bargained with the baker for a loaf of dark country bread. Crispin charmed a cheese merchant for a wedge of Cheshire cheese and a wedge of Stilton in spite of Aurora's protest they couldn't eat that much. Crispin only grinned and said, 'that's not the point.'

A farmer sold them Bosc pears, the fresh fruit a delightful luxury for Aurora. Taking up the last bit of space in their basket was a skin of wine and two glasses Crispin persuaded an innkeeper to part with.

'Ready for a walk?' Crispin asked, looping the basket over his arm.

'Where are we going?'

'Holywell Hill. The original site of the town. We have more sightseeing to do.'

The walk was more like a hike. 'Are you sure you're up to it?' Aurora eyed the upward slope east of the current town speculatively. 'You'd better let me carry the basket. I won't have you hurting your ribs. You can carry it on the way down.'

'It'll be practically empty then,' Crispin noted.

'Precisely my point. You'll thank me tomorrow when you have to sit in a bouncing carriage all day.'

Crispin dismissed her concern with a shrug. 'That's tomorrow. I'd never live it down if any of my acquaintances saw you carrying our basket up the hill and me with my hands empty.'

Aurora relented, but she kept a close watch on him and made sure they took a slow pace. There was no rush anyway. They had all day.

'Holywell Hill used to be lined with inns, but these days only a few remain, such as the White Stag over there,' Crispin commented. 'Ah, here we are. At last.'

He was slightly winded, Aurora noted. It appeared even the redoubtable Crispin Ramsden was human after all.

'Here' was a circle of crumbling ruins of what used to be the St Albans Abbey, built by the Benedictine monks. From the hill Aurora could see the plains spread beneath them for miles. The weather was different up here, too, windier. The breeze blew at her hair and she could appreciate the warmth of Crispin's body where he stood behind her, his hand at her back, the other hand gesturing to the silver strip of river in the distance.

'Before medieval settlers built up here, the Romans built in the valley over there by the Ver River—Verulamium, I think it was called.' He turned her slightly, directing her attention to the opposite hill. 'Before the Romans, the Celts built on that hill over there.' He pointed to the west. 'Prae Hill.'

His voice was close to her ear, low and private although there was no one to hear. 'It has always struck me as interesting how culture never leaves you. The peoples of Italy long preferred to build by rivers, choosing commerce and trade and the lifeblood a river provides a town over the defences of a hill. Even thousands of miles from Rome, the Romans replicated a city based on what they knew. And Englishmen have long preferred the benefits of defence on a hill to a river when it came to building early towns. Have you seen the ruins at Sarum?'

'No,' Aurora said sadly. She'd travelled, but never *to* anything, always *from* something. But Crispin had the advantages of status and wealth. He could travel by choice, yet another difference that separated them, but not today. She firmly pushed those ideas away.

'Sarum was built on a hill. Legend has it the Bishop and the knights stationed at the ring fort fought over the well. The Bishop had had enough so he shot an arrow into the air and declared he would build his own city wherever it landed.' Crispin nuzzled her neck, pushing the windblown strands of hair out of the way.

'Where did it land?'

'The arrow? Apparently where Salisbury is located today, if legend is to be believed. Hungry?'

They ate in the shelter of a crumbling stone wall, the wind passing over them as they lounged on the blanket Crispin had procured from the market. 'Here, try this. Open your mouth.' Crispin leaned over with a slice of pear adorned with Stilton and popped it into her mouth.

Aurora bit into the treat carefully, slowly tasting the mix of flavours, the tangy blue-veined white cheese with the fruity sweetness of the pear. 'Divine, absolutely divine,' she murmured.

'Now, try this.' Crispin sliced a piece of the thick bread with his knife and served it to her with a hunk of the Cheshire cheese. 'If we had a fire, I'd show you how well it melts. But it's still good cold.'

Aurora bit and ate. 'This is no ploughman's lunch. I see now why you wanted two different types of cheeses. I would have pegged you as more practical.'

'I'm practical when I must be and that's been much of the time during my travels. But I love food.' Crispin stretched his long body out the length of the blanket, wincing a little while he shifted into a more comfortable position, his head propped on his hand. 'Most of my warmest memories of travelling come from around a table, a simple table with simple food well prepared. Up in the mountains in eastern Europe, food is life. To eat is to live. The table becomes a source of vital hospitality.'

Aurora nodded, remembering how carefully he'd eaten the stew the first night they'd shared a meal.

He passed her the wineskin and she took a mouthful of the full-bodied red wine inside. 'You are a conundrum to me, Crispin. You're a lord, with lordly connections. You've demonstrated that amply enough throughout this trip. Yet, you thrive on simple pleasures. Who are you, really? What is it that you want?' Aurora dared to ask. In the intimacy of their lonely camp on the hillside, such confidences seemed to flourish.

'If I knew that, I'd have the world by a chain.' Crispin studied her with equal determination. 'What about you? What do you want?'

I want you, Crispin Ramsden, body, mind and soul, Aurora thought silently. What would he do if she voiced such sentiments out loud? Probably run screaming down the hill. They had promised not to make such claims, to hold such expectations, hadn't they? She opted for the safe route of a half-truth. 'I want you, Crispin.'

'Then come and get me,' he growled appreciatively, desire rising in his eyes, turning the sapphires to hot coals.

He'd done plenty of the seducing over the last few days. Now it was her turn. She playfully pushed him back, her hands making quick work of his cravat and shirt. She kissed him hard on the mouth, tasting the flavours of wine and pear on his lips. 'I wonder if you taste this good everywhere,' she murmured in sensual tones.

His eyes burned as he divined her intentions. Her eyes held his, unwavering in their promise. Her hands dropped to his trousers, working of their own accord to free him from the fabric. She took his freed member in her hand, stroking its length, caressing the tender head with the pad of her thumb, watching his eyes darken impossibly as his pleasure mounted. 'God, Aurora, what you do to me.' He groaned, arching into her hand, his tip giving up a bead of moisture coaxed by her touch. She'd been waiting for that, a sign that he was ready for what came next.

Aurora bent to his shaft, kissing it reverently, letting the glistening drop wet her lips. 'Temptress!' Crispin cried out, both pleased by her boldness and aroused beyond all sanity. Encouraged, Aurora held the wineskin over him and dribbled a few drops on to his phallus before moving to take him completely, taste him completely; the tang of the wine mingling with the salt of a man's essence. She thrilled in her own power to bring him such enjoyment, thrilling in the intimacy she could share unabashedly with this man alone. Never had she dared so much.

'Careful, I will not last much longer,' Crispin cautioned hoarsely.

Aurora could feel his body tightening in agreement with his warning. She repositioned herself to take him inside her, riding him slowly out of deference for his ribs. The deliberate pace of her motions brought an exquisite friction all their own, building into a pinnacle of ecstasy that shattered at its apex into a thousand shards of pleasure.

She kept him inside her long afterwards, unwilling to relinquish the moment and all that went with it. Even after she'd taken up residence in the crook of his arm, cuddled carefully and closely to his side, they lay together in abject stillness, neither of them speaking. She closed her eyes and drank in the presence of him, the feel of his hard, muscled body against hers, the smell of him; a gentleman's soap mixed with the musk of a lover's scent intoxicating and as potent as the man himself. She willed herself to remember all of it, saving it all up against the inevitable.

Crispin pushed hair out of Aurora's face, studying the soft curve of her profile in the fading light. The shadows were lengthening and their alcove was losing its heat. They'd have to go back down the hill. Back to reality. 'I don't want to go back,' he said aloud with a sigh, wondering at the words. Did he mean back to St Albans or back to Dursley Park, back to whatever awaited them there?

True, there would be four days on the road before then, but it wouldn't be the same, knowing that each mile took them closer to the unpleasantness of reality. There was Windham to deal with, the unbreakable entail and its myriad of issues to untangle, and the problem of 'then what': When Windham and the entail were resolved, as they most certainly would be, then what? When the next assignment came from London calling him back to his former life, then what?

Aurora found her courage first. 'You're cold.' She pulled at the flaps of his shirt, dragging them across his chest. 'We have to go. The others will be waiting for us at dinner. We've avoided them all day, we owe them at least our presence at supper.' She rose and began straightening her clothes. Crispin wondered if she'd tell Tessa what she'd done in that dress. Irrationally, he wished Aurora had her own clothes, her own gowns, even though he preferred her in her trousers and cut-down shirts. Aurora shouldn't have to rely on borrowed finery. Maybe he'd do something about that when he got home.

It was a husband's right, a husband's duty, to see his wife clothed. A husband.

That was how he thought of himself when he thought of Aurora. Crispin hid a small smile. How ironic—he realised he wanted to make the most significant commitment of his life by thinking of one of the most mundane duties that commitment entailed. He wanted that right and all the others that went with it. Complications aside, he wanted to be Aurora's husband.

He had never thought to arrive at this point with anyone. He must go slowly. He could imagine what Aurora would say. He could imagine what Peyton would say, what society would say. There was plenty to work out, not the least being the direction of his future. Aurora wasn't the only one with issues to settle. This deed would require all nature of sacrifice, from personal to social. There would be dragons aplenty to fight before he'd see the goal accomplished. But for now, he wanted to savour the elation of having reached this momentous decision.

'Why are you smiling?' Aurora queried, absently arranging her skirts.

Ah, he hadn't been successful in hiding it. Crispin gave his grin full rein. No sense to hide it now. 'I am smiling because I have found the answer,' he replied cryptically. 'I know what I want.'

'Are you going to tell me?'

'Yes, but not yet.' Crispin clambered to his feet and began to pick up the detritus of their feast, distracting Aurora with the task of packing.

Predictably the basket was much lighter with the food eaten. The trip downhill was predictably quicker too. In no time at all they entered the warren of streets that made up St Albans.

'The adventure is over,' Aurora said at his side.

'Dinner will be festive,' Crispin reminded her. 'There's still four days until we're home. Who knows what will happen on the road?' He tried for levity, but he felt it too. The adventure was slipping slowly away. He talked of the gaslights that lit the town at night, chatting of their instalment in 1824 to keep the gloom away.

They checked the horses, pleased to see Kildare in rested spirits. They dressed for dinner in a more subdued manner than that in which they'd dressed for breakfast, when the day had spread before them like an eternity.

Downstairs in the hotel dining room, Becher and the others beckoned them to a table. They ate, they drank, they exchanged stories and laughed loudly over each other's escapades. But Crispin sensed the underlying desperation that permeated the edge of the group's good humour. The excitement was over. They would all go back to the mundane. Becher would go back to his post as Captain of the yeoman guard in his quiet hamlet, coming to town occasionally to conspire with Coleman on the next great event. The others would drift back to their country estates and country lives. Some of them would endeavour to go up to London for a while once the Season started. All of them would wait for next year. For them, the only season that mattered was over. The hunt and steeplechase season lasted until March. Then it was flat racing and thoroughbreds and the Jockey Club's obsessive stud book until October when they could start all over again.

Someone brought out a fiddle and Aurora danced gaily with Weston. 'Will you be back next year, Ramsden?' Elmore asked while Crispin watched Weston do a funny jig around Aurora.

'Hard to say,' Crispin replied evasively.

'And Miss Calhoun? Will she be back? Those stables have talent and goodness knows I've never seen a rider the likes of her.'

'Again, hard to say.'

Elmore fixed him with a hard gaze. 'There is no brother, no father, no male relative behind the scenes of Calhoun Stables, is there? Other than you, of course, for whatever that's worth.'

'There is me,' Crispin said staunchly. He would not lie outright to John Elmore or to the others who'd backed him unerringly this week, making so much possible in an impossible world.

'I see,' John Elmore said cryptically, withdrawing back into his chair. 'It's a large gamble she takes, Ramsden. Surely you know that? For her to succeed, men of power and influence will need to make exceptions.'

'I think they will,' Crispin answered evenly. 'You're willing, Dursley's willing, all of us this week were willing. If those are any indicators of her ability to persuade, she stands a chance.'

He watched Aurora make an exaggerated curtsy to a laughing Weston and he felt his earlier elation surge. For whatever else was unclear about the future, he wanted her. He wanted her far beyond the pleasure of her company in bed. He wanted her for ever. For once, the word did not fill him with its usual dread.

Chapter Eighteen

Crispin's mind was made up. *He wanted to marry Aurora.* But he was not so foolish to believe in 'ask and you shall receive'. When it came to the concept of long-term commitment, Aurora was as skittish as he was. Or rather as skittish as he *had* been, he amended silently. He'd made his mind up. There were only the details to work out. He reasoned he would do better to work through them on his own first so that when Aurora threw up barriers to his proposal, he'd have his answers ready.

For that reason, they skirted London on the way home, electing to stay at an inn outside town the end of the first day instead of going to the town house. The last thing Crispin wanted was Aunt Lily and Eva going on about society, a reminder of the social barrier between them. Not that it mattered to Crispin. He moved in society only when need mandated such a choice. But Aurora would not see it that way. He didn't need any more reminders of his title, honorific as it was, or of the family wealth. Nor did he relish the idea of running into anyone from the Foreign Office who might have a new mission for him. Aurora would never see his proposal as sincere if she thought he'd be leaving for far-off parts for an indeterminate length of time.

Those were two loose ends he'd have to wrap up. He'd send a

letter to the Foreign Office, stating his resignation. He'd halt inquiries into breaking the entail. They would live simply at Woodbrook if she chose, although he had wealth aplenty to live in whatever style she desired. Aurora could move her stables to Woodbrook, develop the farm as she wanted with the courtesy of his name behind her. Surely, Aurora would see that marriage to him would free her in ways that were currently beyond her reach. As it had freed him.

The journey home gave him all the freedom he wished to explore the new revelations that had dawned on him during the course of their trip. He'd originally loathed the idea of marriage because it would confine him, but there were no limits with Aurora. He did not have to work to keep up a conversation, he'd not had to play the usual courtship games with trinkets and poetry under the watchful eye of matchmaking mamas who studied his every move, wondering if one of their daughters would be the one to bring the wild Crispin Ramsden up to scratch.

That was not to say there hadn't been a courtship of sorts or that he didn't want to shower her with gifts. He did. He wanted to buy her dresses of her own. He'd wanted her to have Dandy that day at the horse fair. He was thinking of having a saddle commissioned for her as a wedding gift. If she wanted diamonds and emeralds, she could have those too.

'You're smiling again.' Aurora nudged his boot with her foot. She was sitting across from him in the carriage, the light drizzle outside having called a halt to riding outdoors. Beside her, Cousin Beth looked up briefly from her reading to study him.

'I suppose I am.'

'Are you going to tell me what has caused you to smile this time?'

'Not yet.' Crispin continued to grin. He'd become quite relaxed on the journey home now that he was convinced he could change enough of his life to satisfy Aurora. Perhaps he'd settled enough to test the waters.

She leaned forwards now and peered out the window. 'We're nearly there.' Familiar landmarks of Dursley land passed outside.

'It's awkward, isn't it?' she said, her hands folded in her lap, tightly locked together. 'The moment my feet touch the ground it will seem like these last two weeks have never happened. Already, I am thinking what I should do first; walk through the stables and check on the horses, go up to Dursley Park and return Tessa's things.'

'They won't seem like a fantasy if you don't let them become that,' Crispin broke in.

Aurora eyed him sharply. She was trying to read his mind with those green eyes of hers that missed nothing, noted everything. She was suspicious and her suspicions made her cautious. He could see it in the rigidness of her posture, the tight grip of her hands. She was wary.

'You know what I mean, Crispin. It's not the events that are hard to come home from.' She was making an effort to choose her words carefully so as not to embarrass Beth. 'It's pretending that we belonged together, being Miss Calhoun and Captain Crispin Ramsden.'

Crispin leaned back against the cushions of his seat, arms folded across his chest. 'I don't pretend. Have you thought that we do belong together?'

Beth looked up in abject shock, the announcement stunning her out of her well-cultivated aura of complacency.

'Perhaps "pretend" isn't quite the right word,' Aurora answered, doggedly clinging to her argument. 'None the less, our intimacy has occurred in a social vacuum.'

'Nature abhors a vacuum,' Crispin recited absently from some old science lesson of his youth. He knew what she meant. It would do him no credit to affect otherwise. He'd been able to conveniently avoid being a peer of any significant standing among the crowds in St Albans. She'd been able to put on the mantle of respectability there as easily as she'd been able to put on a gown. The social strictures were less severe than in London. In St Albans nothing had mattered in the group of friends they'd carved out except the mutual love of horses.

Perhaps nothing had mattered because everyone had been the same. There were several captains among their group. A few hon-orific peers too, like himself, who bore the title only out of social deference. A pretty, respectable 'Miss' was an acceptable prospect for the men who'd flocked to St Albans: squires, captains, men of some military standing and country gentry. Respectable, but cer-tainly not *ton*nish. Amongst the *ton*, such an association would be shunned a hundredfold. Especially when one was a Ramsden. Yet it occurred to him that both of his brothers had overcome such a standard. Neither of their wives came with impeccable social cre-dentials. Julia had been the niece of a struggling viscount. Tessa had been the oldest daughter of a diplomat who'd run afoul of scan-dal in his last days.

Crispin stretched his legs out, crossing them at his ankles. 'It was not all pretence. We were not lying to anyone.'

'Some people may have created expectations. You cannot tell me your friends did not think you were a serious suitor who was all but affianced to me. There was a certain level of artifice to the image we presented.'

'Only if we allow it to become a deception.' Crispin gave her a lazy grin. 'We could live up to their expectations, Aurora. If St Albans proved anything to me, it was that there was a place for us in this world.'

It was a bold gambit and he knew it, but he wanted the seed firmly planted in her mind before the coach rocked to a stop.

'What exactly are you suggesting?' She was all caution, a skit-tish filly new-come to a bridle.

Crispin gave her his best wolfish smile, brash and confident. 'I am suggesting that you marry me.' Was it his imagination or was

Cousin Beth flipping far too quickly through the pages of her book in a gallant attempt to be unobtrusive? She wasn't the only agitated female in the carriage. Aurora was staring at him as if he was a freak-show oddity.

She found her voice. 'You cannot mean it, Crispin. There are a hundred reasons why I should refuse you right now, not the least being whoever proposes in a carriage in front of his cousin? Honestly, there's too many reasons to refuse and only one reason to accept,' she replied with a shake of her head.

'All you need is one reason.' Crispin was all grave solemnity. Beneath the humour and the teasing, he wanted her to know he was in deadly earnest.

The coach came to a stop in Aurora's stable yard and Crispin jumped down to help her out.

Aurora looked at him archly, letting him hand her down. 'You planned this on purpose. You waited until it would be too late to argue over your ill-timed proposal.'

Crispin laughed. 'Ill-timed is a matter of perspective. I think it was timed perfectly.' He went behind the carriage to untie Dandy and Kildare. He passed the leading ropes to her. 'I noticed you didn't say no.' He winked, jumping back into the coach. The coachman was eager to be off now that he was so close to home after four days on the road and Crispin didn't want to keep him waiting.

'I'll see you tonight. I'll send the gig for you.' He leaned down and kissed her briefly. 'You can tell me what the one reason is.'

He'd managed to fluster her. 'What reason?'

'The one reason you'd said you'd marry me!' he called over the noise of the coach setting into motion.

Incorrigible. Usually it was a word she reserved for naughty village boys and their pranks, but in this case, it fit Crispin Ramsden to perfection. No one possessed of his rightful sanity proposed marriage and didn't give the prospective bride a chance to answer. But that was precisely what he'd done.

And it was brilliant.

Not as a proposal, but as a strategy.

Aurora stood in her stable yard, her small valise at her feet, two horses in hand, and she laughed. That devil! Crispin knew his proposal was preposterous. That's why he'd hedged his bets. He knew she'd never say yes readily, but he didn't want her to say no. That promptly sobered her.

Dursley men appeared from the stables to take the horses. Another one took her bag inside her apartments and she followed him inside, noting the army of men at work in the stables. Good lord, how many men had Crispin conspired to put down here? She was thankful for their efforts. In her stunned stupor, she doubted she was capable of doing the necessary chores at the moment.

He didn't want her to say no. What in blazes was he thinking? Did he think a groom's daughter from Ireland could marry an English lord without society taking cruel notice? Did he think he would be happy with a barren woman ten years from now when he looked at his nieces and nephews and realised how empty his life was destined to be? Worse, did he think he owed her? Did he feel obliged to save her stables now that he'd done so much to put them on the road to respectability and prominence? Did he understand he would be giving up his entire way of life? Did he understand she couldn't allow him to do that? She would not tolerate such a sacrifice on her behalf.

These were all the reasons she could not marry him and there were countless more to add to the list. There was only one reason to marry him—because he loved her. She already knew she loved him, but she could not marry him for her love alone. She'd done that once before, believing that her love would be enough to sustain both of them.

Aurora flopped down on to the worn sofa. She usually refused to think of Jonathon and her first marriage. Now that Crispin had proposed, it seemed impossible to avoid it. Not only was she barren and untitled without any substantial wealth to her name, she was a divorcée to boot. Surely, Crispin must understand all the reasons she couldn't marry him. It was her duty to make him see how unsuitable she'd be. Except for one thing: she wanted to say yes.

'She'll never say yes,' Peyton asserted, drumming his hands on the polished top of his desk, having listened to Crispin's account of the trip to St Albans. 'Of the two of you she's showing the most sense in this matter.'

'She just needs to be persuaded. Certainly there are obstacles that need to be overcome, but nothing insurmountable. You did it with Tessa. Paine did it with Julia.' Crispin was undaunted by Peyton's verdict. Now that he'd made his decision and laid his plans, the way forwards seemed straight and obvious. He was impatient to embrace the future. 'There's a lot of work to be done to get Woodbrook ready for inhabitants again.'

'Already filling those bedrooms?' Peyton's blue eyes glinted mischievously.

'No. I don't think there will be any children,' Crispin replied in tones that brooked no further comment, but he could see the myriad questions in Peyton's eyes. 'Your family and Paine's will be enough for us. Besides...' Crispin waved a hand to indicate a long-past conversation. Peyton would know what he meant.

Peyton shook his head. 'You're not like them. Our parents are not us. You'd make a wonderful father. I watch you with Nicholas and Alexander and I think it would be a shame if you didn't have children of your own.'

Crispin shook his head. 'And I disagree. It's simply not in me.'

Peyton's eyes narrowed in speculation. 'You once said that about becoming a landowner, just a month ago, in fact. And now you're changing your entire life for this woman. You're taking on a property, a wife, the business of a stable. I would urge you to slow down and think this through. Aurora is not the kind of wife society would expect you take. Society may very well turn its back on you for good. I do not know that you can make her acceptable. We must be realistic about her background, Cris…' Peyton waved a hand, his voice dropping off, not wanting to elucidate the issues stacked against her.

Crispin could hear the list in his head: bastard birth, illegitimate connections only to a maternal grandfather, a deceased Irish earl, her barren state, to say nothing of her behaviours.

The comment infuriated Crispin. How dare Peyton pass judgement on him and on Aurora. 'A month ago you were all but begging me to stay and do exactly that and now you doubt my ability to carry it out.' He struggled to remain calm. 'You changed for Tessa. Paine changed for Julia.'

'I cannot speak for Paine. However, I disagree. The one thing I love most about Tessa is that she's never sought to change me. Once I realised that, I realised how much I loved her. I didn't change *for* Tessa. If I've changed at all, it's *because* of Tessa. There's a big difference between "for" and "because".' Peyton opened a small drawer and pulled out an envelope. 'You should think about all you'd be giving up.' He pushed the envelope across the desk. 'This came for you while you were gone.'

Crispin recognised the seal. The Foreign Office. He gave a dry chuckle. He'd skirted London purposely for this very reason and London had still found him. From the looks of the date, his efforts had been in vain. 'You'd think they could survive without me for a few weeks.'

'They'll have to survive a lot longer than that without you if you marry Aurora,' Peyton pointed out.

'I will resign,' Crispin countered swiftly with a tenacity he didn't quite feel at his core. Arguing with Peyton was like fighting a hydra. Defeated on one issue, Peyton brought up another. It was a sensitive issue. The solution to staying at Woodbrook was a practical one, but such a change would be Crispin's largest sacrifice for the marriage he wanted.

'And stay in one spot for years on end? You were not so sure of that a few months ago.' Peyton pushed as if he sensed the seed of doubt Crispin had tried to bury deep beneath his fury over being challenged.

'Yes!' Crispin fairly roared, coming to his feet. His integrity was being questioned. If Peyton pushed him any further on this, he had no compunction about coming to fisticuffs, but Peyton remained immobile behind the desk, giving him no opening for a brawl.

'Dammit, Peyton. Stop being the earl for one goddamned minute and be my brother.'

That did it. Peyton's chair smashed into the wall and Peyton was up, lunging for him across the desk. Crispin took his weight and dragged him over the desk, the two of them tumbling noisily to the floor, the desk ornaments crashing around them.

They punched and they struggled, they kicked and they wrestled, knocking over a lamp stand in their wake. Peyton managed to get him in a headlock. 'I've always been your brother, first and foremost. Who got you that commission? I let you go away when I wanted nothing more than to keep you near so I wouldn't be so alone.'

Crispin delivered a sharp elbow to Peyton's gut and pushed out of the headlock, tripping Peyton up with a swift twist of his leg. 'You've always been too bloody perfect!'

They went down again, Peyton taking him to the floor as he fell. The fight was a long time in the making and it might have gone on indefinitely if Tessa hadn't opened the study door, the twins spilling from her skirts in glee at the sight of their uncle and father locked in combat.

'We wanna play too!' they yelled, jumping heedlessly into the scuffle.

'You most certainly will not!' Tessa's voice acted like a wet blanket on fire. 'What in heaven's name is going on in here? Peyton? Crispin?'

Crispin shot a glance at Peyton and mumbled. 'She's your wife. You tell her.'

'Ahem. Well, it's like this.' Peyton stood up and tugged at his waistcoat, never mind that it was now minus two buttons. 'We were ah, celebrating. That's it. We were celebrating. Crispin is getting married.'

That softened Tessa slightly. 'This is wonderful news. May I assume the bride is Aurora?'

'Yes,' Crispin said, scrambling to stand up beside Peyton.

'We'll celebrate tonight in a *more fitting fashion*.' She shot Peyton a glare of disapproval that nearly made Crispin laugh. He probably would have, too, if the rest of Tessa's statement hadn't garnered so much of his attention.

'Um…about that. Perhaps we could defer the celebration.'

Tessa looked at him quizzically. 'Why? This is great news. I couldn't be happier for you both.'

'Well, she hasn't said yes.' Then Crispin hastily added, 'Yet.'

'She will.' Tessa was all confident assurance. 'The sooner the better, I say. She'll need all the protection she can get once Windham hears you're home.'

Crispin nodded. 'We humiliated him thoroughly without anyone else knowing a thing. He'll be stinging from it for a while.'

Tessa flicked a quick look at Peyton. 'You didn't tell him?'

'I haven't had a chance. We've been too busy—'

'Celebrating,' Tessa finished for him, hands on her hips.

'What's going on?' Crispin's sense of foreboding was on high alert. He'd known Windham would have to be dealt with. Humiliating him at St Albans only increased tensions between Windham and Aurora and consequently himself.

Peyton bent down and scooped up one of the twins who was persistently pulling on his father's trouser leg. 'Eleanor's gone and there's no doubt about who Windham will blame.'

Chapter Nineteen

Eleanor had run. Windham's presence in St Alban's would have provided the girl with the temptation and means to leave. A *frisson* of alarm ran sharply down Crispin's spine, straight to his gut. Aurora was alone at the stables. 'How many men were left down there to watch the property while we were gone?'

'Three watchmen. We had no trouble while you were away.'

'Three?' Crispin's sense of alarm sharpened. 'There were far more than three when I dropped her off.' The stable yard had been full of men going to and fro, carrying out the business of taking care of horses. It had looked a bit over the top, now that he thought about it, but he'd brushed it off as merely being overprotective of Peyton. He'd been too caught up in the emotions of the moment; the strategic proposal, the look of shock on Aurora's face and the fact that she hadn't said no.

Now, through the distance of a couple of hours, he saw the scene more objectively. If his suspicions were right and Windham had planted his own men down there, having done away with the Dursley watch, he didn't mean to wait. He was ready to exact his revenge the moment Aurora returned.

He shot a sharp look at Peyton and did some rapid calculations in his head. It had been two hours since he'd left Aurora. A look-out would need time to deliver his message to Windham. It would be a look-out from the stables so that Windham could ascertain she was absolutely alone. Windham would not want to hazard meeting him there too. Windham would wait and deal with him separately. Then Windham would need travel time to reach the stables.

Peyton read Crispin's concerns. 'At his fastest, barring no mishaps, he would have reached the stables fifteen minutes ago. With luck, he is still en route.'

Crispin spun on his heel, shouting orders that sent footmen running. 'I'll need a fast horse! Don't bother with a saddle. Have him out front in five minutes.' His voice sounded in control, he even sounded logical as he pounded up the stairs to his chambers. He tore through his drawers, flinging clothes carelessly to the floor, extracting the weapons that lay beneath the once neatly pressed garments. He shoved a pistol in his belt, checking to see that it was loaded. He buckled a knife sheathe around his waist. He bent to assure himself his other knife was still hidden in his boot.

'It's a veritable arsenal up here,' Peyton said tightly from the door, but he was no less armed when Crispin turned around. 'I'm coming with you.'

Crispin shook his head. 'No, it's too risky. We didn't know Windham had amassed an army. This won't be two on one.'

'All the more reason I should go,' Peyton replied.

'You're the earl,' Crispin protested. He could not live with himself if anything happened to Peyton. How would he ever face Tessa and the children again?

'Right now, I'm your brother.' Peyton turned from the door. 'We'd better hurry. Do you have your knife in your boot?'

Crispin gave a predatory grin. 'Always. You have yours?'

Peyton answered his grin with a wolfish one of his own. 'Always.'

Two horses pawed the ground outside, anxious to be off.

Crispin vaulted on to the barebacked mount with grim determination. 'Here's to incompetence,' he muttered under his breath, hoping against hope that by some miracle Windham would be way-laid. Crispin kicked his horse into motion and let out a wild yell, bent low over the horse's neck, letting it thunder down the drive. The race for the stables was on.

Aurora put aside thoughts of Crispin's proposal long enough to unpack the valise. She was tempted to change into trousers and a shirt, but decided against it. She'd just need to change back in a couple hours for dinner at Tessa's. Good lord, she was tired of skirts. She'd worn a dress more times in the past two weeks than she had in the whole three years she'd been in Dursley.

Three years! That brought a smile to her face; not the perma-nence of making a home here, but rather all that she'd accomplished. She felt at last that she'd put her life back together after her acci-dent and Jonathon's desertion, after being driven out of other places that wouldn't tolerate her skills. All of those trials seemed worth it if they'd brought her to this place, to Crispin. Now did she dare to believe in love, in a man again? It was tempting when the man in question was Crispin.

Aurora hummed to herself, putting a few undergarments away in her trunk. A glimmer of white caught her eye when she rose. A letter stuck out, tucked between a few of her horse-care reference books kept on a high shelf. Perplexed, Aurora reached up for it.

She recognised the loopy handwriting immediately and cold dread filled her. Eleanor. Aurora sat down on the bed, reading and re-reading the short note over and over in stunned disbelief. She'd not thought the girl would leave. Apparently, she'd thought wrong. Eleanor had taken advantage of her father's trip to St Albans and made good her escape. Fleeing Windham's house could be called no less.

Aurora counted days in her head. Windham had not arrived in St Albans early. He'd only shown up the night before the race, but he'd still had to spend at least three days on the road. There was race day, and then he was sent packing. Aurora hoped Windham's early departure hadn't wreaked havoc with Eleanor's plans. The girl would have been counting on having up to eleven days to effect her disappearance. Would she have built in the possibility of her father returning earlier?

Worry over Eleanor gave way to a new concern. Windham would blame her for Eleanor. Aurora suddenly wished Tessa's gown had pockets, a place where she could keep a pistol. She was feeling very vulnerable. Windham would not let this latest development go unpunished. The thought did spike her worries, but she reasoned that in a couple of hours Crispin would drive the gig down to fetch her for dinner and she could tell him her concerns. She drew a deep breath. What could go wrong in a couple of hours? Windham couldn't possibly know yet that she was home and she had an abundant population of Dursley men in her stables.

To settle her nerves, Aurora took a walk through the stable, stopping to stroke the horses who poked their heads out into the aisle. The stable was eerily quiet. With the exception of the occasional horse sound, the bustle of working men had died away. Everyone had disappeared. True, it was five o'clock and the work day was ending, but she'd thought someone would have come and told her their work was through and the men were off home. It seemed odd that the place could be bustling one hour and still the next.

Sheikh nuzzled her hand, pushing his nose against it, hunting for an apple. 'Your master has spoiled you.' She petted Sheikh's long face.

'He's spoiled you as well.' The cold voice behind her made her jump. She turned sharply, her back against Sheikh's stall door.

Windham!

'What are you doing here?' Aurora asked, keeping her chin up, her voice full of authority.

He continued to advance down the length of the aisle, a riding crop in one long-fingered hand. 'I'm here for you, Aurora. Let's not play games. You have made me look the fool for the last time. You have rejected my honourable suit, you've thrown your lover and his money in my face, stolen a decent steed out from under me, humiliated me in front of people whose respect I desired in St Albans, and convinced my daughter to run away from home and an advantageous marriage.'

'Those things are not my fault,' Aurora answered. 'I had a right to reject your suit. Eleanor has a right to make her own choices.'

'You are too bold to think you can argue with me.' He was nearer now, only twelve feet away. She could see the burn of irrational anger in his eyes. Hands behind her back, she worked the bolt to Sheikh's stall.

'You are the one who is overbold,' she challenged. 'There's Dursley men all over this place. All I have to do is scream.'

A malevolent grin took Windham's face. 'Go ahead. I think you'll find the men belong to me. We neatly disposed of the Dursley watchmen yesterday in case you arrived home early.'

Aurora held his gaze, searching for signs of the lie, but there were none. He was secure in the knowledge that there were no allies here. She was entirely at his mercy. On her periphery, Aurora spotted a pitchfork left propped up next to a stall door across the aisle. 'What do you want?'

'I want a little of what you've been giving to Ramsden. It's my due. My reward for all that I've suffered.'

If she meant to act, it had to be now. If he came any closer, she wouldn't have room to dart. Aurora lunged for the pitchfork. Her hand closed about the handle, but Windham was too fast. He grabbed her about the waist from behind.

'That's not nice, Aurora,' he chided, crushing her against him, half-dragging, half-pushing her towards the wall in an attempt to shake the pitchfork free of her grip.

Aurora screamed, struggling against him. She jabbed wildly with the pitchfork, hoping to jab a tine into a foot. She only had one chance before Windham managed to get an arm about her own arms, effectively impeding any motion from the elbows down. The pitchfork clattered uselessly to the floor.

She fought wildly, trying to kick a knee, trying to stomp on the instep of his foot, but his boots were too high, too thick, and, in the end, too resistant.

In his stall, Sheikh whinnied frantically at the loud noises and the scuffling. His hooves kicked against the door, once, twice and then he was free. Free and skittish. 'Go, Sheikh!' Aurora cried out, still fighting against Windham.

But Sheikh wanted to fight. He reared up on his legs, big and impressive. Shocked, and suddenly cognisant of the danger the big horse posed to him, Windham's grip slackened. Aurora felt his arm loosen and she jabbed an elbow hard against his ribcage. She darted to the side, leaving Windham in Sheikh's path.

Sheikh would trample Windham and she would swing up bareback like a circus rider as he passed. They would both be free. Aurora tensed, waiting for the moment. Time slowed, Windham drew a gun and the moment was lost. She instantly assessed what he meant to do.

'No!' She gave up her freedom and launched herself at Windham, trusting Sheikh would not trample her too, trusting that Sheikh would turn and run out the open end of the stable, run straight to Crispin.

Windham had always underestimated her and this was no different. He'd not expected her to re-engage. Caught off balance, they both went down together on the hard stone floor. The gun flew out of his hand, misfiring loudly into a hay bale. Aurora cursed her skirts. They tangled about her legs, making it difficult to wrestle a grown man. It didn't matter—the misfire brought men running to Windham's assistance. She was no match for Windham plus four.

In short order, her hands were bound and she was efficiently marched into her quarters where Windham summarily kicked the door shut, barking orders that chilled her to her core. 'Get ready to fire the building.'

'No—' Aurora whirled on him '—you can't mean to burn it! It's stone, it won't burn.'

'Enough of it will burn.' He pushed her into a chair. 'But not yet.'

'Free the horses.' Aurora fought the rise of panic that edged her voice.

Windham smugly took the chair across from her. 'You must bargain for them. How many of them are there? Twelve? Counting that beastly Kildare and the one your lover stole from me at the horse fair.' He smiled evilly and leaned the short distance to her, his face too close to hers. 'What twelve things would you be willing to bargain with?'

Aurora thought frantically through her list of meagre possessions. 'My mother's pearls.' She'd worn them the day she'd married Jonathon. They were perfectly matched and of great value to her both financially and sentimentally, all she had of a mother she'd lost when she was too young to remember her.

Windham scoffed. 'What would I do with pearls? I can buy far better gems.'

Aurora stuck to her offer. 'They're worth two horses, the mares at least.' They were likely in foal, but she wouldn't tell Windham that. He would only hold such knowledge against her.

Windham shook his head, running the ever-present riding crop down the side of her cheek. 'I'm not interested in that sort of bargain, Aurora. You have stolen my daughter from me with your radical ideas and indecent lifestyle. In doing so, you've taken something very personally valuable from me. I would take something personal from you in exchange.'

She didn't need to be told his intentions. She'd known from the start all that Windham had implied and all that he wanted. He wanted her body and her pride and she had no choice but to give it to him. It was the only guarantee she had that the horses would survive.

'Take off your dress, Aurora, and I'll let the mares go.' His eyes burned with naked lust now that the pretence of negotiation was gone.

Aurora's hands trembled at the front buttons down the bodice. She should be thinking about a strategy, how to maximise the opportunity, but she couldn't think past the horses, past the shame he was so wantonly inflicting on her. To her dismay, she couldn't work the buttons effectively with her bound hands. She hated asking him for anything. She held out her bound hands.

A knife appeared in his hands from a coat pocket and he slit the bonds. 'Make it good,' he growled, flopping down into a chair and prepared to watch. 'Hurry up or I'll shoot something for good measure.'

Her freed hands went to the first button on the high collar of Tessa's gown. Then the next.

'Don't act like a nun,' Windham hissed. 'You're not a nun for Ramsden.' He was losing patience.

Aurora slowly pulled her arms out, one by one, from their sleeves as if they were tight gloves. Windham's pupils dilated. She'd miscalculated. She had not meant for such a movement to tease, she'd only thought to use it for a delay, but it had heightened his level of arousal.

She worked the fastenings of her skirt, finally letting it skitter to the floor, leaving her in chemise and petticoats. 'Free the mares,' she whispered huskily, finding some courage amid her fear. 'My dress is off. I want Dandy out next.' Three horses down, nine to go. She wanted to know Kildare was safe, but he was the prize. Windham would not let him go without a large forfeit from her. She rather hoped things would not get that far, that Crispin would come before they reached that point.

'Take down your hair and I'll let Dandy go.' Windham gestured to the man in the doorway awaiting orders.

Aurora raised her arms, reaching for the pins holding the twist in place. She shook it free, letting the long fall of hair cascade around her shoulders. Windham rose and came to her, seizing a length of hair, bringing it to his nostrils and inhaling deeply. 'Lavender. Such a delicate, womanly smell.'

Aurora cringed and instinctively tried to step away. He captured her with an arm and dragged her against him. 'I'll be touching a lot more than your hair before we're through,' Windham answered. 'How well you play the innocent with me, such a potent aphrodisiac. Does Ramsden know what a consummate whore you are? What will he think when I tell him what we've done in here, in the very bed where he did the same thing?'

'It won't be the same thing.'

Windham made her pay for the retort. His hands fisted in the cloth of her chemise and ripped the fabric. Aurora gasped in terror. The nightmare got worse by the moment. She felt naked in her petticoats and shredded chemise in a way she'd never felt naked with Crispin even when she'd not worn a stitch. Instinctively, she crossed an arm over her chest, a futile shield against Windham's glittering eyes.

'The horses, I'll want two of the stallions,' she braved, trying to slow him down, but Windham had had enough of negotiating.

Windham sneered. He crowded her until he'd backed her into the bed frame. 'I find I grow weary of bargaining. I'll make one last bargain. Get on the bed and Kildare goes free.' He pushed her and she fell back on to the mattress. Sure of her compliance, Windham took a moment to undo his flap. Aurora seized the opportunity. She rolled to the other side of the bed and inelegantly scrambled off it, putting the bed between her and a furious Windham.

His eyes narrowed. 'Perhaps we'll have a lesson in discipline first. I will enjoy taking the crop to you.'

This was it. She'd have to fight, but with what? The bed and Windham stood between her and the door into the other room. Where was Crispin? Had a rampaging Sheikh raised any sort of alarm?

Windham smacked the crop against his hand and confidently moved around the foot of the bed. Aurora took the only avenue open to her and dived across the bed. If she was fast enough, she could gain the door.

She dived.

Windham lunged. Bigger, stronger, he felled her, his body effectively pinning her to the mattress. Aurora kicked and struggled, her efforts only serving to frustrate Wickham. He delivered a hard, stinging blow to her cheek, dazing her, subduing her. She clung to awareness with the last of her tenacity. She had to remain alert. She could not protect the horses unconscious.

There was nothing left to do but beg. Perhaps he'd planned it that way, knew it would be the final blow to what remained of her dignity. He'd taken her clothes, he'd rendered her helpless. He'd put her at his mercy. Surely that was enough. Aurora felt a tear of desperation slip out of the corner of her eye. 'Please, please don't do this. You've already humbled me.'

'Save your pathetic efforts. Pretend I'm Ramsden.'

Aurora clenched her jaw, felt his hand snake up her leg, bunching the petticoats as it went, felt the intimate press and hardness of his body, of the phallus that had risen so thoroughly in response to his crude requests. She shut her eyes, feeling each tear. Never had she been so helpless. Never had she had so little recourse. Not even her body was hers to control.

'Mr Windham!' A man dashed into the room. Her mortification sank to new lows at the thought of onlookers witnessing the débâcle. Windham made no move to ease from her, to hide her exposed body from the new arrival.

'There's riders on the horizon. If we're going to fire the place, we'd better do it now. There won't be time if we wait.'

'Damn! Throw me some rope.' Windham pressed down on her, making breathing difficult. 'I can finish with you later, Miss Calhoun. The choice is yours.'

The man returned with rope and Aurora realised what Windham intended. Unable to stop him, Aurora watched Windham loop the rope about her wrists and leash her to the bed frame. 'No, you can't mean to leave me here!' She started thrashing the moment he levered off her.

'Hush, Aurora.' Windham looked down at her, taking one last leer at her exposed breasts. 'The knot's not so tight you won't master it before the fire reaches you. If you want to escape, you will. Or perhaps you cannot live with the shame. Surely you don't expect Ramsden to want you now? There's not much to look forward to once you walk out this door, except knowing that I am waiting to finish what we've started.' He gave her a malevolent smile. 'Well, it's not for me to decide. I will leave you to your ponderings.' He took an exaggerated sniff of the air. 'Ah, smoke. Don't ponder too long.'

Aurora pulled herself up into a sitting position, the better to work the rope. Windham was right. The knot was loose enough to untie if she focused her thoughts, but it was hard to fight back her desire for haste. She had no way of knowing if Kildare had even been let out. Windham was a wholesale murderer dressed in gentlemen's coats.

She could smell smoke. She could hear the frightened neighs of the horses that were left. From the source of the sounds it seemed her captors had started at the end closest to the stable doors. The horses that were left were all in the stalls furthest from the door, with the least chance of rescue if the fire caught. Aurora struggled with the knot; it started to give. The smoke was thickening now. Dammit, they must have started the fire right outside the apartment doors, right in the centre of the stable. Fire wouldn't burn stone. It would burn the hay, the wooden stall doors, the beams that supported the roof. She had to get to the horses. The knot was almost undone.

'Smoke!' Crispin yelled, flying into a stable yard full of panicking horses, at least it seemed that way. In all likelihood there were only five horses. Their shrill calls of fright to their comrades still inside the stable lent a sense of chaos to the macabre scene. Crispin jumped down and smacked his horse on the rump, sending him out of the stable yard and away from the bedlam. Without hesitation he ran into the building, Peyton behind him. They'd come across Sheikh moments after leaving Dursley Park and they'd ridden like the devil to cover the distance.

'Aurora!' Crispin called out, raising a hand to ward off the smoke that threatened his vision.

Peyton checked the stalls they passed. 'They're empty. The remaining horses must be in the back. We'll not get to them this way. It's too far.'

Crispin nodded, still scanning the smoky interior for Aurora. Had she fallen and landed in an empty stall? Was she the one who'd freed the horses? How had they got out? 'There's a wide barn door at the other end. If you can open it from the outside, we can reach the horses. I'll check Aurora's apartments.'

Peyton nodded and dashed back towards the entrance. Crispin knew he'd have to work fast. The flames were dangerously close to closing off any entrance to the apartments. Worse, flames licked at the beams supporting the roof. If the roof went, he'd be trapped. He had two minutes, not a second less if his judgement proved right.

A faint call reached his ears. He took one last look at the threatened beams and darted inside the apartments. 'Aurora! I'm coming!'

He found her in short order and swiftly cut away the remaining circuitry of the knot. It was obvious from the state of her that Windham had put her through an ordeal. He clutched Aurora to him, his anger soaring in primal waves of fury. How dare another attack what was his! But Windham could not be his concern now. Aurora's safety came first. She found her feet and together, they pushed their way back towards the corridor, Crispin hoping desperately the way was still clear. Ash fell from the ceiling, hot cinders flaking to the ground like snow.

He shielded her as best he could. They were lucky, it could have been worse. They would make it. He could just make out the open stable door ahead of them.

Suddenly, Aurora stiffened. Coughing and gasping, she managed one word. 'Kildare.'

Crispin shook his head frantically. 'There's no time. He may have got out.' He barely had enough voice left to utter that much. But then he heard what must have drawn Aurora's attention earlier: one last whinny in the centre of the stable. Peyton had saved all but one.

'No. Aurora, we can't. It's too risky,' he croaked with all the sternness he could muster, but Aurora jerked away from him and ran back into the inferno. He knew in the core of his being he'd never be whole again if Aurora did not survive. Crispin cursed hoarsely. Love was a damnable thing. There was no choice but to follow her.

Chapter Twenty

It was all a blur after that. Even years later, Crispin would remember little of what transpired after he followed Aurora back inside. He remembered ripping off his shirt and blindfolding Kildare; Aurora collapsing, her hands seared from handling the hot metal bolt on Kildare's stall. He remembered throwing her face down over Kildare's back like a set of saddle bags. The rest he recalled only thanks to Peyton, who caught him as he staggered out into the daylight, horse in tow. He remembered Peyton's arms about him and then nothing more. But he would never forget the fear that had drenched him; fear that he would lose her, that he would lose himself if he failed to protect her.

Physically, he'd come out of the fire remarkably unscathed with the exception of some minor burns on his chest, sustained in the last rescue. Aurora hadn't been as fortunate. Crispin glanced across the room where she lay dozing in the big bed. Three days since the fire and she was still pale, still exhausted. Her long hair was shorter now by three inches, having been singed. Her hands were wrapped in white bandages. The doctor assured him she'd recover full use of her hands, that she'd be able to hold reins again with no problem, but still the bandages were stark reminders of how close he'd come to losing her.

Of course, he wasn't surprised. Aurora obeyed no rules and was stubborn to a fault. That was why he loved her. That was why he hadn't left her side. Part of him feared he could still lose her. Not in the physical sense. She was out of danger from any subsequent ill effects of the fire. He feared he could lose her in other ways, that she'd never agree to his proposal now that the stable was gone. The loss was devastating. He'd gone down to survey the ruins, to see if there was any chance of rebuilding. He'd had nothing good to report upon his return. With that news, Aurora had seemed to slip a further from him.

Aurora stirred on the bed, deciding to wake up. 'You're still here,' she murmured at the sight of him in the window seat.

Crispin strode to the side of the bed and sat down on the edge beside her. 'Of course I'm still here.'

'I'm sure you have better things to do than sit in my room all day. You should go do them, Crispin. Tessa has a houseful of servants to wait on me.' She gave him a soft smile.

'I'd rather be the one to wait on you.' Crispin reached for a glass of water and held it for her. Her bandages made certain things difficult for the time being.

'I feel silly,' she said self-consciously, water dribbling down her chin.

'You're just used to being independent.' He set the glass back down. 'The weather is good today. Why don't we walk down to the barn and check on the horses?' He wanted to get her up and moving, wanted to get her out of this room and re-engaged in life. Something uncertain flickered in her eyes, but she reluctantly agreed. Crispin smiled his relief. One step at a time.

'There's so many of them!' Aurora exclaimed over the crowded stables. Peyton's facilities were indeed full to capacity in order to make room for Aurora's horses, but it wouldn't last long.

'The stables at Woodbrook will be ready by the week's end.

We'll move the horses then,' Crispin said, easing into the things he wanted to discuss with her.

She looked at him curiously. 'You're staying, then?'

'Did you forget I've got a wedding on the horizon?'

Aurora sat down on a hay bale. 'I don't recall actually accepting and you don't have to marry me now, Crispin. You needn't feel any obligation or pity.'

Crispin began to interrupt, but she waved him into silence with her hand. 'I know it looks like the perfect solution. I've got nothing. The Calhoun stables are irreparable. I've got nowhere to go, nowhere to put up my horses and you've got a house and a barn just waiting to be filled. But you should get married for better reasons than that.'

'I asked you to marry me before all this happened,' Crispin reminded her.

'Everything is different now.'

'Nothing is different,' Crispin countered. He could see her prevaricating. What could he tell her that would persuade her this was the right path? She should know by now that she could trust him, that he didn't seek to change her. He wanted her just the way she was.

Aurora peered up at him. There was no other man equal to Crispin Ramsden. Did he have any idea how tempting it was to say yes? To let him share in her burdens? Those broad shoulders were more than capable of doing so, but she could not allow it. He would only end up being shamed by her. Windham had promised as much. 'You're wrong, Crispin. Windham—' she began, twisting a piece of straw between her fingers.

'Windham is a snake. He will be dealt with,' Crispin cut in.

Aurora shook her head. 'You cannot go around slaying all my dragons. I've fought too hard to become independent to let a man solve all my problems. Whatever happens with Windham, I want to be part of it. I deserve that. I've earned that. But it won't stop with Windham. I'm a divorced woman, Crispin. Even if I had rank, that would be enough for society to condemn me. I am an absolute liability to you. We can't hide that from society for ever. Someone will find out.'

'Peyton has voiced these concerns as well,' Crispin said flatly. 'But I've told you more than once that I don't care. I've never been one to put much stock in society's silly rules.'

'It's not just about you, Crispin. It's about Tessa and Peyton, Petra and Thomas and Eva with her début. The scandal would affect them if you married me. I don't think they'd be as nonchalant about it as you are. You feel you have nothing to lose.'

'I could lose you, Aurora. That is unacceptable. How another man let you get away is incomprehensible to me.'

She sighed and shook her head. 'Do you see why I hesitate? I've tried marriage to a peer before, Crispin. I can't pretend to be other than I am. My mother loved foolishly and gave birth to a bastard daughter. I loved foolishly and ended up divorced.

'Those kinds of things matter in your world. It is why I must keep you at arm's length when it comes to any long-term commitment.' *And the fact that I love you beyond reason. I could not stand to see you hate me.*

'I'm not him,' Crispin said succinctly, closing his hand over hers where it lay on the railing, careful of the bandages. 'By the time those bandages are off and I can slip a ring on your finger, you'll know I am worthy of you, Aurora. I'm not a boy wet behind the ears. I am a man who knows his full measure. If I was not capable of upholding my vows, I would not propose something as enduring as marriage. May I ask the vicar to call the banns?'

The moment stretched out endlessly. Never had a three-lettered word carried so much import. 'Yes' meant more than an acceptance of the proposal, it committed her to a new way of life, one that was shared with a partner. It committed her to some level of re-engagement with society. What that level would be remained to be seen. Along with the re-entrance came the possibility of hurt and rejection. Saying yes committed her to taking that risk for Crispin's sake and the sake of the family she'd inherit through marriage. She had no doubt Crispin knew what he was asking of her. Her life had always been about risks and she was no coward. She took risks because they were worth taking and no risk to date had been more worthy than the one Crispin was asking her to take now. Suddenly, the choice was simple.

Aurora smiled. 'If you're willing to take the chance, I am too. Yes. I'll marry you.'

Some men persuaded with words, but words were often rendered meaningless in her experience. Perhaps that was why so few men had appealed to her over the years. Crispin Ramsden persuaded with actions.

Dursley Park thrummed with vibrant purpose over the next three weeks. Crispin took up residence in the library, commandeering the long reading table for his workspace. Correspondence flowed steadily out into the world. Aurora would leave her bedchamber each day just to see what he was up to. Petra and Tessa were giddy with excitement and apparently full of secrets that caused them to laugh whenever she walked into a room.

Crispin's energy was infectious and she recognised it did much to return her to good spirits. The loss of her stables had been difficult to face, the horror of the ordeal with Windham even more so. But all that was swept aside in the wake of Crispin's enthusiasm. He wouldn't say more about whatever grand plan he'd set in motion, only that she should trust him. And to her surprise, she did.

The horses were moved to Woodbrook and Crispin began to spend long days away from his table in the library, returning each night at sunset, a tired smile on his face. Her bandages came off the day after the banns were read for the third time. The next day,

Crispin presented her with a pair of specially made riding gloves and hoisted her up on Kildare. 'We're going for a ride,' he said with a playful spark in his eye while he adjusted the girth on Kildare's saddle for her.

It was the first time she'd ridden since the fire and the day was glorious. Somehow, March had bled into early April without her notice. Green had returned to England. Roadside hedges bloomed in a profusion of colours. Aurora flexed her newly healed hands around the reins, feeling the tight skin stretch. She revelled in it. It was the feeling of health. Beneath her, Kildare protested the sedate pace, fighting for his head, and Aurora gave in, eager to taste the wind and celebrate her freedom. 'Race you!' she called to Crispin.

'Aurora, wait, you don't know where we're going!' Crispin laughed.

'Better catch me, then!' she called over her shoulder.

They were going to Woodbrook. Aurora didn't know, of course, until they turned into the lane with its freshly painted sign reading 'Woodbrook Manor and Horse Farm.'

'You couldn't break the entail?' Aurora asked, sliding off Kildare in the yard.

Crispin came around to catch her, planting a kiss on her cheek. 'Didn't *want* to break the entail, after all,' he corrected.

The place was quiet today, but Aurora could see signs of construction. Timber was piled to one side where a shed was being built. Fencing around an outdoor arena looked new and other projects were progressing from the looks of things. 'So this is where you've been spending your time.'

Crispin grinned. 'Do you like it? Come, I'll give you the tour. If I know you, you'll want to see the stables first, the house second.'

She laughed. 'How'd you guess?'

'That first day in the road, you were more worried about Sheikh than me. I knew right then who had priority with you.'

It was almost overwhelming. Aurora doubted any other woman in

England would get teary-eyed over a stable, but she did. Everything was of the finest quality. Her horses could not expect better accommodations. Neither could she expect a better training facility. 'We'll win St Albans every year,' she whispered in awe.

'We'll breed champions here, Aurora. This is the start of a whole new life for us, a life together.' Crispin's grip tightened on her hand and she winced a little at the unconscious pressure. Was that a tremor she'd heard in his voice? It had been so slight as to be hardly noticeable. Perhaps he'd merely swallowed the wrong way.

He let her gape at the indoor arena a few moments longer before ushering her over to the house. 'Here, try the key,' he said solemnly, pressing the key into her hand.

Aurora fitted the key into the lock, nerves fluttering suddenly in her stomach. She pushed the door open and stared in amazement. 'This is incredible.' Now she knew what Tessa and Petra had been doing. They'd been creating a home for her. Aurora stepped inside. Walls were freshly painted a pale yellow. Braided rugs dotted the floor in cheery colours. 'And furniture, too!' Aurora exclaimed. A yellow-and-blue print sofa and matching overstuffed chairs framed a white-mantled fireplace.

She wandered from room to room. She marvelled at the kitchen, which Crispin assured her would have a cook. 'We won't have to live on toasted cheese and stew every night,' he joked.

She ran her hand along the smooth surface of the dining-room table, and commented on the dishes already arranged in the china cabinet. 'Not exactly my wooden plates, are they?'

Upstairs, guest rooms were in serviceable order. The master's suite was spotless and perfect right down to the comforter turned back on the massive carved bed. 'It looks like it's just waiting for us.' She gave Crispin a mischievous smile.

'It certainly does.' He made a sweeping gesture towards the bed. 'After you, my love.'

An afternoon spent making love did much to dispel the nerves

Aurora had felt at the door. She was fully cognisant of the great gift Crispin had given her. He'd given her back her life, her dreams. With Kildare and Sheikh to stand to stud, she could breed to her heart's content. With the protection of his name and his connections, she could re-establish her riding academy for women and never worry about malice destroying it again. It was not clear if they'd ever have social acceptance outside their little part of the world, but that was of secondary concern and they would have to grapple with it later. This was not a fairy tale where the prince could magically remove all her problems, all her obstacles. That was fine with her. She didn't want the fairy tale. A woman should be able to take care of herself.

More importantly, she understood that his actions said what his words could not and they were all the more meaningful because of it. *I love you.*

For the first time since the proposal, she saw what it had cost him to commit to marriage. Her acceptance was only part of the investment being made to this relationship. When he'd said this was the beginning of a whole new life for them, he'd not meant only her. He'd meant himself. There'd be no more moving around, no more dangerous assignments from the Foreign Office. His world was changing as assuredly as hers was.

'You've laid the world at my feet, Crispin,' Aurora murmured drowsily, snuggled against him in the big bed.

'I've laid Woodbrook Manor at your feet, Aurora,' he corrected teasingly. 'But if you want the world, I'll try to give you that too.' Crispin dislodged her and sat up. He reached for his discarded jacket and rummaged through it. 'I've been waiting to give you this.' He produced a small velvet box tied prettily with a pink ribbon.

The ring. Aurora knew what it was before she opened it, but that didn't stop her from gasping. Yet another display of his thoughtfulness. The ring was a simple band of gold containing three small diamonds. It was a ring she could wear beneath riding gloves, a ring to wear every day while she worked without worrying that it would snag on a harness. 'It's perfect.'

Crispin took it from her and slid it on to her hand. 'There's another surprise for you in the wardrobe.'

Aurora tossed him a saucy look. 'You just want to watch me walk across the room naked.'

Crispin grinned and laid back against the pillows, folding his arms behind his head. 'Well, that too.'

Aurora opened the wardrobe and stared. She'd been staring all day. She'd been overwhelmed all day. Crispin had arranged everything perfectly. This was no exception. 'My wedding dress,' she said simply. 'I was going to ask Tessa for one of her dresses.'

'You'll have your own gowns from now on, starting with that dress there. Not that you need to wear them, mind you. You're welcome to your trousers, but your clothes should be your own.'

'How did you ever manage this?' Aurora stroked the soft silk of the ivory gown.

'I wrote to Eva in London. If anyone knows dresses and sizes, it's Eva. She saw to all of it. I'm glad it pleases you, as far as dresses go anyway.'

Aurora fingered the celery-coloured ribbons that trimmed the sleeves. 'I'll write to her and thank her. This has been an extraordinary day.' She hung the dress back in the wardrobe and climbed back into bed, snuggling against Crispin's warm form.

'Are you happy, Aurora?' His strong arm came around her, a hand idly fussing with a length of hair.

Oddly enough, with all the miracles of the day, she couldn't give him the answer he expected. She opted to answer with a question of her own. 'Are you?'

'I have you, don't I?' Crispin whispered, rolling her beneath him. Aurora said nothing, but she was not easily fooled. There were a lot of questions in bed with them and very few answers.

Chapter Twenty-One

There was one more issue to wrap up before the wedding, one more loose end that needed tying: Gregory Windham. With Windham squared away, Crispin would have done all he could to ensure a smooth transition for Aurora. She had not made it easy.

True to her word, Aurora insisted on being part of the plans to serve out justice to Windham. Crispin would have spared her the discomfort. He would also have preferred to have settled the issue more decisively with his fists, but Windham needed justice that would legally cast him out of society on a more permanent basis. In this instance, naked revenge would not help Aurora's cause.

Although he would have liked to have Aurora step aside on the matter, her help proved to be invaluable in building the case against Windham. She had a familiarity with the situation that he did not. She knew who to seek out to acquire the testimonies needed to build the case, cutting down their preparation time drastically. Together, they gathered depositions from Mackey the blacksmith, who'd been more than eager to tell the earl and his brother what transpired between him and Windham, especially the parts where Mackey had refused to contribute to Windham's scheme any longer. 'I had nothing to do with burning the barn,' he'd said contritely. 'That was all Windham's men. By that point, he wasn't using village help any more. We'd had enough.'

Mackey had put them on to his assistant, Ernie, who confessed to the night attack with a beet-coloured blush. Ernie also mentioned meeting in the tavern's private room and that led them to question the tavern owner, who recalled the names of the men who'd come to meet with Windham. Aurora immediately recognised the names as belonging to her students. There were letters and interviews exchanged until the pattern of Windham's method was clear—he'd played the concerned citizen with these parents, preying on their concern for their daughters' and wives' well-being for his own benefit, subtly encouraging them to leave the academy. These letters came with post-scripted apologies over Windham's chicanery and some even with promises to pursue lessons once they returned to the area; a small sign of hope in regards to the campaign for social acceptance.

Most significant of all, there was Eleanor's letter, saved from the fire only by luck and charred around the edges, bearing witness to her concern that, if she left, her father would extract retribution from Aurora. The letter had been dated a week before the fire.

By the time they were done, they'd built a devastating case against Windham. Crispin would have preferred that the case never be aired publicly. He hoped the visit he and Peyton paid Windham would suffice for justice.

'Do you have all the files?' Peyton asked, swinging up beside him on to a sleek grey stallion.

'Yes.' Crispin patted the saddlebags. 'The copies are in your safe. I hope Windham sees reason and we have no cause to use them, however.' Crispin was grim. He cast a parting look up at the window of Aurora's room at Dursley Park. He had not told her that he meant to confront Windham today. This was for him to settle and he feared Aurora would insist on coming along. There were times when a man had to be allowed to do things for those he loved.

A familiar voice called out from an upper window and Crispin grimaced. This was not going to be one of those times. 'Wait, Crispin, where are you going?'

He looked up to see Aurora leaning over the casement. He did not dare lie to her now. 'We're going to see Windham,' he said with straightforward seriousness.

'Not without me you aren't.' Aurora slammed the window sash down and Crispin knew she'd re-appear at the front door in two minutes, the precise time it took to gain the entrance from the upper hall.

'At least she didn't shout at you for not telling her,' Peyton offered.

'Not yet. She will.' Crispin frowned.

Aurora gained the front steps, calling for a horse and slightly out of breath. He had only a few minutes to dissuade her before a groom arrived with a mount.

'Aurora, you don't have to go,' Crispin began. 'Any obligation you have to see justice served has been fulfilled. You've gathered testimonies, listened to difficult conversations about what has been done to you all for one man's revenge. You don't need to do any more. Let me handle this.'

'I will see this through to the end, Crispin.' Aurora's determination was obvious and redoubtable. 'He attempted to debase me in the most demeaning of ways. He meant to break my pride. He meant to break me. He has to know that he did not succeed. I want him to look me in the eye and know he failed.'

Crispin knew the argument was lost. Or won, depending on how one looked at it. A horse arrived saddled from the stables. He tossed Aurora up and they were off on what was to be the final leg of their journey before they could take the walk to the altar.

They arrived in the early part of the afternoon when Windham was sure to be home. They were readily received and ushered into Windham's office. Crispin thought Windham looked rather the worse for the wear. The man's face was haggard, pale, his eyes ringed by dark circles. Perhaps waiting to confront Windham had had its benefits. His eyes widened at the sight of Aurora with them.

'Expecting us?' Crispin asked coolly as he drew out a chair for Aurora, emphasising the courtesy due a lady. He and Peyton each took a chair on either side of her in front of Windham's desk.

'I've been expecting *you* for weeks,' Windham confirmed Crispin's suspicions. Windham had thought they'd come much earlier and the waiting had taken its toll. 'Not her.' He jabbed a finger at Aurora. 'I want her out of my house. She's a Jezebel who's brought nothing but trouble to my home.'

'She stays,' Crispin answered with steel. 'She's the reason we're here and an important witness to your crimes.'

'I know nothing of crimes. There have been no charges,' Windham growled.

Peyton intervened and redirected the conversation. 'As someone of magisterial authority in these parts, I've been been investigating the fire at Miss Calhoun's stables,' he said objectively. 'We're here because it seems you've had quite an adversarial relationship with Miss Calhoun and her own testimony puts you at the stables the day of the fire.'

'She's a whore. No court will believe her lies and I'll swear to her questionable morals. I have witnesses, too, you see. I have men who will vow they've seen you spend the night in her bed, Ramsden. I'll tell them about the divorce in Ireland,' he sneered at Aurora. 'Did you think I didn't know? I know every dirty secret about you, my dear. Miss Calhoun isn't even your legal name.'

Aurora stirred beside Crispin, meeting Windham's eyes evenly. 'No, there are grounds to claim that my legal name is Baroness Ashtonmere. Since the divorce that's become a bit muddled and I prefer to go by my maiden name. My former husband prefers it too and I am happy to oblige.'

Crispin grinned at Windham's discomfort. The man who'd craved a title, who'd put Aurora down because her lack of one, had been served a very just desert at Aurora's hand. He'd have to scold her a little later, though, for keeping that bit of information from him. Not that her title mattered. In all likelihood it was defunct as Aurora had suggested. Still, some people in society would settle for any title at all when it came to conferring acceptability.

Crispin reached for the files, ready to add injury to insult. 'As for those men who'd claim I'd spent the night, I have depositions from them regarding what they were doing on private property in the middle of the night to know such details. They and others also attest to your intense dislike of Miss Calhoun.' He pushed the file across the desk. 'Look through it carefully. There is bountiful proof that you have attempted to ruin her business in hopes of forcing her to leave the area. There is also more damaging testimony from Ernie and Mackey about putting glass in Dandy's stall. Currently, we've not mentioned the disappointing episode at St Albans, but that could always be brought up,' Crispin said in falsely congenial tones.

There was a long silence while Windham went through the files, scanning the assembled documents.

'This would be scandalous indeed if it went to a public trial. Surely that cannot be what you wish.' Windham pushed the file back towards Crispin. 'I've heard the banns called. If you mean to marry her and make her respectable, you cannot wish to see her made the centrepiece of a trial where her dubious background will become an issue.'

Crispin shrugged at the threat. 'I am not a man of convention, Windham. I do not care about scandal. It will not change my feelings for my wife. I do not live among society and their opinions matter little to me.'

Crispin leaned forwards, his stature menacing. 'I do, however, care that justice is done. I will not allow my wife to live in proximity to a man who secretly covets her body and has attempted to force himself on her in the most crude of ways. A trial is nothing to me.' Crispin leaned back in the chair, hands steepled confidently in front of him.

'But you have a daughter,' Peyton put in. 'Eleanor would be painted by the same brush that taints you. A trial cannot be what *you* wish.'

'Eleanor is gone,' Windham said with dead eyes. 'Aurora Calhoun has inspired her to flee her marriage.' Anger simmered behind his flat grey gaze.

'Regardless, wherever she is, her reputation is all she has to recommend her. I would think we all must attempt to protect her in any way possible, give her the chance to make her own way. The world is harsh for a woman alone,' Peyton said smoothly.

'To that end, because of my bride's friendship with your daughter, I wish to offer you a deal.' Crispin's gaze was cold. 'You have two weeks to organise your affairs. Then you embark for Australia, not to return upon pain of immediate arrest for arson, attempted rape and the other sundry list of crimes you've committed against the future Lady Aurora.'

Windham's reaction was not what Crispin had been hoping for, but rather the one he was prepared for. 'I will kill you for this!' Windham leapt across the desk for Aurora, a dangerous blade glinting from nowhere in his hand.

Aurora's excellent reflexes saved her the worst of it. She managed to throw herself out of her chair and catch the blade on her arm, but Windham was off balance and went down with her. She fought back with her fists, flailing and punching, anything that would keep the dangerous blade from finding purchase. Rescue was immediate. Before the blade could strike again, Windham's weight left her and the fight turned as Crispin dealt him a facer, his own blade in his left hand already drawn from his boot.

Windham grappled with Crispin, but the older man was no match for Crispin's anger or expertise. Within moments, Crispin held his blade against Windham's throat. 'Now you're bargaining for your life,' Crispin growled. 'Australia, or this knife across your throat. It's no less than you deserve.'

He could sense Windham's fear. 'Australia,' the man croaked.

Crispin released him with a shove. 'Two weeks. You're gone before my wedding. Peyton, be sure to remind him that we know Governor Arthur quite well.'

Crispin sheathed his blade and gathered Aurora to him. He escorted her out of the room to look after her injured arm, thankful it was only a small nick. Peyton could settle the details. His own temper was running too hot to be of use, but he was relieved none the less. Aurora would be spared any scandal and Windham would be a world away, unable to harm her. There was nothing left to stand in the way of marrying Aurora and taking up life as a gentleman horse breeder. Peyton would be thrilled to have him nearby. Aurora would be delighted to re-open her school. All that was left to do was post his resignation letter to the Foreign Office and await his bride at the altar. The loose ends were wrapped up. So why did he feel something was missing?

Chapter Twenty-Two

'What is the matter with me?' Aurora stepped down from the ottoman in Tessa's rooms, carefully lifting the hem of her wedding gown so that she didn't disturb the pins Tessa's maid had used to adjust the length. She stared at the woman in the mirror, the woman who would marry Lord Crispin Ramsden in two days and take up residence at Woodbrook as Lady Ramsden. Life was a long way from the three-room cottage she'd shared with her father in County Kildare, a long way from the small apartments she'd kept at her stables.

'Wedding jitters?' Tessa ventured a guess from the *chaise* where she rocked the baby. 'Everyone gets them.'

'Did you?' Aurora stood still to let the maid unbutton the exquisite dress.

'Well, to be honest, no,' Tessa admitted, then hastily added, 'Our circumstances were different, though. Jitters or not, there was no going back. We had a baby on the way.'

The addendum didn't assure Aurora. 'If you weren't sure, you wouldn't have married Peyton no matter what the situation. I know you too well, Tess.'

'I see.' Tessa handed the baby to a maid and smoothed her skirts, gathering her thoughts. 'You have doubts about Crispin?'

'No.' Aurora was confident on that score. In the weeks since accepting Crispin's ring that afternoon at Woodbrook, she'd sorted through her feelings, her nerves, countless times, looking for the source of her anxiety. 'But something's not right.' Aurora slipped into robe and sat down next to Tessa.

'Maybe it's the ring, the idea that this is for ever?'

'No.' Aurora twisted the gold band on her hand, studying it. 'Crispin has demonstrated that he loves me as much as a man can love a woman and beyond that even. Perhaps that's what bothers me. He's given up everything that matters to him.' She shook her head. 'He didn't come home to Dursley Park looking to stay and start a life.' Her mind was whirling now. She'd known from the start how much he valued his freedom, how he'd thought he'd be bored if he stayed in Dursley too long. He was a man used to wandering. He'd put that aside for her.

'He changed himself for me, Tessa, but I never wanted that. I never asked for that.' She knew now what was wrong and she was desperate to find him. She should have questioned this earlier. 'I have to find Crispin. I won't have my happiness purchased at the price of another's freedom.'

'The gown…we're not finished,' the maid protested.

Aurora shook her head. 'It won't matter. We won't need it.'

Crispin needed fresh air. He'd promised Peyton he would spend time looking at some legal documents with him this afternoon, but he wasn't ready to go inside. In two days, he'd be a married man, finally succumbing to the parson's mousetrap like his brothers before him. His freedom would be gone. Never again would he have the freedom to do as he pleased, to wander the length of the empire, to dance at gypsy campfires high in the mountains of countries waiting to be formed. In two days, he'd become Lord Crispin Ramsden and take his place in English society, whatever that place might be. Just as he had feared he would that day months ago when Peyton had first taken him to Woodbrook.

All that he'd abhorred about commitment had come to pass with two substantial differences. It had happened far more quickly than he'd anticipated. And he had Aurora in exchange for what he was about to give up. That was far more reward than he'd imagined. For Aurora, he'd give up everything. He'd not lied when he told her he'd give her the world.

He'd have a wife and a business that would bring him pleasure. Sheikh was a fine horse with prospects and it wasn't as if Aurora wasn't giving anything up either. As Lady Ramsden, she'd never race at St Albans again. She'd have to limit her steeplechasing to hunt parties and private endeavours, but they would be together and they'd have their own world somewhat apart from society at Woodbrook. It would be enough. More than enough. Any other man would begrudge him his success. He was marrying on his own terms, something not every man in England could claim.

And yet he had not sent his resignation from the Foreign Office. He'd penned it, folded it, and put it in a dresser drawer right next to the letter containing his next assignment. As he'd expected, it was to South Carolina to monitor the growing unrest in America over the slave trade, an issue that was fast coming to a head in the British Empire as well. There was a horse farm he'd be leasing for the duration of his two-year stay, although that stay was likely to be longer.

The very thought of horses seemed to conjure Aurora out of nowhere. She was dressed in trousers and one of her cut-down man's shirts, walking with grim determination down the path towards him. He smiled at the sight of her, his blood already heating. Oh, yes, this should be enough, he thought. He would make it so.

'Crispin, we can't get married,' Aurora blurted out, taking him completely off guard.

'I don't understand.' Crispin tried to focus his thoughts. Was something wrong with her dress? With the flowers? The church? What did women worry about before a wedding?

'Don't you see? I can't have you giving up your freedom for me. I don't know why I didn't see it sooner. Maybe I just didn't want to see it.'

'Aurora, wait. Slow down. You've got cold feet.' He reached for her hand and gripped it.

'Crispin, you feel it too. At Woodbrook, I asked if you were happy and you couldn't answer me. When we walked into the house, I felt your hand tighten on mine like it is now and your voice trembled.'

Crispin gave a harsh laugh. He couldn't deny her intuitions. 'I've always wondered what it would be like to have a woman know me, to truly know and understand me. I thought I'd like it. It was always the standard by which I rejected everyone, until you. You know me too well, Aurora, and I rather wish you didn't.'

Aurora wasn't daunted. 'I know you because I know myself. We are two wild hearts, Crispin. Marriage and tradition aren't for us.' She tugged at the gold band until it came off. 'Take it, Cris. I love you too much to hold you. There are some horses that aren't meant to be tamed.'

Her eyes watered, liquid moss.

He stared at the ring in the flat of his palm. He had his freedom. She'd understood his need as clearly as he had understood himself, but she was only half-right. 'I need you too, Aurora. My freedom isn't worth much without you. Maybe we aren't cut out for tradition, but I'm sure I'm cut out for marriage to you.'

'Well, we can't have both. Take your freedom and run, Crispin. I won't be strong for ever.'

Crispin regarded her for a long moment. He could not leave her. He would regret it to the end of his days. He knew it deep in his bones just as he knew there was still something fundamentally flawed in their future plans. A bold thought came to him. It wasn't the marrying he held any reservation with. With a newfound clarity, he spoke slowly as the thoughts came to him. 'Why do we have to choose? Why does marriage have to mean tradition?'

He thought of the letter in his drawer. 'Marry me. I've got a posting to South Carolina. Come with me. I'm to be a respectable horse breeder and it's meant to be more permanent, danger free. I love you and that's all that matters as long as you love me too.'

'And leave Woodbrook?' she teased, but he could see from the dancing lights in her eyes that her relief was nearly a palpable thing.

'Petra and Thomas can put it to good use until we decide we're ready for it.' Crispin grinned, his blood humming as his improvised plans took root. He felt alive, the dread of the past few days easing from his shoulders while he spun possibilities with Aurora at the paddock fence.

'I hear America is a more open society,' Aurora ventured.

Crispin nodded, understanding the root of her concern. There was no sense in leaving England if her antecedents would make her a pariah in the New World as well. 'The people there put great stock in what a man can do instead of who he is and what family he was born into. Where we're going, there's supposed to be some fine plantation homes, but the men who built them are only a generation away from having lived in log cabins in the woods. These planters are self-made men and many of their wives are self-made women.'

Aurora smiled at his reassurance. 'A place to re-invent myself sounds good.'

'Well, I wouldn't re-invent too much. I do like you just the way you are.' Crispin reached for her, kissing her full on the mouth. 'I think we've solved the riddle of our cold feet. Rather, you've solved it, Aurora, my brave girl.' He winked. 'If you hadn't spoken up, we would have started a life we weren't meant to live.'

Two months ago he'd never have believed this moment was possible. Now, he was happily awaiting his wedding to the most vibrant, stubbornly independent woman alive. Life was an adventure once more, the only way he knew how to live it.

Aurora tilted her head to the side, studying him in earnest. 'What are you thinking, Crispin?'

'Aurora, I'm thinking that I never saw you coming.'

Two days later, Aurora entered the small stone chapel at Dursley Park on a late sunlit spring morning, radiantly turned out in ivory silk, a crown of spring flowers in her dark hair, her arm looped through the Earl of Dursley's to make her way down the aisle amid the gaze of those gathered to witness the wedding.

There were friends among those assembled: Petra and Thomas, Eva and Aunt Lily who'd journeyed from London for the occasion, along with Catherine Sykes and her parents. Letitia Osborne had come, too, confessing that she wouldn't miss a chance to see the parish's bachelor vicar perform a wedding. Who knew, she'd giggled, it might put him in a proposing mood.

Aurora knew they were there. She was grateful for their presence and all it signified, but while all eyes were on her, she had eyes only for the handsome man at the altar. Crispin Ramsden waited for her, a man of uncommon strength of character, who loved her unconditionally and was willing to be her partner in life on entirely unconventional terms. His presence in her life was a blessing she had long stopped looking for.

Aurora blinked hard against an errant tear. Characteristically prepared for any circumstance, Peyton discreetly passed her a handkerchief. 'You make him happy, my dear. Shall we?'

She would remember for the rest of her life the joy that surged in her step by step down that aisle, her happiness growing greater as the distance to Crispin diminished. By the time Peyton placed her hand in his, she was full to bursting. Crispin looked at her with blue eyes that mirrored the joy of her own and smiled.

The vicar began the service, but the words were for the others assembled. They were lost in their world, emerging to recite their vows.

* * *

'You were right, the first day we met,' Aurora whispered softly during the final prayer before the service concluded.

'About what?'

'You said there were no other men like you and you were absolutely correct.'

At that moment the vicar intoned the words that ended the ceremony. 'By the power of the Church of England, I now pronounce you man and wife. You may kiss the bride.'

'Ah, my favourite part,' Crispin murmured, moving to take her in his arms. 'I have it on good authority I kiss better than I ride.'

'Thank goodness for small miracles,' Aurora breathed as Crispin took her in a kiss that would long be remembered as the finest wedding kiss Dursley had ever seen.

Outside, an open carriage waited to take them to the wedding breakfast at Dursley Park and yet another carriage waited to take them later on the first stage of their journey to Southampton and the ship to South Carolina, the ship to their future, where Kildare and Sheikh would have first-class accommodations for the duration of the voyage.

Hand in hand, Aurora walked the aisle beside Crispin towards that future. She smiled up at her husband. Who would have thought that the best way to tame wild hearts would have been to let them run free?

Epilogue

Aurora and Crispin Ramsden stood at the rail of the sleek schooner that would take them across the Atlantic to Charleston, South Carolina and into their new life. The breeze off the water blew Crispin's dark hair back from his face as he waved to the figures on the wharf. Tessa and Peyton had come to see them off, all three of the boys gathered around them; the baby in Tessa's arms and the twins climbing on Peyton. Crispin swallowed hard. He had not anticipated such a reaction to this farewell.

'Miss them already?' Aurora asked softly by his side.

'We'll see them again,' Crispin said staunchly. 'I've already got summers planned for those scamps when they're old enough.'

'The assignment's only for a few years.' Aurora smiled up at her husband.

Crispin shrugged. 'You never know. I feel like South Carolina might be the right place for us. A new world, a new life where we can decide who we want to be.'

'I know, I feel it too.' Aurora's voice was edged with excitement.

Crispin waved one last time. It had been a whirlwind month. Gregory Windham had kept his word and disappeared quietly to Australia before the wedding. The wedding had been perfect; small and simple in the old family chapel, attended by friends they'd made in St Albans and by family. Petra and Thomas had been thrilled to take over Woodbrook and awed, too, by the generous wedding gift of the farm. Everything had fallen into place.

'Eleanor's out there somewhere—I hope she's all right.' Aurora sighed as Peyton and Tessa finally slipped from view.

Eleanor Windham was the only loose end Crispin could do nothing about. There'd been no word or sign of her since her disappearance and he knew it weighed on Aurora's mind, that Aurora felt some responsibility for the girl.

Crispin wrapped an arm about his wife's shoulders, still marvelling that he'd found the one woman in the world that could understand and fulfil him so completely. 'She'll be fine.'

The decision to leave had been a hard one to make, but the right one. There were plenty of people in South Carolina who were only one generation away from their common roots, who were more interested in what a man could make of his life than where he was born. In South Carolina they'd have a chance.

'Shall we go check on the horses?' Aurora asked after a long silence. In the large hold below, Kildare, Sheikh and Dandy would be settling in to their new quarters for the next twenty days.

Crispin nodded. 'It's always the horses first with you, isn't it?' he teased.

Aurora cocked her head and looked up at him, her green eyes dancing. 'Unless you have something better in mind?'

'As a matter of fact I do.' Crispin caught her mouth in a full-bodied kiss. 'The horses can wait.'

Aurora laughed at him, her arms about his neck.

Crispin hugged her to him and looked out over the water to their future, fully confident that the greatest adventure was the one that lay ahead.

* * * * *

DANGEROUS LORD, INNOCENT GOVERNESS
Christine Merrill

Daphne Collingham is convinced that her cousin died at the hands of her husband, scandalous Lord Timothy Colton, so masquerades as a governess to discover the truth. But suspicion and provocation go hand in hand as she becomes the dangerous lord's ultimate temptation…

CAPTURED FOR THE CAPTAIN'S PLEASURE
Ann Lethbridge

Fearsome Captain Michael Hawkhurst lives to wreak revenge on the Fulton family. When he captures Fulton's spirited but virginal daughter Alice, Michael faces a dilemma—should he live up to his scandalous name and take his revenge, or will his honourable side win out…?

BRUSHED BY SCANDAL
Gail Whitiker

Nothing's more important to beautiful Lady Annabelle Durst than protecting her heart. However, when faced with a family scandal, she must risk her reputation and her heart in order to persuade the disreputable Sir Barrington Parker to help..

LORD LIBERTINE
Gail Ranstrom

Notorious Andrew Hunter finds a diversion from his dissolute life in the form of the mysterious Lady Lace. Unable to tell if she is innocent or an experienced temptress, he is determined to seduce the truth from her. But is he ready for the secrets he will uncover…?

Mills & Boon® Hardback
Historical

*Another exciting novel available
this month:*

HONOURABLE DOCTOR, IMPROPER ARRANGEMENT

Mary Nichols

A woman worth fighting for!

Dr Simon Redfern has risked his heart—and his reputation—over a woman once before. So when he meets Kate Meredith, who is helping a ragged child, he's shocked to find himself longing to make the warm-hearted young widow his wife...

Despite family disapproval, Kate volunteers to work at Simon's children's home, and her growing feelings for him throw her into confusion. For, longing to have children of her own, she has accepted another man's proposal. But Simon is the only man she can now contemplate as their father...

REGENCY

0212 HB HDIA

Mills & Boon® Hardback Historical

*Another exciting novel available
this month:*

THE EARL PLAYS WITH FIRE

Isabelle Goddard

A game of cat and mouse

The young Richard Veryan was heartbroken—and bitter—
after unrivalled beauty and childhood friend Christabel
Tallis jilted him three weeks before their wedding.

Six years later, and toughened by adventure overseas,
Richard—now a lord—is very much his own man. But
when he and Christabel meet once again dangerous
temptation hangs in the air.

Richard sees his chance to teach Christabel a lesson.
He'll prove to her that he can still command her body,
mind and soul—then *he'll* be the one to walk away...

Mills & Boon® Hardback Historical

*Another exciting novel available
this month:*

HIS BORDER BRIDE
Blythe Gifford

Royal rogue, innocent lady

Gavin Fitzjohn is the illegitimate son of an English prince
and a Scotswoman. A rebel without a country, he
has darkness in his soul.

Clare Carr, daughter of a Scottish border lord, can recite the laws
of chivalry, and knows Gavin has broken every one.

Clare is gripped by desire for this royal rogue—could he be the
one to unleash everything she has tried so hard to hide?
Those persuasive urges have stayed safely
dormant—until now…